BOSSY MR. WARD

SHARON WOODS

Cover Design: Wild Love Designs

Editing: Susan Gottfried

Proofreading: April Bennett

To everyone who believes in true love...

Prologue

JOSHUA

STARING ACROSS AN OLD wooden desk into my father's gaze, my head thumps inside my skull as I watch my dad's small, thin lips move. I can't understand his words; it's as if he is speaking underwater. I scrunch my forehead, trying to concentrate on reading his lips, but I can't for the life of me lip-read.

I shouldn't have drunk so much scotch last night at the party. It was a regular boys' night that quickly got out of control. As usual, I let myself get loose. With no work commitments or girlfriend to answer to, I don't know when to stop. I'm not complaining. I love my easy, free life. But the hangovers every week are getting harder to bounce back from.

I'm slumped in one of his worn office chairs. I watch as he rubs his eyebrows with his hand, rests his elbows on top of the desk, and blows out his cheeks, frustration written on his face. I haven't had the best relationship with my parents. They wanted the so-called perfect child, not the rebellious party boy they got.

If they gave two shits about me, they would have talked to me. But I was invisible to them. I think I was born for the society picture, not out of love.

Love—what is that?

I wouldn't know what it feels like to be truly loved. People see the outside, the pretty face, the family money, the carefree attitude I put on, but underneath the façade is darkness. Deep loneliness hidden deep under layers.

I scan the office, noting the mess, the papers piled up on his desk. I shrug it off, blaming my drunken state that I must be seeing shit.

Rubbing my hands over my face, I say, "Dad, what did you call me here this early for?" Irritation is laced in my voice.

He rises, snatching his glass full of whiskey off the desk and taking a big swig. "It's eleven in the morning, for god's sake. Look at the state of you. Every week, you do this to yourself. You need to grow up."

I sigh, leaning back, taking in his profile. He looks out the window, talking to it instead of me. He barely looks at me. I shake my head. He seems to have aged, his gray hair more white, his black suit a little big for his small frame.

My head throbs and I snap. I would rather be on my couch, recovering, than sitting here. "What did you call me here for?"

He picks up a piece of paper and shoves it out to me. I move a little too quick and wince. I want to get the fuck out of here. I snatch the paper from his hands.

I peer down and my brows furrow. *What the fuck?*

I blink rapidly. *Surely not.*

It's a contract.

For the business.
The family business.
He transferred it.
Into my name.
Joshua Ward.
Effective immediately.

My mouth slacks and I try to think of what to say, but nothing is forming coherently in my mind.

I thrust my hand to the back of my neck and squeeze the tension that's building up, hard and fast.

I clear my throat. "Why?" I whisper.

I want to say more, but that's all I can think of right now.

My heart is beating erratically at the news and the contract that I'm currently glaring at. "Why?" The words leave my mouth again as I lean back into the office chair in shock and take in my old man. I squint as I try to read his face for answers.

"It's time, son. I'm not young anymore. I can't do this forever." He continues looking at the window and not at me.

Lie.

He is hiding something. I'm certain. I lean into the right side of the chair and rub my hand along my chin, trying to figure out what it is. As if glaring at him long enough will make him spit it out. *I wish!*

I lift my chin in a sudden thought. "It's sudden. Effective immediately? Why not prepare me—show me how you run the business?"

My dad stands and rounds his chair to the drink trolley. He turns and lifts the glass into the air in a silent offering.

Bile rises in my throat. I shake my head. *Fuck, that hurts.* I cease immediately and he shrugs before pouring himself another large helping of whiskey. He takes a large gulp of the amber liquid.

He cradles the glass as he returns to his chair. I notice his eyes appear red and dull.

Maybe it is the right decision. I just wish he hadn't thrown me into the business like this. A little warning would have been nice.

"Your mother and I are taking a trip for six to twelve months. Change of scenery." He stares out the office window and takes another large sip. Something is on his mind.

I shift, sitting up in my chair. Raising a brow, I say, "You're serious?"

His gaze meets my hard eyes. "What is your issue, son? I thought you would be happy taking over the business."

I think about his question. Am I happy? I sigh. "Of course I am. Just not like this. And this soon. But it's not like I have many choices. How much time do we have before this...trip?" I ask.

"Six weeks."

I slap my hands on my thighs, not giving a fuck about my head. "You expect me to learn everything in six fucking weeks? You're crazy, old man...Gahhhhh," I growl, sitting back in my chair.

His body straightens and his eyebrows draw close together as he says, "Do not speak to me like that. You will show some respect. You will be fine. You're young; you will find better and new ways to run the ship."

My jaw thrusts as I hold back another outburst. We don't speak as he drains his glass. I watch him stalk toward the alcohol trolley and lower his empty glass. He swings around and walks over to me. He stands beside me, resting his right hand on my shoulder, and squeezes. "I'm tired. It's time I get home. Your mother will be expecting me."

I nod, scared that if I open my mouth, I'll disrespect him. And I'm not wasting my breath. My sore head is quickly turning into a migraine.

I hear him walk to the door. It creaks open before I hear the click shut. *Asshole.*

I inhale a deep breath through my nose and stalk around the desk, dusting my hands across the top surface. Papers fly in every direction.

I take a seat in my new chair, scanning the room. Old white paint, dark brown carpet, and a small window looking outside at houses. It's a small, run-down building. The computer needs an upgrade desperately. My dad insisted that upgrading was a waste, but I don't agree.

Now that I am to take over, things need to change.

As I scan the office, I think about the recent projects we have lost to our competitors. My gut twists and I need to dig deeper.

I tear open the drawers and pull the paperwork of all our current jobs out and pile everything onto the desk. Some papers hold on top of the pile, but a few slip straight to the floor.

Once all the papers inside the office are on top of the desk, I sift through, making two piles.

Keep or throw. My stomach grumbles, reminding me I skipped dinner with a fling I have been seeing this week.

It's close to two in the morning by the time I finally get ready to leave the office. I've been here all day, trying to make sense of everything, and I pick up one final paper that had slipped off the desk and landed on the other side.

I crouch down and scoop it up. As I stand, I scan the contents. "You asshole," I say out loud. So this is what he wasn't telling me; I knew he was hiding something… Scrunching the paper in my hand, I pull out my phone and click on James' name, bringing the phone to my ear. It doesn't take long for him to answer.

"Josh?" His voice is gravelly and I wince.

"Shit. Sorry. I didn't even think about the time when I called you."

"No, no. It's fine. What's up?" he asks.

"My dad left me with the family business, effective immediately. The asshole is going on a holiday in six weeks for six months, maybe a year. I don't know how to run a business, James—a failing one at that." I squeeze my eyes shut at the last statement. The paper in my hand has angered me further.

"It's okay. I got you. I'll be there in five minutes. You at the office?"

I sigh loudly. "Yeah."

I hit the end button and shove the phone back into my pocket.

I step to the drink trolley and pour myself a good three fingers of scotch, the one thing he still had—expensive liquor.

I move over to the chair and pull at the drink, the amber burning my throat before my head reminds me I'm still hungover.

I lower the glass to the table and sit down again while I wait for my friend James. I crinkle the paper and stare at the eviction words. Staring back at me. Mocking me.

Fuck!

CHAPTER 1

AVA

Six months later

MY DESK PHONE RINGS, scaring the crap out of me. I work as a receptionist for a printing company. "Good morning. Ava speaking. How may I help you?"

"Ava, it's David. Could you see me in my office when you finish with the orders?"

"Of course. I won't be too long," I answer.

"Take your time."

I hang up. I've been working with David for a few years now; I enjoy the peace of the small town I live in. And there are only a few of us who work here, so I can be myself.

Twenty minutes later, I rise and wander over to David's office. I knock on his doorframe.

He looks up from his computer with a half-assed smile. Uneasiness churns in my stomach. "Ava, come in. Please take a seat."

I frown at his comment. He doesn't ask me to sit down. Ever. Sweat forms on my palms and I rub them quickly down my ripped blue jeans.

"Okay." I step inside and sit down on the chair opposite him. I sit straight, waiting for the reason for his call.

He rubs the back of his neck before gazing at me. *Shit. He looks serious.*

"Ava, I'm so sorry to have to say this, but we have to close the business."

My hands cover my gasp. "What. Shit. Why?" I mumble through my fingers.

He hangs his head. "I know it must shock you, and trust me, I tried to avoid this, but financially the company is now in the hands of administrators."

I blink rapidly, trying to process his words. *What the fuck am I going to do for money now?*

Feeling my heart beating in my throat, I try to concentrate on breathing in and out, trying to calm the panic that's rising. My breaths are shallow yet audible. I'm unable to talk, my mind going over the same thoughts. How am I going to get through this? I can't go back there.

"Are you okay, Ava? Would you like a glass of water? Ava?" He asks again, louder this time.

I would rather have alcohol, but I know we don't have any here in the office. I nod slowly. His chair drags across the floor as he rises, and heavy footsteps walk to the water fountain. The water trickling sounds like my bleeding heart. The footsteps begin again as a shadow appears in front of me. I slowly raise my head to see David has the cup held out in front of him. Grabbing the cup slowly out of his outstretched hand, peering down at the clear liquid, I raise the plastic cup and chug the water back, draining the cup. The cold water coats my warm throat. *So good.*

David steps back around to his chair.

I offer a small smile and talk in a quiet voice. "Thanks." I continue to concentrate on breathing in through my nose, out through my mouth, feeling my shoulders relax with every breath and my heartbeat regulating.

He clears his throat, gaining my attention. "I'm giving you two weeks' notice. If you find another job before that, I will understand. You're a fantastic worker and I'm happy to be called as a reference."

My lips tip up. "Thanks, David. I appreciate that." I hesitate before adding, "What will you do?"

He takes a deep, audible breath and leans back in his chair. His gaze meets mine. The sadness there makes my cold heart break.

"I don't know, Ava. Truthfully, I don't know."

"Well, shit." A nervous smile appears on my lips.

He laughs, but it's not his carefree laugh. It's a broken cackle. "I will miss you. You kept this place in order. Hell, you kept me sorted. I just couldn't keep this place afloat. I'm sorry."

His eyes return to his computer and I swallow. "You are a significant person and boss. I'm sure something better is out there waiting for you."

He raises his chin to glance at me, offering me a genuine smile. The surrounding air is quiet, so I stand. "I better get back to work."

He nods and also stands, walking around the desk and toward me. I instinctively take a step back, not wanting any physical touch. I cross my arms, spin around, and wander back to my desk, lost in my thoughts about my future.

The next few hours drag. I work, but it's not as productive as I usually would be. Not like I have to try very hard now. I will be jobless in two weeks. *Fuck. What will I do?*

A few hours later, I clear my desk and make my way home. I pick up the cheapest bottle of wine from the store, not giving a shit that cheap wine causes the worst hangovers. I need alcohol tonight. It might help this numbness I'm feeling disappear. That, or it will help me sleep.

As soon as I enter my apartment, a lump forms in my throat. I hate that I could be looking at moving out of here. *My home.* It's a warm and safe place. Entering the kitchen, I pull open the cupboard and scan the contents. I don't have the energy to cook a fancy dinner, nor do I have the funds.

I spot a packet of noodles. *Bingo.* I grab them and begin preparing them. While they cook, I connect my phone to the Bluetooth speaker so I have music playing softly in the background, then I open the bottle of wine and pour myself a decent helping. Taking a sip, I scrunch up my face. *This shit is awful. Fuck.* I stir the noodles, which are almost done, and take another large mouthful of my shitty cheap wine.

My phone rings as I lower the glass and choke on the awful shit, then twist the volume down on the speaker so I can answer the call. Pulling out my phone, I check the display. Mom's name is flashing. Even though I hate myself right now, and I hate that I could disappoint her, the need to tell her about my day has me answering it.

"Mom, your ears must have been burning. I was going to call you tonight." I step back to the kitchen.

"Oh, no, they weren't, darling. What did you want to talk to me about?"

Raising the wine, I take another large sip, needing the liquid courage. I stir my dinner before flicking the stove off. "Are you sitting down?" I ask quietly.

"No, but what happened?" Concern is laced in her voice.

A sour taste hits my mouth. I am hating how I'm about to let her down, that David sacking me is a disappointment to her. A heaviness enters my heart and I blow out a breath I hadn't realized I had been holding until she speaks.

"Darling, tell me. You have me worried sick here," she begs through the phone.

I squeeze my eyes shut, then open them. "Sorry. I was turning my dinner off. David called me into the office today and said he is closing the business." I hear her gasp. Tears form behind my eyelids. I'm glad she isn't here because I would be a basket case.

"Oh, darling. I'm so sorry."

"It's not your fault, Mom." Pinching my lips together for a moment, I finally say, "I have two weeks to find another job."

As I glance around my one-bedroom apartment, my heart hurts. I love this place. I'm settled here and my paychecks keep me living here independently.

"No wonder you're upset, darling. But there is a reason. Things happen in your life for a reason. There is a better opportunity out there. I believe that," she offers.

My eyes fill with tears. I still don't believe this is happening. I love how she always believes in me, but right now, I'm feeling numb and not optimistic.

Desperate to change the subject so I don't start sobbing on the phone, I say, "Thanks, Mom. I hope you're right. Anyway, enough about me. What are you doing?"

"I was going to see if you wanted to come for dinner Sunday night? Darling?"

I am having trouble responding; my mouth is opening but no words are coming out. After a beat, I sigh, "Yes. That sounds good." I would rather be by myself. Alone. But then all I will do is think about my jobless situation. And she would insist she comes to visit. At least this way, I won't have to cook.

"Okay, good. I'll cook one of your favorites."

I close my eyes at her sweet gesture. Any food is my favorite, but there are definitely a few dishes that stand out. I feel weak, like I need to sit down. "Mom, I better eat my dinner before it gets cold."

"Good idea. Are you sure you will be okay tonight? Do you need me to come over?" she offers.

"No thanks; I'll be fine. I'm tired and will crash soon."

"Okay. Call me if you need anything. I love you."

My heart thumps at those words. "I love you too...Bye." I hang up and retreat to the stove to serve my noodles. Scooping up my bowl, fork, and glass of wine, I carry them into my living room, lowering my butt to the floor, my food on the coffee table and wine beside it. I stab the noodles with the fork. I try to eat but my throat thickens, making it hard to swallow. Deciding against eating, I push the bowl aside and drink the wine instead.

A few glasses of wine later, my veins are now filled with alcohol. It's warming me from the inside. Feeling hot, I peel off my sweater, leaving me in my tank top and leggings.

I search the television, looking for a show or movie to watch tonight. Scrolling aimlessly through the stations, I find nothing. I flick it off and open my mom's old laptop. I power it up and continue to drink. By now I have had too many, but I'm cradling my last glass as I scroll through job ads. I stop on one that sounds simple enough. I sit up straight and the wine sloshes around in the glass and over the edge. *Fuckin' hell.*

I lift my finger up the glass and wipe the wine up, sucking the residue into my mouth. I don't want to get this over my white couch or rug.

I squint as I read the job description.

Personal Assistant required for an expanding electrical company. That sounds easy.

I shrug at myself on this cozy night. Scrolling through, I read each duty.

Able to work as part of a team
Facilities management and maintenance
Schedule management and meeting coordination

Coordinating and organizing project manager

Office management including stationery, mail, greeting clients, couriers, and more

It all sounds easy enough. I can support a project manager with daily tasks. *Piece of cake.*

Feeling a little buzzed, I set the wine down on the coffee table. A little smirk plays on my lips. I fill in a new version of my résumé. I'm smiling to myself as I add some cheeky extra words and side tasks. I have never done them, but it makes me sound more experienced.

I need money and a job desperately. With no other options and only two weeks to find something new, I laugh at how ridiculous I sound on this résumé. But the website has nothing else that's suitable.

An icy shiver runs through my spine. The thought of getting kicked out of here has me hitting send. I close the laptop, drain my glass, and my eyes become heavy. Unable to concentrate on the TV, I switch it off and climb onto my sofa, snuggling in as my exhaustion takes over, and I pass out.

When I move the next morning on the couch, my head feels like it's about to explode. I groan out loud at no one. *Fuck. I feel sick. Stupid cheap wine.* Without lifting my head up, I reach for my phone.

I can't remember a thing about last night. I seem to have lost all recollection of events. My fingers touch my cell. *Yes. Found it.*

I lift it up in front of my face and squint as the light from the screen blares back at me. *Ahh, so fucking bright.*

I blink rapidly until my eyes adjust. My thumb moves aimlessly over my socials and I catch sight of my email icon, showing one new message. Frowning, I click on it and open my emails, sucking in a breath as I read the subject line to the one email.

Job Interview from Ward Electrical and Infrastructure.

I rub down my face, trying to wipe away the sleep and foggy brain. *What?*

Shifting my weight on the couch, sitting up a little, I try to understand if it's a spam email. I need a closer look. I haven't applied for any jobs. *Right?*

I open up a browser and google the company's name. Sure enough, a website pops up. And as I scan, it seems legitimate.

So, the next question is how?

I rub along my brow, trying to remember and finally deciding to check my sent emails. I have a niggling feeling in my stomach. *Did I apply last night?*

Clicking the folder, it opens up and sure enough, there is the application I sent off. *Fuck.*

Moving back to the inbox, I reopen the email and read the contents. Job interview means I'll need to look professional. I groan. But my stomach grumbles, reminding me I also need money for necessities. *And better wine.*

As I continue to read, I see a comment stating it's a phone interview. *Thank fuck.*

The interview is scheduled for ten a.m. on Thursday. If I'm successful, I start Monday. Maybe Mom is right about her signs. If I get this job, then I'll know for certain that it was meant to be…but at the moment, I'm not convinced. Surely someone is going to come busting through my door and tell me I have been punked.

My shoulders drop and I relax back onto the couch with a loud sigh.

Closing the application, I swing my legs off the couch and sit up. I grip my head with both hands, wincing from the movement. Waiting for the waves in my head to settle, I stay still before getting up and sorting myself out with some food before work.

Thursday arrives, and after work, I sit at my dining table, waiting for the phone to ring. I chew the end of my pen. I hardly slept last night, tossing and turning. Not having much experience with interviews, I was mulling over all the questions they might ask me. I stayed up and googled all the standard interview questions, as well as the business.

My pen repeatedly taps on the paper, my stomach fluttering with nerves. The phone rings. *Shit. It's time.* I pick it up and stare at the screen, not answering until a few rings. I don't want to seem desperate, even though I *need* this job.

I swipe the pad of my finger across the phone, bringing it to my ear. "Hello. Ava speaking."

My tone is the sweet professional one, not my regular, relaxed tone.

"Hi, Ava. This is James calling from Ward Electrical and Infrastructure. How are you?" A deep voice speaks into the phone. It's rich, confident, and sexy. I'm still nervous, but now a tad of excitement shrills through me.

"I'm good. Thank you for asking. And you?"

"I'm excellent, thanks. Now, I'm calling about the job for the assistant position you applied for."

"Yes," I say back.

"Are you okay if we begin the job interview now?"

"Sure." I shuffle to the edge of the chair and twirl my hair around my finger. I stare down at my paper. My heartbeat picks up speed.

"Why do you want this position?" he asks.

My mouth drops open. Straight to the point, no bullshit approach. I like that. I like it a lot.

"My previous company is closing. Having previously worked for them for the last eight years, I need a job and I'm experienced in the position you require."

"You are, and you have had no other workplaces?" He seems to be taken aback.

"No, my previous employment was the one and only. Oh, and the odd jobs when I had spare time."

The add-ons to my résumé have returned to haunt me. I really could kick myself for making that shit up right now. Hopefully, I don't get caught out by the lies. Surely I would have been interviewed on my work with David alone. I don't know why I lied. *The booze, you idiot. This is why you don't drink so much. And especially with no food.*

"Very good," he mumbles. I can hear the faint scratching of a pen gliding across paper.

I sit back a little, my shoulders still tense and sitting up around my ears. I'm waiting for the next question.

"What do you think you can bring to the company?"

I answer, "I'm creative, timely, and organized."

A pause and then he chuckles, "Perfect. Thomas, who you will potentially be reporting to, needs that. A lot," he drawls.

Oh god. I hope this Thomas isn't a slob; I'm not a cleaner. I can organize the office for a better system for working. But I don't want to be cleaning up after a male. I shake my head at the thought. *Gross.*

Luckily, David was tidy and understood my quirks.

"What do you know about the company?" he asks.

I hear a rustle of papers in my ear. When it stops, I answer.

"Ward Electrical and Infrastructure specializes in the electrical design, cabling, project management, information technology, and technical services. They provide these services to the construction industry, public transport, and the corporate sector," I answer without a pause.

"Impressive," he mumbles. "Are there questions for me?"

I rub my brow with my free hand, not expecting that question and feeling a tad stupid for not being able to think of anything. My brain is coming up blank. "Ugh, no. Not at this stage, thanks."

"Well, you sound like you would make the perfect assistant to Thomas, so congratulations. I'll email you now with a formal letter of offer and more important details about the company. If you can come to the address on the date provided, someone will welcome you in."

An enormous smile appears on my face. *I did it. I found a new job.*

"Wow. Thank you," I breathe.

My mouth opens and shuts, but nothing else leaves it, so I just slam it shut again. I wish I could talk, but I'm shocked by how I scored a job quickly after David sacked me.

"You're welcome. Goodbye, Ava."

"Goodbye." I rip the phone away from my ear, hanging up and staring at it out in front of me. I take a few big deep breaths as relief washes through me. Then I call Mom.

CHAPTER 2

JOSHUA

I'M STANDING IN FRONT of my mirror in my bathroom, adjusting my gray tie. It's early morning and I'm getting ready for a full day's work in the office. I smooth down my tie, feeling the silk under my palms, and then begin running my hands through my hair with some product.

I walk out of my bathroom to my front door, knowing I won't be back until it's dark. My refresh button started when I was handed the business. I'm not interested in a messy playboy life anymore. A chill runs down my spine at the memory. What fun, but dark, times, drinking away my life. No goals. No motivation. I only fucked and drank until I passed out.

I check my emails on my phone on the way to my car. I read as many as I can until I run out of service and then stuff my phone into my suit pocket. I will answer the others at the office.

James and I spent last week interviewing and hiring staff. All the positions filled easily. Having James assist me with the interviewing and hiring of staff meant the entire process was smooth and quicker than with just me alone.

Some applicants lived farther than thirty minutes away, so we did those over the phone.

I pull into the space reserved for me at my building and dial James.

"Morning. I'm here," I say.

"Okay. I'll walk over now. See you in ten." I hang up and answer a few more emails on my phone before stepping out of the car and waiting for James to arrive.

I lean my elbow against the new reception desk. I have a stupid, proud grin on my face as I take in the space.

James strolls into the building, calling out, "Morning, sunshine."

I laugh. "You're happy today. Did you get laid last night?"

"Of course." He elbows my ribs on our way to the elevators. We are inspecting my office for the last details before we officially start. The small business my dad started is going to be an empire.

We are stepping into the elevator when I say, "I need to get laid. It's been a week." I peer at James, whose body is relaxed and unfazed. His hands are stuffed inside his pockets.

He rolls his eyes. "I thought you were going to say longer. You are so dramatic. A week isn't that long."

"As if you can talk, Mr. Threesome," I mock. Because he is a notorious playboy too, and threesomes are a must. Every damn time. I don't know where he finds them. He can't keep the same woman; he has the same issue I have. They want more.

He throws his head back with a chuckle. "Not my fault if they offer. How can I say no?"

I don't know how they offer, but I'm not a threesome guy. Don't get me wrong: I love sex, but I don't enjoy threesomes as much as he does.

"You can't," I shrug.

"My point exactly."

The elevator doors open and James holds out his hand, gesturing for me to walk through the doors first. I step onto the same gloss tiles as downstairs, the office style all the same throughout. Level twelve is all my office, so it's a massive open plan, with my desk to the right behind clear glass doors that define the reception area. I love the see-through aspect but it has the option to be frosted for meetings.

James whistles. I tilt my head up and watch as he scans the room. "Check this office out."

I chuckle, "Amazing, isn't it?"

As I enter the office, I walk around my desk, running my hand across the tabletop. Dropping down into the chair and leaning back, I stretch my legs out over the desk, and link my hands behind my head.

A smirk plays on James' lips. "You cocky shit."

My face splits into a smug grin. Pushing myself back up, I lean on the desk as he stands inside, peering around at the furniture. There is a bar to his right, all stocked with the finest liquor—for meetings and clients, of course.

A couch sits near it in case I need—No idea why there is a couch there, to be fucking honest.

The room is stocked with papers, filing cabinets, computers; everything I could need. We will meet all the new staff tomorrow, including my new receptionist. James and I agreed she wasn't allowed to be young, no matter how experienced. The distraction isn't something I need right now when I'm setting myself up.

I lift my chin and take a deep breath as I take in the last moments of peace. The next time I'm in this office, it will be filled with staff.

"Want to grab coffee?" I ask James, who is still wandering around, checking to make sure everything is in order and moving anything that isn't in perfect alignment. I shake my head. *Such a perfectionist.*

He swivels so he is looking at me. He offers a curt nod. "Yeah, good idea, but then I gotta get back to the office."

His office building is next door to this new swanky home of Ward Electrical. His, of course, is larger and intimidating.

Nodding, I say, "Okay. Let's go to the café across the street."

Striding toward the elevators, I follow James out the door. He looks up from his phone. "I have this meeting with a nightmare client tomorrow."

I chuckle at his bored tone. We arrive at the traffic lights, waiting to cross the road.

"Why are they a nightmare?" I ask.

"The list of demands is a joke. Some of the shit they expect from the company is ridiculous. But you know the shit I have to deal with," he breathes.

I laugh. "That I do. But that's why you get paid well."

The light turns green. We are reaching the café James and I have been meeting in regularly. It's trendy and relaxed but still has the city vibe.

I'm passing the pickup order line when a brunette turns unexpectedly and crashes into me, causing her to collide hard with my chest. The hot coffee splashes over the top of her cup and straight onto my shirt.

"Fuck!" I shout from the pain. Glancing down at where the pain is radiating from, I take in the brown liquid now covering my light blue shirt. I pull the shirt off my skin. But the burn is still there.

"Oh shit. I'm so sorry. I didn't see you there," she stammers.

I let go of the shirt, frustrated. "No shit. You should watch where you're going!" I spit, the pain from my chest pissing me off and, on top of that, my shirt is now ruined and it's only ten in the fucking morning. I'm going to look like a mess for the rest of the day. *Fuck*!

I had dressed to present a dominant image to my clients today. Why would they want to offer me work if I can't look professional? I'm seething.

"Excuse me? You could do the same." With a sharp tone, she spits the words right back at me. My gaze shoots up to meet the eyes of the stranger. I blink and my mouth pops open in awe. *Beautiful in the most unique way.*

My breath catches and my hands still on my chest before I slowly slide them down and tuck them into my pockets. My eyes gaze over her body from top to bottom, memorizing every bit. Her hair is brown, but the front pieces are platinum blonde. Her stormy gray eyes stare back at me. She has black eyeliner framing them like a cat, making the gray stand out.

My gaze drops to her lips. *Fuck me.* They are full, pink, and luscious. I just want to feel how soft they are—and drag her lip between my teeth. My dick is getting hard, irritating me further because, on top of the mess I'm wearing for the day, I'll be horny and edgy too. *I need to get laid ASAP!*

I drag my gaze back to her eyes and her eyebrow lifts, waiting for an answer. Shit. I didn't reply to her snarky comment. *Busted.*

"Really," I choke out.

"Yes. You could stand back a little. Give people personal space. Now you owe me a damn coffee." She crosses her arms over her chest.

I pop a brow. Is she kidding? *What a smartass.*

My blood boils. Her smart mouth is really pissing me off. "I don't owe you shit. I'm the one saturated in coffee, darling," I drawl.

Her arms tighten and her jaw ticks. "I'm nobody's darling. Don't insult me," she orders.

My teeth grind together. "I'm not buying you shit," I spit back just as quickly, standing a little taller as I do.

She points at me, poking my chest with her finger. "You're a stuck-up prick. Fuck you."

I swipe her finger away with my hand.

"Thanks for the charming comments," I say as I brush past her. It's a damn shame her shitty attitude sours her beauty.

I spot James in the back corner, at a table by himself, talking on his phone. His head is down;

he's looking at the table. Clearly, he missed what just happened. I march up to his table and overhear the tail end of his conversation.

"I gotta go. I'll talk to you later. Okay. Yep. Bye." His gaze meets mine and I watch as his brows crease and he points at my shirt. "What the fuck happened to you?" He chuckles, irking me further.

I growl back, "Don't you fucking start. Some idiot just spilled her fucking hot coffee on me and then told me it was my fucking fault," I continue, "because I was in her personal space and how I owe her coffee... which, I did no such thing. I was walking past, minding my own damn business, when she walked into me." I blow out my cheeks, frustrated.

James throws his head back and lets out a deep, throaty laugh. "Is she still here?" He looks around me, moving his head to either side to check out the shop. "I will buy her the coffee, just for pissing you off and not just apologizing."

"Asshole," I say with a smile, knowing if she hadn't left the café, he would follow through with that threat.

Chapter 3

Ava

My mouth hangs wide open as I process what just happened. What the fuck was that? *Asshole.* I twist my head to watch him march over to the back corner like a little child throwing a tantrum. He joins a table that is occupied by another slimy, stuck-up suit. Ahhh, men suck. Especially the ones in expensive suits. They think they are entitled, with their family money and coffee-sipping jobs. They wouldn't know hard work if it slapped them in the face. Or what it's like to live paycheck to paycheck and worry you're about to lose the apartment you're renting.

No. They fucking don't have the same life concerns like the rest of us.

My mouth closes and I grind my molars together. Gazing down at my now half-empty latte, I huff. I can't afford to buy another coffee and losing half of it on his shirt is such a waste. Bringing the cup to my mouth, I sip the remaining coffee, which is decent. Even half filled.

Looking around the shop, I spot an empty table and chair near the window at the front.

Needing distance between the jerks and wanting to look out at the street, I walk over and pull out a chair to take a seat. Feeling the annoyance still pumping through me, I tilt my head slightly to peek a side glance in the boys' direction. They are talking and nodding. I sit here, still seething at my loss of coffee. Rolling my eyes, imagining the shit talking they must be exchanging, I drain the cup. Lowering it to the table, I peer out the large window and watch the traffic and pedestrians walk by. After a few minutes, I rise with no other reason to sit here any longer, and besides, I badly want to get away and put distance between myself and the men. Stepping over to the rubbish, I pause for another peek. The powerful men are now laughing and sipping coffees as if nothing serious is going on in the world. Only themselves. Having seen enough, I tear my gaze away, dump my cup in the bin, and exit the café.

I walk outside, where the fresh crisp air hits my skin, helping cool my heated skin. Moving to the side of the sidewalk, I reach inside my bag, digging around to locate my phone.

Ah-ha. There it is. Pulling it out, I search through my emails to locate the address for my new job.

Hopefully, my boss Thomas isn't a stuck-up asshole like that guy, no matter how hot that guy is. Talking of attractiveness, Thomas better not be good eye candy because it will be hard to act professional, working with an attractive man every day. I never had to worry about that with David, my former boss. He wasn't ugly, but he never made me fantasize or want to cross that forbidden line.

Finding the address on my phone, I peer up, realizing that it's the building directly across the road. My head cranes up and I take in the large modern mirrored building. It's not as tall or overbearing as the tower beside it, but it's intimidating, making me shrink.

It will take adjusting to go from a small-town office to a large building. The offices here will be filled with workers. I swallow past the lump that's formed in my throat. I'm pushing myself here by working in an office of this size, but I can't afford to be picky. I need a job.

After looking around, I toss my phone in my bag and hitch it a little higher on my shoulder and begin walking to the train stop. I don't have a car; I'm saving for a condo deposit first. It's important for me to own a condo, to become financially stable and build a future for myself. It will be hard work, but isn't that life? The thought of everything being able to be taken away makes bile reach my mouth. I shiver with old memories entering my mind.

Catching the train back home, I walk inside my apartment, dump my keys on the counter, and flick the kettle on before throwing myself on the couch and tossing a blanket over me. It's a cold winter day and I need to defrost after the walk from the train stop to my building.

I call my friend Gracie while I wait for the kettle to boil. "Hello. How are you?" I ask when she answers my call.

"I'm good. What about you?" she asks.

"Well, I went to the city today. To check out the new job."

"Oh, that's right. So, how is it compared to David's Printing?"

"Other than being in the big city? The building is massive." I pause. "I'm worried about how many people will work there. I hope I can adjust okay." I thrum my fingers on my lips, thinking of this town, my quiet life. I barely go out and when I do, it's usually Gracie's work. I'm an old soul who likes to keep to herself. The thought of the city frightens me, but losing this apartment scares me more. I have had enough loss in my life. I don't want any more.

"I think you need this. To be honest, you're too young to be so isolated."

I know she is right, deep down. But I can't change. I keep busy so I don't have time to think or feel. Wanting to change the topic, I ask, "Anyway, are you coming over before work for me to do your makeup?"

"Duh. Yes, of course I will. Give me some time. I'll order some food and have it delivered to your apartment."

"Okay, I'll see you soon." I hang up. Being without a job, I can't exactly argue about her paying for dinner.

I get my makeup ready on my kitchen counter and have just finished lining up the brushes when a knock comes at the door. I pause to answer it, thinking it's Gracie. But it's the delivery guy with our food. Taking the bag, I carry it inside and begin laying it out as I eat, not wanting to eat a cold dinner. Another knock comes and I know it's Gracie this time. I get up and open the door.

"Food's here." I cover my mouth as I finish chewing.

"That's good because I'm starving and I'll need fuel for work." She moves toward my stools, dragging one out and sliding up.

I laugh, "Let's feed you, then I'll do your face." I walk around to the opposite side of the counter, picking my food back up.

I have been friends with Gracie since I was a teenager. She is a little more outgoing than me, but still in some ways is a quieter person, like me. We bonded during the hardest times in our lives.

I shovel more food into my mouth and continue setting out the rest of the makeup.

Gracie takes her bowl. "I don't know why you don't publish all these videos on YouTube. Make some extra money."

Shaking my head at her silly idea, I say, "It's not a job I can make real money from. I need a stable job. A regular and consistent income to afford my condo."

She nods as she stuffs rice in her mouth. I spin around and grab two glasses from the cupboard and the water out of the fridge and pour us some water. I push a full glass to her, then I have a drink to wash down the food. She lifts her glass, sips, then speaks. "Thanks. I know, but even just for fun. You're so talented."

I lower my glass back down and eye her suspiciously. "Of course you would say that; you're my friend. You have to be supportive."

She peeks up from her bowl with a raised eyebrow. I chuckle at her side-eye. "Okay, well, maybe you would be honest. But still. No thanks."

But I'm thinking about how it would be fun to do it as a job, rather than a corporate job. I'm remembering the assholes from earlier today.

"I found the cutest coffee shop today. Across the road from my new building. When I can afford it, I will be there daily, grabbing a latte. The only downfall is the amount of guys in suits," I groan.

Gracie finishes her bowl, chewing her last bite. I hold my hand out. She places the bowl in my hand and I wash it, then let it air dry. She shuffles back in her seat and twists to make it easy for me to apply the makeup. "I love guys in suits. Like a hot guy in a suit, all intelligent and shit. That's so bloody hot."

I wander around the counter and step in front of her, beginning the process of applying the makeup. "Yeah. I will admit a hot guy in a well-fitting suit is something else. But, today I bumped into one with my coffee and it spilled down the front of him. And when his pretty mouth spoke, he turned ugly. The stuck-up attitude was a turnoff...I asked him to buy me a fresh coffee. I sure as hell can't afford another one and he flat-out refused."

My body tightens from the memory of his rudeness. He really got under my skin. But the vision of his stomach is causing hot flushes from my chest to my cheeks. Flashes of the wet coffee stuck to his torso enter my mind, making my body tingle. I shuffle my feet. I can't deny that when his blue shirt clung to his abs, my pulse skipped a beat inside my chest. His body is something I have only had in my dreams. I wonder what those abs would feel like under the pads of my fingers? Or even what they would feel like under my tongue. A new flush floods me from head to toe, my body filled with scorching heat. Of course, the men in suits in this city are all full of themselves and treat women like trophies.

Clearly I need to get laid, if my thoughts are drifting to that asshole and how he would feel inside me. I definitely need to release some frustration. I haven't been with anyone in a long time. I shake my head to try to rid my brain of dirty thoughts.

"So, he didn't buy you one?" she asks. Her eyes are closed; she is enjoying being pampered by me. By the end of this, she will be asleep. It happens every time.

"No, he was blaming me for bumping into him. He was the rudest prick. So I only got half a cup of coffee. And it was a damn good latte. Such a waste."

"The city. It's full of coffee lovers, so the coffee has to be good. I will have to venture out and have a coffee with you on one of your breaks."

My lips perk at the offer. "Yes, that would be awesome! How's the bar?"

Gracie has worked in the same bar in our town for as long as I can remember. She enjoys working there, and being small and full of locals, it's easy.

"Same. Same. Nothing exciting is happening. But the boss lady is nice to me, so I can't complain," she mumbles through her tired state.

I nod and concentrate on her makeup while she rests.

My alarm chimes beside my head. I groan. Throwing the blanket up over my head, I stay under the covers for a little longer. When the second alarm goes, I push back the covers and climb out of bed. Rubbing my eyes with the backs of my hand as I break into a yawn, I stumble my way into the bathroom and turn the tap on. I throw handfuls of cold water on my face, trying to wake myself up.

I moisturize before applying my makeup; I have always enjoyed being creative and different. My style is unique, standing out in the sea of faces. I mix up my hair and makeup as often as I can to fit with how I'm feeling.

Today, for the first day of my new job, I add some waves into my hair before dressing in my skinny tan pants and white shirt. I run my hands through my soft and tousled hair. When I'm happy with the style and the way it's sitting, I head to the train stop. It will take forty-five minutes to get there. While I stand and wait, I plug my headphones in and begin blaring music through my ears.

I catch the train to the same spot I practiced on Friday.

Arriving at the building, I pause to take a deep inhale, trying to calm my trembling body.

You got this!

I roll my shoulders back and look around as I enter and approach the reception desk. A mature woman with dark shoulder-length hair, glasses, and a white shirt is busy typing away on the computer.

I clear my throat when I approach. "Hello. My name is Ava Johnson, and today is my first day working here."

Her head lifts and she offers me a warm smile. My shoulders ease at her gentle tone. It has a calming effect on me.

"Good morning, Ava. It's a pleasure to meet you. I'll find your name in the computer system."

I dip my chin. "Thanks."

Her fingers tap on the keyboard.

"Found you. Level eleven. You're working with Thomas Dunn." She glances back at me.

Smiling, I move away from the counter, glancing around. "Thanks. Err, where are the elevators?"

"Oh, right. Sorry." She gets up, leans across the counter, and points. I follow her finger. "Just down the hall to your right. You can't miss them." She lowers back down to her chair.

"Okay, thanks." I hitch my handbag higher on my shoulder and wander down the hallway. I spot the elevator and quicken my pace. It's a silent workplace, and the elevator is empty too. I walk inside and click the button for the eleventh floor, noting the floors only go to twelve, so I guess they left twelve for the CEO.

Level eleven is only one down. My stomach drops at the realization. *Oh shit.* I'm working for someone pretty important then. Squeezing my eyes shut, I hope he isn't a stuck-up prick. *Please don't be an ass.* The doors slide open when I arrive on level eleven and the most stunning floor comes into view. My eyes bulge as I take it all in.

The same glossy tiles are up here, and there are only two desks on this floor, one behind glass walls and the other in the open. No surprise as to which is mine—I am the assistant, after all. But this is elegant; the desks match. Someone neatly arranged and organized all the stationery on my desk, which makes my heart sing.

Wandering slowly around the room, I take it all in. When I arrive at my desk, I pull open the drawers to look around. There are a few notebooks and files, but it's otherwise empty.

The computer is the top of the range Mac. *This is real money.*

I pat the monitor. I smile. The timber cupboards, which match the desks, catch my eye. I open them to see what lies behind each door. More files, books, and stationery. I am bouncing on my toes in this dream office; let's hope it's a dream job. Once I finish snooping around, I trek back over to the large window and peer outside. The view is spectacular. I watch as people walk around below. When I hear the elevator chime, I push away from the window in time to see a handsome man walk into the office.

A fluttery feeling enters my stomach, but I force a smile. "Hi, I'm Ava. You must be Thomas?"

He dips his chin with a smile to match my own. "Yes, that's me. Lovely to meet you, Ava. Have you just arrived?"

Thomas looks about mid-thirties. Short brown hair and brown eyes. He's wearing a crisp navy suit and white shirt and a matching navy tie. He radiates warmth and affection. Relief floods my body and I begin to really relax.

"Yes, I just had a brief look around. This is spectacular."

"It really is. Joshua did a brilliant job. Maybe we should grab a coffee and get to know each other. We will work closely together. It will be good to get to know each other."

Definitely a brilliant start. Offering to buy me coffee is better than David already.

I smile wider. "That sounds great."

"Let me flick my computer on and check for any urgent emails and then let's go."

"Okay." Watching him walk into his office, I swivel and ponder what I should do. When I look at my desk, I decide to figure out how to turn the Mac on. I lean around to inspect the monitor and find the button, then click on it, but I'm interrupted. I jump at the sound of his voice. "Are you ready?"

My eyes flick up to his face and I nod, figuring I can work it out when we get back. "Yes." I clutch my bag and follow him to the elevator.

"So Ava, tell me about yourself."

I inwardly groan, hating these types of questions, but I guess he is trying to get to know me because we will work closely together. Still, I can't help but hate talking about myself.

"Not much to say, really. I'm twenty-six. Single. No pets. The last job I had was a printing company, and I was there from the time I left school until recently. I'm really grateful to have found this job."

It's surface talk, and it's information I'm willing to share right now.

"Why did you leave?" he asks.

"I only left because it closed down." My voice is strained as I speak through a restricted throat. The nerves are holding me back.

We walk side by side on the ground floor. A few of the office workers are walking down the corridor now, so he speaks more quietly. "Oh, that's sad. Did the nose hurt?"

"Yes, a little." I touch the metal ring through my nose. "It's not an issue, is it?" A sinking feeling washes over me. I didn't think about it with David because I got it after I worked with him for a few years.

Shaking his head vigorously, he says, "No. I don't care as long as you do your job. It's a judgement-free zone here." He lifts his hands in the air in surrender.

I nod but say nothing. It's quiet for a beat before he talks again. "I have two girls. Lily, who is five, and Rose, who's two. And a fun fact about me is I have ink." He gestures to his chest. My mouth falls open at his confession. "No piercings though." His tone is light.

I giggle at his fun nature. He seems warm and easy to talk to.

"Wife?" I ask. Mentioning his kids has me wondering about the type of wife he would have.

He shakes his head. "She passed away."

My stomach drops. *Fucking Hell.* Trust me to stick my foot in it. I close my eyes. "I'm sorry."

"Don't be; it's a valid question." We exit the building and wait at the lights. I swallow hard, feeling awkward.

"Did you organize our desks?" I ask, hoping he is neat.

He chokes out a laugh. "No. I wish I could take the credit, but it was Josh and James. They set this building up. I'm so proud of Josh."

"So you're messy?" I ask as we walk down the sidewalk.

"No way, but I'm not obsessive, if that's what you're asking." He turns to look down at me.

"Oh, good. You had me worried for a second. I'm obsessive enough that I don't know how it would work with two neat freaks working together."

He reaches for the door handle to the café, opening it and offering his warm, open smile as I walk past him. Stepping inside the shop, the vision of Friday enters my mind—the coffee incident. I shake my head vigorously, trying to clear my head, and focus on reading the menu.

Thomas comes up to stand beside me. "What would you like?" he asks, breaking through my lost thoughts.

I turn my head to look up at him. "Are you sure?"

"Yes. I'm the boss and part of that is to look after you."

My heart swells. He is such a friendly boss. I'm already loving my first day. It can't get any better.

"A latte," I answer through a smile.

He dips his chin, proceeding forward to join the line. I stay where I am while he orders and pays, then returns to stand beside me again as we wait for the order to be called.

"Thanks for paying. You really didn't have to do that," I mumble.

"I don't mind. Really."

I nod, not wanting to explain to him my personal struggles on day one. It's not airing your dirty laundry day.

Our order gets called out. We step forward and take our cups and wander back to the office. He talks about his girls, and hearing the stories has me smiling wistfully. We enter the building and he gets stuck chatting with another employee. Rather than stand around awkwardly, I gesture upstairs; he nods in approval and I step away, walking to the elevators and riding back up to our office, sipping my delicious coffee.

My first agenda is to learn how to use the computer. When the elevator opens, I wander to my desk, take a big sip of the nutty coffee, and place it down next to the notepads. Opening the bottom drawer, I put my bag inside and close it, then search around for a damn manual for the computer. *Ah-ha. Got it.* Opening the ridiculously small manual, I begin reading the instructions. I'm absorbed in reading when I hear a deep male voice exit the elevator. My back tingles with familiarity. My gaze lifts and widens at the sight. *Fuck off.*

I sit back in my chair, raising my eyebrow. *No way.*

"I gotta go," he mumbles into the phone to whomever it was and doesn't bother waiting for a response before hanging up. I roll my eyes.

Jerk.

"What are you doing here?" His eyes bore into mine, anger rolling off him. I cross my arms over my chest, popping it out confidently.

"I work here." A smug grin twists on my lips. And I swear I see steam leave his ears.

CHAPTER 4

JOSHUA

WHAT. THE. ACTUAL. FUCK.

She rolls her fucking eyes at me. God, this woman gets under my skin.

"I didn't hire you," I spit.

She chuckles at me. Which makes me grind my teeth.

"Clearly," she mocks.

Dropping her gaze back to the desk, she returns to reading the papers in front of her. Dismissing me.

This woman is infuriating. Doesn't she know who I am? The motherfucking CEO.

She is the rudest person I have ever met, with no respect for me or her fucking job. I'm vibrating with anger.

I step closer, glaring down my nose at her, looking at the metal ring protruding through her nose. When she just spoke to me, I saw a flash of silver metal on her tongue. Doesn't she realize that it's not appropriate for this workplace? I'm trying to turn my dad's shitty failing company into an empire.

I could kill James for hiring her. She is the opposite of what I wanted here. This is my fresh start to prove to myself that I'm not worthless. I want to make a good impression, not to look like teenagers run the fucking place.

Fuck my life. What a mess.

People will assume I'm the same irresponsible party boy I used to be. Not the man I am today. Since I took over, I don't go anywhere near parties, late nights, or the antics I used to. I have cleaned my act up.

The elevator opens and I turn my head to watch Thomas stroll across the floor. An easy smile plays on his lips.

I'm still boiling hot; the anger is still blazing under my skin. "Thomas, I need to talk to you," I spit through clenched teeth.

His eyebrows furrow, clearly trying to understand why I'm pissed. But I refuse to say anything in front of *her.*

He wanders past me to his office. "Yeah, come." His head tilts toward his office.

No way. Not happening here. She cannot be within earshot. She will try to listen for sure.

"In my office," I say curtly before I storm off toward the elevator, not waiting for his answer. I need to put distance between us and return to my space where I can calm down. *She's a fucking bitch.*

Inside the elevator, I push the button for level twelve and lean back against the wall, eyes closed, jaw thrust upward. I'm taking slow, deep breaths, trying to calm my racing heart.

My temper calms as more distance grows between her and me. The doors open and I march over to the large window in my office, leaning my hands on the window ledge and gazing out at the world passing by. Watching people go about their day, I wonder what they are thinking about. Where they are going. Trying to take my mind away from what just happened. I spot a family in the park's corner, playing together. The mother is smiling and watching as her husband plays ball with their two boys. A weight in my chest hits me but I can't tear my gaze away.

A throat clearing behind me is the only thing breaking my stare. I whip my head around to see Thomas standing behind me. He has stuffed his hands inside his pockets and a frown is on his face.

"What was that about?" he asks.

I return to people watching outside for one last glance before I push off the ledge, spinning around to face him. "I don't understand how she works here. I didn't hire her." It's not really meant to come out so bluntly, but it's how it comes out. Touching the base of my neck, I give it a squeeze. *Fuck me. A drink is tempting right now.*

He looks at me with a blank look. "You would have had to have. How else did she get the position?"

I'm opening my mouth to speak, but he cuts me off to finish, "And what's wrong with Ava?"

My lips twitch at her name. It's different, like her.

And how can he not see what's wrong with her?

"I didn't. Fuck... James... Fuck... He hired her." Rubbing my face with my palms, I move away from the window and begin walking over to my desk. I bend over, letting my head fall forward, and clutch the sides of the desk with my hands.

Fuck you, James. Seriously. Fuck you.

Thomas blows out a breath. "I'm so confused right now. What is going on?"

I lift my head and then stand up. My eyes bore into Thomas'. His brows squish together and he crosses his arms over his chest as he waits for me.

"James helped hire," I sneer.

He offers a small nod. "Ah, okay. I get why you didn't know about her then. But I don't get why you're so angry?"

Cursing under my breath, I say, "I ran into her at the café and she spilled her coffee all down the front of me. Her attitude toward me was disgusting. She doesn't represent my company at all."

Thomas lifts a hand out in a *stop* gesture. "That's totally unfair. You're judging her on an accident. Ava seems sweet."

He puts his hand back over his chest.

What? Sweet... How?

"What's that mean?" I ask, my upper lip curling back.

"She seems really nice, and the poor girl just lost her job. Give her a break. Let her prove herself."

Surely we can't be talking about the same girl.

"You cannot be serious," I growl.

"Deadly. You aren't replacing her; don't you dare think about it," he huffs, waving a finger at me. Why is he standing up for her? I really don't fucking get it.

Pushing the thoughts aside, I say, "I will if I have to. I'm watching her."

If he thinks I am joking, he is kidding himself. I'm working too damn hard to build this business up and make something of myself—and in the process, stick it to my dad. How dare he hand me a sinking ship? What kind of sick parent does that? Why am I so surprised?

Dragging a hand through his hair, he says, "Now that you have finished your little tantrum, are you ready to do some work today?" He teases as if I am one of his girls.

Taking a cleansing breath, I nod, trying to not take it out on one of my best friends. "Sure. Let's talk."

I drag out the chair and take a seat. "What projects are you working on that we should discuss?" I ask, flicking my gaze from Thomas and then back to the monitor.

"I want to pick your brain on Park Lane. That's the project I want to focus on today. I have a meeting with the builder later today." He leans forward in his chair.

I dip my chin and click my mouse, bringing up the client's file. I whistle and say, "Look at the profit margin for us." My gaze meets his as our smiles form in unison. There is pride in his eyes. "Great job. We needed this for our startup. Plus, I gotta pay James back for what I borrowed."

"Yeah, I get that. I'm glad you're happy. I'm completing the contract, but I will get them to sign it today if they agree. Lock them in while we can." A knowing grin is on his face.

"Yes, exactly. Love your work, man. You are killing it already," I say with a gleam in my eye.

To work with your friends is always a risk. But Thomas isn't a party boy or lazy. He is a single dad of two young girls, focused on working hard and providing for his family. I knew the fresh start was what he needed after his wife died. He is a brilliant father, and he has stepped up in the role of both mother and father. I'm glad I could convince him to take my offer. I won't let him down. I'm going to turn this doomed business around. I have the best support, so failure isn't an option.

"Thanks, Josh. I'm really enjoying myself here. You have started something truly special here. Entrepreneur life is totally suiting you. I'm proud of you."

I smooth my shirt down, feeling my heartbeat racing at that word. *Proud.*

It feels strange to hear. I haven't heard it used about me before. Clearing my throat, I say, "Thanks, bud. Now get back to work and stop sucking up to the boss." I laugh a little too loudly.

I watch as he rises, a satisfied smile on his face. "I do need to prepare for Park Lane."

"Good idea." My phone chimes in my pocket. Reaching for it, I pause as I stare at the screen. Reading the word *Dad* stills me. I stare at it, unmoving.

What the fuck does he want?

"You all good, Josh? You're pale. It's like you have seen a ghost."

"Hmm?" I glance up and offer a tilt of my lips and a nod. He turns and I watch him step out of my office. The phone is still ringing in my hand, reminding me of what caused me to freeze. I return my gaze to the phone. It goes to my message bank. He won't leave a message; he never does.

I clench the phone tightly, holding my breath. I hate the power he has over me. I don't want him messing with my head anymore. But he knows how, even by not talking to me verbally. Just knowing he called rattles the fuck out of me. A message—*Dad missed call, but no message left*—pisses me off, snapping me out of my funk.

Why call then, dickhead? Leave me alone.

Leave me alone. I toss my phone on the desk and pinch the bridge of my nose and push out slow, deep breaths to calm down.

When I'm feeling less edgy, I prop myself back up tall and return to my monitor.

After a few hours of work, I'm still tense. Needing both the tension eased and a pleasant distraction, I decide to text one of my regular hookups, Candice.

Candice and I see each other when I need relief. We both know it's casual, with no strings attached. There are definitely no feelings and she knows we are not in a relationship. It's purely for sex. We meet at a hotel, hook up, and leave separately. There is no sleeping, cuddling, or kissing.

My phone beeps a reply. She agrees to meet at the usual time and place. At least going to sleep will be a little easier tonight. I put my phone away and return to my work.

Ava

The following week, Thomas is on the phone. My hands are still on the keyboard, not wanting to make a sound. My ears prick up, trying to listen in.

"Josh, I got them to sign the contract." A few mumbles.

I can imagine Joshua is smiling. You can hear the pride in Thomas' voice. My own lips twitch into a smile. Thomas deserves the recognition.

"Yeah, I will. We have a meeting tomorrow morning so we can discuss what we need and run through details. I want to get home tonight," he responds.

There is an enormous gap, so Joshua must be talking. I wish I knew what he was saying. I don't know why I'm listening. I shake myself and start typing out some notes and tables for labor/workers, timeline, schedules, equipment. This job has been a surprise. I didn't think I would love it as much as I do. Helping Thomas above the usual reception duties gives me a challenge I crave. I'm hungry to learn more about sketching and the math of drawing up plans. I would love to offer help in the design process. So I try to learn everything offered to me. Thomas can see I am eager to learn, so he allows me to assist with every aspect of the job he can so far.

This new project is a huge win. It's an enormous job in the city.

"You need to settle down with one person. I don't understand the no strings attached," I hear Thomas rebut, moving around the office, opening and closing drawers. Packing up.

No strings attached.

He chuckles. "I'm fine. Well, have a good night."

A pause.

"Okay. Bye."

He hangs up and I return to my desk chair. I don't want Thomas to have any reason to fire me. And eavesdropping isn't a great look, knowing Joshua already wants me gone.

But just like I thought, Joshua is an egotistical player, a full of himself playboy, running around having sex with anyone with a pulse. Gross.

I hear Thomas's chair dragging across the tiles and he picks up his keys. His shoes click against the tiles. I gaze up into his eyes and smile. "You off now, boss?"

"Yes, and so should you." He moves past me, waving and walking toward the elevator.

"I am. See you tomorrow," I call out. I'm not in a hurry to get home. There isn't anyone waiting for me. I spend the next few minutes printing the schedule for tomorrow, then lay it perfectly straight down on my desk, marking and highlighting the important details. I power down the computer and collect my bag out of the desk drawer and walk to the elevator, checking my phone. No missed calls or texts so I stuff it back inside my bag and ride the elevator down.

When I step out of the building, my mind and body are tired from the day. I'm excited by the prospect of going home and relaxing on the couch. I think about what I can cook for dinner. Needing something fast without buying takeout, I decide on pasta.

I see it has been raining; the roads are wet. Moving to the sidewalk to stand and check the train time, I glance around and freeze when I spot a white sporty car pulling out of the parking lot. The license plate reads WARD.

My blood pressure rises at the sight. That rich motherfucker. Would he know what it's like to catch a train? I bet he doesn't. Spoiled little rich fucker.

I'm back to seething about him.

I stand on the side and watch as he takes off, his wheels spinning muddy water all over me. Splashing into my face, hair, eyes, and all over my green top and skinny black dress pants. I rub my eyes with my hand, trying to remove the disgusting water from my eyes. Blinking my eyes open, I try to see where he took off to, but it's too late.

He drives off, reeking of money while I reek of trash from the dirty water his stupid car flicked up all over me. I hope his dick doesn't work tonight. I pray he can't get it up and it flops. My mouth twists in a sick, twisted grin at the vision.

Running my hand through my hair, grimacing at what I must look like, I walk with cold, stinky clothes to the train station. The clinging, wet clothes make me shiver down to my bones. It's fucking freezing. When I step onto the train, a passenger's eyes rake over my appearance, making me flinch. I hate Joshua even more at this moment.

Arriving home, I run upstairs and storm through my apartment, banging every door and cupboard possible. I'm mad that I had to take the long ride home on a train like a drowned rat. I turn the faucet on in the bath. I need to soak in a warm bath and defrost my frozen state. I'm still so wound up, I could snap.

Picking up my phone to call Gracie, I clutch it between my face and shoulder while I pour myself a big glass of wine. I try not to drink during the week, sticking to only weekends or occasions. But after today, I feel like it's an emergency. My hands tremble as I pour, causing the liquid to spill out of the glass.

I take a big gulp as I hear the ringing in my ear. *Please pick up.*

"Hello, miss. Did you just get in from work?" Her voice comes down the line, making me instantly feel better already.

I lower the glass and say, "Yeah. I just walked in now. I'm running a bath but I need to vent."

A giggle slips out of her mouth. "How come? Tell me."

"So, I'm currently standing in my kitchen, covered in wet, dirty water. I look like a drowned rat." I scrunch my face when I look down at the state of my nice clothes.

"Ew, why? Did you fall over?" I can imagine her face scrunching up in horror.

I draw a breath and release it before I speak. "No, nothing like that. I was leaving work when Mr. Fancy Pants, a.k.a. big boss, drove out in his expensive car and splashed water over me."

She gasps, "Not on purpose, I hope."

"No, definitely not. He is a dick, but not in that sense. I'm just so mad. I guess I should be lucky he isn't my direct boss. I couldn't stand working under that rich playboy."

"Ugh. He sounds like a nightmare. So your boss is still good then?"

Thinking about Thomas, I smile. "He is great, so kind. I'm lucky to have found another easy-going boss."

"Is he single?"

I giggle at her interest. "No; I've heard him on the phone with his girlfriend. But even if he was, he isn't my type at all."

He is definitely too sweet for me.

"You don't have a type," she laughs.

I scoff, "Untrue. And, hey. You are worse than me."

"I don't have a type. I just want a guy to wine and dine me. You are the one claiming you have a type," she teases.

"I do. I prefer a rougher man with tattoos." Just thinking about it has me flooded with warmth. I swipe the glass off the counter and take a good sip. Talking about my type is turning me on.

I touch my lips as I try to think of the last time I had sex. The fact that I can't remember tells me it's been way too long. Clearly my body is letting me know I need to let off some pent-up sexual tension.

"Good luck finding that. That's very specific."

"I know. But I can still dream..." I moan.

"Okay, I gotta run. Mom's calling out for dinner."

My shoulders slump and I wish I weren't about to eat dinner alone. Some days, the past is harder than others.

"Shit. Yes, I have to run. The bath is running," I say in a monotone.

Grace laughs in my ear, "It's probably overflowing by now."

"I hope bloody not. I will talk to you soon. I gotta run." Not waiting for her to say bye, I hang up the phone and make a dash to the bathroom, rushing to the faucet. I turn it off. Relief floods my body. It isn't overflowing. But only just.

I lean over and release some water. I grab some candles from the kitchen and light them, putting them into the bathroom. Then I top my glass of wine up and carry my glass and phone back to the bathroom. The cedarwood and leather from the candles hits, relaxing me. Flicking on my music to play through my phone, I lower my glass beside the tub after taking a big gulp, and then strip. I sink down into the bath. *Ahhh, this is amazing.*

I close my eyes and lie down and lower my head back. My breathing slows down to deep, even breaths. I let myself relax after the day I had. The warm water relaxes my sore muscles. Lying here, listening to the soft, relaxing music, I allow myself to not think, to just enjoy some me time. I grab the body wash and begin washing myself. As I wash my breasts with soft strokes, my nipples harden around their piercings. The desire from earlier returns and my body is still full of sexual tension. To help me relax tonight, I chase the release.

My head tilts back, eyes closed and lips parting. My hands glide over my body, slowly and for the intent of pleasure.

I squeeze both breasts in each hand and rub my thumb across a nipple. It sends a shudder through my body. I move one hand across my stomach while the other stays on my breasts, tugging gently on my nipple. Asking for more pleasure. My legs feel weak and part. My knees hit the sides of the tub. My hand, which had been gliding over my stomach in the warm water, finds my clit and begins to rub in hard circles. When I'm needing more friction, I glide it farther down and find my hot entrance. The water doesn't help keep me wet, but the pleasure is too much to get out of the bath right now. So my hand playing with my breast drops to my clit to continue the hard rubbing and the other hand inserts a finger and my mouth drops all the way open as I move my hand roughly in and out. The slight biting pain from the water intensifies the pleasure and keeps my hips pumping. I add a second finger and the stretch intensifies. Fuck, I'm close.

My breathing increases and I pump my fingers harder, wishing I had that tattooed, toned, sexy-as-fuck guy helping get me off. I vision him taking me there and that's all it takes and I'm moaning loudly and coming hard on my fingers.

I remove my fingers and clutch the bath, my chest rising and falling as I recover from the climax. I clean myself up and get out of the bath.

I blow out the candles and take the glass to the kitchen, pouring it down the sink. Bringing myself to pleasure took the tension away; I no longer need the wine. I feel calm and sedated, ready for bed. I skip dinner and grab some much-needed sleep.

Waking up with determination and an extra spring in my step, I put on a cream-colored tight power suit. It's a high-neck, all in one piece. It hugs my body in the best way and has matching high heels. My hair is in a tight, sleek bun and my bronzed makeup applied perfectly this morning. I'm feeling sexy and fierce, ready to take on that fucker.

I roll my shoulders back as I ride the elevator to twelve instead of eleven. I know he gets here early. I have heard Thomas mention it before. Which is good because I want a discussion without an audience.

His assistant, Linda, won't start until I do, which is nine. But I'm here early. I wanted to get a seat on the train. I would have hated standing the whole forty-five minutes. I'm here to intimidate and confront Mr. CEO Joshua Ward.

As I strut across the tiles, my cream high heels click. His head, which is buried in his laptop, lifts at the sound. A flash of surprise flickers across his face before a frown settles. He's assessing and trying to understand why I'm here. I can see the wheels turning in his head.

I tilt my chin up a little further and plaster on a fake cheesy smile, moving to stand directly opposite his desk.

"Good morning," I drawl in a sickly sweet voice.

He grumbles and eases back into his office chair, eyeing me suspiciously. His gaze doesn't move from my face.

My eyebrow raises, waiting for his proper good morning. I clear my throat.

His eyes narrow. "Morning, Ava. How can I help you?" he says in a sharp tone. He's not enjoying my unannounced visit.

"You know that fancy sports car you drive?"

His pinched expression tells me he is trying to understand where I'm going with this conversation. He leans to one side of his chair and props one hand under his chin. Holding his head up, he glares at me.

"Mmmm."

Not an answer, but I don't have it in me to argue about that. He is acting like a child.

"Well, yesterday when you drove out of the parking lot, you splashed dirty water over my expensive clothes."

He doesn't need to know how much they cost; he just needs to pay for the damage. Own his shit, and stop acting all rude and important.

"I didn't see you," he snaps.

"I was standing on the sidewalk." I cross my arms over my chest, refusing to back down. "You need to pay for the dry cleaning."

"You aren't serious? How do I know you aren't making this shit up? You expect me to take your word?"

"Yes. I'm not lying. I don't lie. Check your cameras." I fling my arms up to the corners of the room, where the cameras cover every aspect of the building.

"I will. If you're right, I will give you the money." He speaks the last part through gritted teeth.

I nod curtly, not wanting to waste any more breath on the bastard; I spin on my heels and exit his office. Feeling his eyes on my back, I pause and peek over my shoulder, catching him perving on my ass before his gaze flies back to meet mine. His cheeks flush pink at being caught red-handed, checking me out. At this moment, I'm happy with my outfit choice. I want to high five myself.

"Second thought. I'll bring the clothes tomorrow and you can have them dry cleaned."

I bite the inside of my cheek to prevent a laugh from escaping and I saunter to the elevator without waiting for his answer. The elevator opens and I break out into an enormous grin. I walk into my office to begin the day.

Stepping onto my floor with the biggest shit-eating grin, feeling impressed with myself, I walk toward my desk.

"Wow. Ava, you look beautiful." I blush at Thomas, who is walking through the door.

"Thanks, boss." I take my seat. As he pauses next to me, he eyes me, his hand leaning on my desk.

He lifts his chin and asks, "How come you are dressed up? Am I missing something?"

A flush begins on my chest and hits my cheeks. I'm suddenly feeling a tad silly for being overdressed but I remember the way I felt not a moment before: the look on Joshua's face and how he wasn't able to talk back like his usual self.

I'm feeling tongue-tied, so even if I wanted to tell Thomas about his friend, I can't. It seems petty and stupid. But Joshua's reaction was priceless.

"I'm meeting someone for drinks after work." I look down at my desk before returning to meet his kind brown eyes.

"Oh nice. Is it a boyfriend?" he asks genuinely.

Shit! He thinks I'm actually meeting a guy. *Fucking hell.*

I don't lie, but it slipped this time. I'm meeting absolutely no one. I want to confess, but I don't.

"No chance. Just drinks." I sound convincing even to myself.

"Well, we better not stay late today. What's on this morning's agenda after emails?"

Opening our online planner, I take a quick glance. "Meeting for Park Lane in the boardroom," I read and then glance up.

He pushes off my desk. "Okay, let me get started and return some emails and phone calls. Can you let me know when it's time to go?"

"Sure, boss." I turn my head back to the screen and the next hour passes quickly.

"Boss, are you ready?" I call out when it's time.

"Yep, let's go."

I pick up the notes, contracts, and plan for the designs. Thomas waits beside me, palm open, to take some folders. I pass him the ones he will need, then I straighten, knowing I'm about to see *him.*

Thomas walks to the elevators and I follow closely behind. We arrive at the meeting room and my nerves pick up. I pinch my lips together as I pass his office, remembering how I felt this morning: powerful and sexy.

I take a deep breath and pop my chest out as we enter the room. Every floor has similar tones and furniture. This room has a large white glossy table with many gray office chairs, which are mostly occupied with staff and their assistants. I have met no others on a personal level. I speak on the phone or say hi in passing, but no friendships have formed. My life comprises of coming to work and going home.

A large television is mounted on the wall, a picture of Park Lane displayed on the screen.

When Thomas moves to the side to greet his coworkers, I offer a small *hi* and a wave.

I feel the energy shift in the room and I move at the sound of his deep voice in conversation. My gaze locks on Joshua's. I suck in a breath. I'm not expecting him to be glaring at me. I match his glare with my own, not folding under his intense stare. His jaw ticks and he tears his gaze away.

Good.

I focus back on my job. A few more people enter the boardroom, so I offer more hellos. And when everyone is inside, *he* clears his throat. It's rough, causing a tingle down my spine at the sound.

Stop it, you traitorous body.

Snapping out of it, I step toward a chair and pull it out, taking a seat and strategically laying out all the folders, papers, and pens. I'm ready for the meeting.

Sitting here, I feel a part of a team. A real team. Next to Thomas, the kindest of bosses, who is helping me learn. It's a shame his friend, a.k.a. Mr. CEO, is a dick. I can't deny he saved an impressive company. And I enjoy working here and am super glad to not work under him.

For five minutes, there is chatter and rustling while people take their seats. *He* takes his position at the head of the table and the noise instantly ceases. Everyone is seated and focused on what he will say next. You can see their awe of him.

I can't deny he oozes sex and power. Sitting opposite him across the table, I can take a good long look. His charcoal suit is perfectly cut to fit his body. I bet it's expensive. It reeks of designer. It would probably pay for a few months' rent. His freshly shaved, chiseled jawline complements his tousled brown hair. But the thing that makes my heart skip a beat is his piercing blue eyes. They can tell a story.

He's an asshole, remember.

Doesn't mean I'm blind. He is sexy and I can't deny it. I just hate his personality; he is entitled.

"Good morning, everyone. So today's meeting is focused on the recent job we won, Park Lane."

His voice cuts through my daydream.

"To get started, let's get Thomas to talk about the builder details first." He gestures toward Thomas, who pushes back his chair and stands. He greets the room. I look up at him and give him a huge smile, showing my teeth.

"Good morning, everyone. Park Lane is an apartment complex...but it involves the entire street." The room gasps. One building is a lot of work, let alone a whole street. This was a big job to win over the competition, as it's a rare situation to have offered in construction.

"We need to split the workers to each side of the road because they will build them one at a time, but both sides are going at the same time," he says.

As he continues talking, I quietly rise from my chair and step over to set the television up, knowing I'm close to *him*. I can feel his eyes on me. I don't know if he is staring or checking me out, but I smirk.

This is fun. Torturing him is fun.

I'm definitely going to need to keep choosing outfits like this. I feel on top of the world right now.

I turn on our presentation, which immediately displays images of the new buildings. We want to present a clear picture of what it will look like, so we show the designs in full to get accurate feedback for our work and then to discuss the budget.

As soon as Thomas ends his speech, I return to my chair. Everyone is clapping as I take my seat.

Thomas leans in to me. "Thanks for that video. It was better than I imagined. You have some creative skills. We are going to have to give you more creative aspects of the job. You are clearly more than capable."

A satisfied smile erupts on my face. "It was my pleasure. I love being creative. And you know I would love to try anything."

He dips his chin and then answers a question that someone has asked.

The meeting continues on to discuss workers and the budget. I take notes and keep order so we can make sure we stay on track and implement any new ideas that are suggested at the meeting.

When I get back, I'll add the notes to the computer so we can both see the folder.

Joshua stands and wraps up the meeting and explains we have another meeting next week to discuss the next stage.

"Great job today, Ava."

I beam back at Thomas. "Thanks, boss."

Stacking the papers on top of each other, I scoop up the contents on the table, then turn.

"Great presentation, Thomas. You are killing it. This role was meant for you." The hairs on my body stand from *him* being so close.

My body goes rigid.

Wasn't just Thomas, dickhead.

"Thanks. But I can't take all the credit. Ava here made that awesome video."

My face flushes hot with the compliment. Joshua's eyes meet mine. His teeth clench and then he grunts, "Great job."

I hold back a laugh. He didn't expect it to be me who did it and he hates the fact he has to compliment me.

I'm full of surprises.

Feeling a sense of victory, I shuffle the stack of files and lift my chin to face the boys. Joshua is standing beside Thomas, talking, his hands stuffed inside his pockets. Flicking my gaze between them, I interrupt. "I'll head back to the office to get started."

Both of them stop talking and their gazes and attention focus on me.

"Okay. Meet you there," Thomas answers. I focus on Joshua, but he says nothing. Swiveling, I saunter out, swinging my hips a little harder, knowing Joshua checked my ass out earlier and in case he is again now. I'm going to have to put more effort into my walk. I don't know why that makes me happy or why the fuck I care, but I do. I feel a little confident as I walk my ass back to my office.

CHAPTER 5

AVA

A WEEK LATER, I check the time and frown. I have been working away, answering emails and forwarding Thomas the ones he needs to deal with.

Where is Thomas? It's after nine a.m. He isn't here, and I haven't heard from him. The office is quiet with just me in this gigantic space. I prefer having him here, making noise. To fill in some time, I set off to grab a cup of tea from the break room. Carrying the steaming herbal tea back to my desk, I falter.

Joshua.

He is standing with his broad back to me. I feel my pulse quicken inside my chest. I push my chest out and strut in, clenching the cup.

"What do I owe the pleasure?" I drawl in a mocking tone. Before he can answer, I speak again. "That's right; you're here to grab my clothes for dry cleaning. I brought them here for you. I was going to visit your office to drop them off."

He scowls. "No. I'm not here about that."

I have to bite back a grin. I know damn well he isn't here for that. He won't waste his time standing in my office to give me an apology, even if I deserve one. My body vibrates when I brush past him. His wide stance takes up too much room.

"Well, I'm assuming you watched the cameras and saw I wasn't lying."

I know how much I'm being a smartass right now, and how I love riling him up. It's becoming my new hobby.

His jaw ticks and I patiently wait for his answer. Rounding my desk, I set my cup down on the desk next to my monitor. He is standing stiff as a board. I ease back, refusing to sit down until he is out of the office.

"No. You weren't lying," he says through gritted teeth.

I smirk, satisfied I'm making him suffer.

"So, you will take the clothes. And have them dry cleaned and returned." I'm not giving him an option.

I lean down to the bag I brought in with me today and thrust it out in front of me. He is staring daggers at me and I'm holding back a laugh. Instead, I have a smart-ass grin on my face. Fuck him.

He snatches the bag from my hand and I have to bite down hard on my cheek to stop myself from laughing. So dramatic. It's comical.

"Fine," he spits. "I'm not here about this. I'm here to let you know one of Tom's girls is sick. So he needs to take some time off."

I let go of my cheek and gasp, at the thought of something bad having happened.

"Is everything okay? What happened?"

He shakes his head vigorously. "You know I can't tell you. I will tell you that everything is okay. But it's not for me to say. It's personal information."

What?

He can't be serious, putting his CEO hat on when he feels like it. It grinds my gears.

"Come on, Josh. Don't be like that," I beg. I'm trying to be nicer, so he will tell me. But looking at his face, he looks more pissed off. I throw myself down into the chair. My stomach is churning.

What has happened to one of the girls?

"We are not friends; we are colleagues. It's Joshua," he demands.

Internally, I roll my eyes at him. And, taking a big sip of my warm tea, I try to calm myself down, but I'm feeling myself becoming angrier every second.

"Okay…Joshua. What am I supposed to do?" I peer up at him. He seems so tall as I sit down.

He lets out a frustrated breath, glancing down at the floor, then back at my face.

"I will need to fill his place," he grunts.

My mouth pops open. "Oh."

I'll be working with *him*. Every day.

Fuck my life.

"Yeah, oh. You will need to run me through the plans for the week so I know what's going on and can plan my week accordingly," he explains.

"Oh, okay." My breathing increases and my palms sweat at the thought of giving a rundown of everything Thomas and I have organized. I hate this. Chaos. Everything is out of order.

People are sick. I need everything back to how it was.

I try to get my brain to work, but it seems to be blank. Why can't I think right now? I reach out and take another sip of tea.

You can do this. This is time to prove yourself. Your time to shine.

Clearing my throat, I peer back up. Joshua is unmoving, watching me with intense scrutiny.

Shaking my head, trying to clear it, I return to my computer and pull up the information I want. "Okay. Here is the folder with everything about Park Lane. I can send it to you but I will run you down the brief points and set up... If you would like?" I ask.

"Please." He offers a curt nod before moving around to my side of the desk and standing next to me. Then I begin.

"These are the daily tasks." I move my mouse around to use it as a guide as I talk. "This is workers: their names, qualifications, and emergency contacts. This one is a budget: weekly, monthly, and then an overall broken-down budget table.

"Here's the timeline, so we stay on track and keep note if we are behind. This folder is meeting minutes, and we share an online calendar. Thomas and I can both enter details and see this." He leans in closer to the monitor, peering over my shoulder. The invasion of my personal space allows me to inhale his scent.

Fuck.

And fuck if it isn't my favorite smell ever. A smell that brings me pleasure. And the other night, the aroma that surrounded me as I brought myself to orgasm. A shudder runs up my spine.

His cedarwood is mixed with something else. I take a deeper inhale, and as my nostrils flare, I remember. It's cardamom. And god, it's damn delicious. I'm going to need this in a candle. Mental note: Buy cedarwood and cardamom candles this weekend.

"Ava?"

Oh shit. He has been speaking to me, but I haven't been listening. I have been too busy sniffing him. *Concentrate, Ava. Mind out of the fucking gutter.*

Slapping myself back to reality, out of dreaming, I open up a few planners I had organized. Specifically, this week's.

"Sorry. Here is today's plan, and I also have this week's," I mumble.

He's still close to me and I feel like I need space. I wish he would put some distance between us. He must read my mind because he steps back and begins walking off.

"Okay, can you email it all? I will read over everything. And then I will call you. I'll get you to come up and we will figure out today's plan. If you don't mind responding to as many emails as you can, and any you can't, forward them to my email and I will take care of them?"

I suck in air that isn't filled with his scent and then answer, "Sure thing."

He offers nothing back, just turns and exits the office, and I glare at his back. My gaze doesn't leave his frame. I watch him enter the elevator. And when he is out of sight, I pick up my tea, drinking it until it's finished before getting started on the emails.

My desk phone rings. "Hello. Ava speaking."

"Ava. It's Joshua. Can you meet me in my office now?" his deep voice says in my ear.

I peek at my work as I speak. "Okay, I will just pack up. I will see you soon."

He hangs up and I hold the receiver out. Hang up tune. I am grimacing at the phone as I hang it up.

Rude prick.

I hit send on the email I was working on and put my computer on sleep mode. I pull open the drawer and reapply my lipstick. Happy with my appearance, I head upstairs. As I ride the elevator, I feel a flutter in my stomach.

When the doors open, I see an older woman who must be his assistant, Linda.

It surprises me she isn't young and hot. Instead, she looks to be mid-fifties, with a short blond bob and minimal makeup. As my heels click on the tiles, her head lifts and an enormous smile appears on her face.

"Good morning, love," she says.

I break out into the biggest grin and say, "Morning." I swallow the lump that's in my throat.

"What's your name?"

"Ava. And you?" I pause in front of her desk, my hands clutching a file.

"Linda. Are you here to see Joshua?"

I nod. "Nice to meet you, too. And yes I am."

"Is he expecting you?" Her face is blank of any expression. She's just asking as part of her routine job.

"Yes. I work as Thomas' assistant. He called me to come up," I explain.

She dips her head. "Okay, love. Well, you go right in and we will have to have a break together and get to know each other. Assistants unite." She winks playfully.

My heart swells and a genuine smile breaks out. "That would be lovely. Thank you."

She smiles back. I slowly turn and walk to Joshua's office. He's so engrossed in something on his computer that this time, he doesn't even hear my heels on the tiles.

Straightening up, I knock on the glass. "Knock knock," I sing.

He swivels his head around and gives me a quick peek. "Hi, Ava. Come in." His tone is sharp.

I walk in and he gestures to the empty chair in front of him behind his desk. I sit down, placing the file neatly on my lap. I wiggle to sit up tall in the chair and wait for direction. I have a quick look around. The drink trolley is impressive.

Would he offer me one?

I need one desperately. Being around him makes me edgy. I bring my focus back to him.

His uncertain gaze lands on mine. "I looked through all the notes and I'm impressed by how well organized everything is. Is this your idea?"

I squirm in my chair and grip the file on my lap tighter, feeling my heart pounding a little faster.

Compliments, ah.

"Yes. Ugh... Well, we have a few projects at the same time, and Park Lane being the biggest, with multiple buildings, I figured it was only fitting to have it organized." I slam my lips shut after the ramble.

As I glance around at his messy, disorganized desk, I squeeze my eyes shut and remember it's not my desk and refocus on the plan for today.

He nods his approval. "Okay. So, we need to go through the plans. Then let's go down to the site and check that we are on schedule."

I watch his lips move and mutter, "Okay."

He turns to face the computer, clicking the mouse until he brings up the daily planner. I already have my file open and am ready to take notes. He turns, moving papers and folders, a crease etched in his face. He's clearly looking for a paper pad and a pen.

How does he expect to find anything on his desk?

I hold up mine, bringing his attention up. Relief washes over his face. "Yes, good idea. You take notes."

He then reads them aloud while I write them down. It only takes us a few minutes and then I close the file.

"Now that's done. Why don't we go down to the site and check out the progress?"

"Good idea," I reply. He stands and grabs his wallet and phone. I follow.

"Bye, Linda," I say as I pass her.

"Bye, love. Nice to meet you," she coos.

I smile.

"Linda, I'm just going to Park Lane with Ava. I won't be long. I have my phone but I'll bring you back a coffee."

"That would be lovely. Take your time."

My brows lift at the offering. I'm surprised he can be nice. I mainly get the asshole version. This version is...different.

In the elevator, neither of us speaks, but the electricity vibrating between us is strong. Arriving on the ground floor, we walk out into the foyer and then step outside. I immediately suck in the fresh, crisp air. My nostrils flare, clearing his scent from my nose. He has this sickly intoxicating smell and it's too good to be that close to him. It fucks with my head.

Why couldn't he smell like my dad or some ex-boyfriend that would make bile rise from the back of my throat? Not make me want to jump his bones whenever we aren't fighting.

"Will you be okay to walk the block?"

"My legs aren't missing, so I'm good." I can't help the smartass reply. He brings the spitfire attitude out of me. It flies out before I can slam my mouth shut.

He shakes his head but doesn't bite back. *Shame*. He walks on and I match his step as we walk side by side.

The city is buzzing and with all the people around, I feel my throat constricting and my ears ringing, but I push forward, knowing it will take time to adjust to city life. Even though I work here, it's still overwhelming. The crowded buildings, the busy streets, the constant noise. It's a vast difference from my last office in my hometown.

He opens a black car door that's parked to the side and waits for me to get inside. My eyebrows draw together. Whose car is this?

"It's my work car. I have a driver so I can work between meetings. James insisted I get one and now I know why. I get a lot more work done in a day."

"That makes sense." I step forward and slide into the back and buckle in. He follows and closes the door.

"Hi, George. Park Lane please."

He has manners. Who would have thought?

"Yes, sir."

I clasp my sweaty hands in my lap. Being in the small space with him is hard; his sexy smell wafts around me and I play with my tongue ring to keep a knowing smirk away. The night in the bath where I self-pleasured to his smell enters my mind and I feel naughty as I sit beside him. I side-eye him and look at his thick, muscled thighs. His hands match mine in a vicelike grip, but his legs are parted. For a second, I imagine how his thick fingers would have felt instead of mine. His hands part and rest on his thighs and I turn my head to my window, looking out and closing my eyes for a second, trying to get a grip on my craving to be touched by him.

Pulling up to the site, we exit the car. Joshua tells George to wait and that we won't be long.

Walking around the site side by side, we talk to a few workers and note any concerns, but after the assessment, we are happy with its progression and return to the car.

"George, back to the office now."

"Yes, sir."

He pulls back into traffic and I keep my gaze out the window, not trusting myself to not check him out. I don't think I have met someone as handsome as him. The warmth my body feels around him is something new. I wonder if he has ever had sex in here. I'm sure his boy George could share a few stories. My jaw clenches at the thought. Why the fuck do I care so much? We arrive at the front of the building and exit the car.

"Let's grab our coffee."

"Sure." I walk beside him, and on our way, we pass a person sitting on the street, a hat on the ground in front of him and a sign for money beside it.

Joshua pulls out his wallet and hands over multiple twenties. My mouth drops open and I blink rapidly. Rubbing my eyes, I think, *It can't be.* The generosity mentally numbs me.

"How are you?" Joshua asks the man, who is wearing jeans and a red checkered shirt. The man's face lights up—at the money, but mainly at Joshua. He seems surprised Joshua is asking him questions. And to be honest, I'm thinking the same way.

Who are you, Joshua?

"Not too bad. Thanks for this; I'm going to go get some food." The man's broken smile shows.

"What's your favorite food? I might tell you the best place to find it," Joshua continues.

"Italian, for sure." The man is clutching the money in his hand. He has a flat gaze as he looks up at Joshua.

"Yes, me too. Love an excellent beer and pizza with the guys. Well, Giuliano's is two blocks, but it's worth it. You're making me want to get some now." Joshua's soft laugh erupts. He is talking to this homeless person like he is a friend he has known for years. I'm standing behind him, watching the exchange, my arms crossed over my stomach tightly, giving myself a warm hug. A lonely tear slides down my face. I quickly swipe it away with the back of my hand.

"You can come," the man offers.

"Unfortunately, I have to get back to the office. But next time, sure."

The guy beams and I can't help but smile too.

"That's okay. Next time, hey."

"Next time." Joshua nods.

Reaching for my wallet, I grab any money I have spare, and drop it in. It's not as much as Joshua, but it's something. I wave and we walk off to the coffee shop. And I'm still lost in what just happened. I'm a walking zombie, not paying attention to where I'm going. I just follow his frame. My brain is replaying what just happened.

When we arrive at the café, he holds open the door for me to pass. "No spilling coffee on me today, please," Joshua jokes.

"Ha! That was your fault. All I did was turn around," I say with a cheeky grin as I enter.

"You took off without looking," he counters.

"I did not. Anyway, I'm not arguing with you because neither of us will back down."

A soft giggle slips my mouth, knowing he is right. Both of us are so headstrong.

We move to the counter and he orders two coffees before turning to me and asking, "What would you like?"

"Ah, a cappuccino. Thanks." The unexpected generosity of him buying me and Linda a coffee causes my heart to swell. I watch as he pays before we take our order and leave.

Waiting at the lights to cross, he gets bumped by a passerby walking the opposite direction. "Are you fucking kidding?" he mutters under his breath. I look over at him and he is dusting his jacket down with his hand, where his coffee spilled.

"I'm sure Daddy will buy you a new one," I joke, elbowing him. His head jerks toward me, his nostrils flaring. I turn away quickly and sip my coffee, trying to understand his sudden attitude change.

The rest of the walk is in awkward silence. As we approach the building, I ask, "Did you want me to go back to my office?"

"Have some lunch and then we can look at what we need to order for the site, later in my office," he answers sharply.

He carries the coffees for Linda and for himself into the elevator. I trail behind, but since I want to hit the break room, I leave the elevator at level ten. "See you soon."

He says nothing, but I wander off not giving a fuck.

Joshua

I'm confused by her. She bosses me around like she is the CEO. The way she can push my buttons and not give a fuck intrigues me, yet irritates me at the same time.

The arguments have been one of my highlights. Her cream jumpsuit last week had me hard. Painfully hard. Like, how old am I? That I get hard over a woman just by what she is wearing, but that jumpsuit did something to me. Her ass especially; I wanted to bite it or spank it. Or both.

If I'm honest, I went home and pulled myself off in the shower. Otherwise I wouldn't have gotten any sleep. She knew by wearing that damn outfit, she was hot as fuck. It left me speechless. Her confidence is sexy. But it's a shame she has such a poor attitude.

Anyway, she isn't my type, so I push it aside, needing to focus on my company. I can't have any distractions, not when I need to prove to my parents I'm worthy and not useless.

Once I'm back behind my desk, I cannot believe what she sent me this morning. It's beyond any organized system I have ever seen. Linda is damn good, but holy shit, this girl is an organized queen. I'm disorganized and messy. But it works.

Her system made it simple to find what I needed and also I found the to do list without sifting through files and folders for an hour.

She really is a surprise. Now it makes sense why Thomas raves about her. I'm still not impressed by her outfits or behavior. But I cannot deny this shit is good.

I email back to the ones she forwarded to me earlier and didn't respond to. It doesn't take long, and it's done. Moving to the plans for tomorrow, I read through them, trying to get on top of the to do list.

My phone vibrates. Opening my phone, I read the text.

James: Are you free to watch the game on Saturday?

Joshua: I'm free. Will be there.

James: Need a lift?

Joshua: No thanks, I'll drive.

James thinks the complete switch from drinking heavily on weekends to only a few beers with friends will end. He offers to drive me every time. But my answer is the same. No.

CHAPTER 6

AVA

RUNNING LATE FOR DINNER at Mom's, I rush off the train and to her door, knocking on it before entering. I'm out of breath, huffing and puffing.

"Mom, it's just me," I call out. The waft of warm, delicious food hits me.

"Come in. I'm just in the kitchen."

Making my way to the kitchen, I dump my bag on the counter, then step over to her. She is stirring a pot of pumpkin soup. Every week when I come over, she cooks one of my favorite dishes. She removes the wooden spoon from the pot and I take the opportunity and kiss her cheek.

"Smells good," I say, pulling away. She strokes my face. I smile at the touch, and heat radiates through my chest.

"It's almost ready. Can I get you a drink?"

"Wine?" I plead.

"Of course. Take a seat; I'll grab us one." I wander to the kitchen stool and take a seat. But getting off work late meant I was standing for fifty-five minutes. Sitting down never felt better. I start to relax.

I lean my forearms on the counter as I watch Mom move effortlessly around the kitchen, pouring two glasses of wine and handing one to me. Sitting up, I take my glass, holding it out. We cheer and I take a good sip. Fruity dry white wine.

"Thanks. That's good."

"How was work?" she asks, swiveling back to check on the soup.

"My boss's child is sick at the moment. So I'm working with the big boss, the CEO. He is so rude and kind of a jerk." I explain the issues with Joshua.

"Oh, that's a shame. Is he like that with everyone?"

I think about that for a second before answering. I haven't seen him engage with anyone other than Thomas and Linda. Who he treated nicely.

"Not that I have seen," I answer honestly.

"At least it's only temporary, if he is filling in. But are you happy there minus him?" She is standing across from me, drinking her wine.

With a nod, I say, "Definitely, even with him. It's amazing. Thomas allows me to learn so much."

"Oh, that's good to hear, darling." She lowers her glass to the counter and steps over to the stove.

"How was your day?"

She fills our bowls with soup and carries them to the dining room. "Come in here; let's eat while it's hot."

I slide off the stool, grabbing our glasses, and walk to the table. The dining room is small and cozy, filled with Mom's small round table. It's older than I am. I hand Mom her wine and take my place, taking a moment to get comfortable.

"I went to the homeless shelter to help with the lunchtime rush," Mom says.

I take my first sip. "Mmm, this is great. Thanks, Mom...I need to come and volunteer. Since I started this new job, I have slacked and I feel bad. How about this weekend? I could come and help?"

Mom is spooning soup into her mouth before offering a kind smile. "Darling, you're allowed to be busy. I'm retired. I have the time to volunteer."

Lowering my gaze back to the soup, I continue to eat. Mom talking about volunteering makes old memories flash back, replaying some of my darkest times. *Sitting in my room, but really it's the attic in their house, my stomach rumbling and I'm shivering from the cold and trying to wrap the single dirty blanket around me tighter. They refused to let me eat their food; I remember being so hungry and wondering if this was all my life would be. I decided after a few months of neglect to pack up and move to the streets. My parents would have been livid if they knew I did this. But living with my aunt and uncle was no longer an option. I didn't have any other family or friends to call. So I packed my stuff into one bag, including the only photo I had of my parents. I wandered the streets until my feet couldn't handle it anymore and I found a park bench to curl up on and try to sleep. I was drifting off when a touch on my shoulder frightened me awake. I scurried up and my body tremored. "Sorry to startle you, darling."*

The same voice is in my ears right now, trying to calm me down.

"Ava, can you hear me?" Mom is asking me. Her voice sounds like it's so far away. Even though I know I'm at her house, I just can't help but stay frozen in place as I take quick, shallow breaths.

My chest tightens from the memories and a wave of nausea hits. I have barely managed a few mouthfuls of food, but I feel like I want to vomit.

"Ava, take nice, slow breaths. In through your nose and out through your mouth. I'm right here. You're safe." She is stroking my arm as she hugs me from the side, offering comfort, knowing I need the safety of her arms right now.

The rapid, quick breaths finally slow down. My mouth opens and closes to say something, but I don't have the energy to speak.

"Come on, let me help you on the couch. You need to rest. I will bring you over a glass of water."

I tilt my head up and down slowly. She pulls me out of my chair, then takes my hands in hers and guides me to a standing position. I shuffle my heavy feet, feeling dizzy, and lean on her to help me. When we reach the lounge room, I flop onto the couch and lie down on my side. Mom lifts my head and pops a pillow underneath it, then grabs a blanket and covers me. My heavy lids close, exhaustion taking over.

I wake in the morning, feeling lighter. I stretch, sore from not moving out of the same position I fell asleep in last night.

Swinging my legs off the couch, I hear the television mumbling and I wander to Mom's room. I stand in the doorway and see she is propped up on pillows in her bed, watching the television and sipping from her mug.

"Morning."

Her eyes shift to me and she lowers her mug to the bedside table. Getting out of bed and coming to stand in front of me, softly stroking my upper arms, she asks, "Are you feeling better?"

I nod. "Yes. Much."

"Come, let's make you some tea and breakfast. You barely ate dinner last night."

Her mention of food has me salivating. "Good idea."

She wanders off, so I pick up her mug. It's still half full so I bring it to her in the kitchen.

"Toast and tea will be plenty. Here, you finish your tea. I'm fine to cook toast and make myself tea. I promise."

Her brows raise as she reads my face. I chuckle. "I'm fine. Seriously." She nods and takes her mug out of my hand.

I make some chamomile tea, avoiding caffeine, and grab some bread, lifting the loaf, silently asking if she wants some. "Please," she says.

Tilting my chin, I swivel and pop some pieces in the toaster. While it's cooking and my tea is cooling, I look around. "Mom, have you seen my phone?" I ask.

"I put it just on the hallway table with your purse."

"Thanks." I collect my phone and read the time. "Shit. I'm so late. Joshua will probably fire me." My eyes widen and my body temperature rises at the knowledge I could lose a job I really enjoy.

"You must have needed to rest and I'm sure when you speak to your boss, he will understand, darling."

Shaking my head vigorously, I say, "I'm new, and now Joshua is going to think I'm lazy. I'll definitely lose my job."

"I'm sure he will understand if it's just a once off," she replies, her voice filled with calm hope.

I grumble, not sold on that. Joshua is an asshole.

I open my emails and type out a quick email to the dick himself.

To: Joshua Ward
Subject: Running Late
Message: Good morning Joshua,
I'm running a little late to work. I will be in as soon as possible.
Regards,
Ava

After I send the email, I have breakfast, shower, and dress in the spare clothes I keep at Mom's house. I come out of the bathroom in tartan pants, a black crop, and a black jacket. "Mom, are you ready?" I call out as I enter the kitchen.

"Coming. I'm just popping on my shoes."

"Okay. I will do the same." Once my boots are on, I grab my bag, checking my phone while I wait for Mom.

No new emails. My stomach twists.

I'm so dead.

"I'm ready."

It only takes twenty minutes to drive in, making it close to ten when I arrive.

An empty feeling sits in the pit of my stomach as I ride the elevator up.

I don't want to lose my job.

I'm going to have to beg to keep my job. Joshua will have a field day with me begging. I can imagine his smug face as I do. Internally, I groan, but if that is what I need to do to keep this job, then that's what I'll do.

Exiting the elevator, I dump my bag in the drawer and turn on my computer. Opening the emails, I begin responding to them.

When I'm finished, I don't delay another second. I walk upstairs to check in with Joshua.

As I exit the elevator, Linda's wide smile welcomes me.

"Good morning, Ava. What do we owe the pleasure? Joshua didn't mention any meetings." She takes a peek at her computer, obviously checking her schedule.

"No, Thomas is still away, so I wanted to check in with him."

She sits back in her chair. "Go ahead; he is inside his office. I'll be due for a break soon. Did you want to come have a coffee with me?"

I smile at her. "That would be lovely. Yes, thank you. I'll see you when I get out." I'm riding on so many emotions right now. It's been a rollercoaster day, and it's not even close to ending. I don't know if coffee is the smartest thing, but I want to join Linda.

"Okay. Wish me luck," I laugh.

A slack expression appears on Linda's face, but I shrug it off and strut to Joshua's office.

Let's get this show on the road.

I pause before I knock on his door.

"Come in," he calls out loudly.

I roll my shoulders back and pop my chest out. *You got this, Ava.*

I open the door and close it gently behind me, stepping closer to his desk.

I stare at him as I enter. He turns, meeting my gaze, and his lips twitch. And his blue eyes narrow.

He glances at the wristwatch, clearly checking the time. *Asshole. I know I'm fucking late.*

My lips purse. I sent him an email. No need to be dramatic. But of course he has to.

"You're late," he grunts.

No shit, Sherlock.

"I sent you an email," I challenge.

"Ava." His tone is sharp with a warning.

Whatever, dickhead. I cross my arms.

Would he like me to tell him I had a moment because of past issues? No, that would be personal and highly inappropriate. And he would look at me differently. Everyone does when they find out about my past.

I'm confident and hardworking. Yes, I was late today, but I stayed late every day to make sure my work was done. I go above and beyond my duties whenever possible.

I say nothing back. I just glare down my nose at him, biting down on my tongue ring. I refuse to waste my breath or potentially risk losing my job by biting back at his insults. I just pull out the chair opposite him and sit down. Crossing my legs and sitting up straight, I am ready to begin work.

"What are the plans today?" I ask.

His stormy blues squint back at me. "We need to meet the builder. There seems to be something wrong with the designs."

I gasp, "Oh no. How bad?" My fingers touch my parted lips, waiting for him to explain.

His eyes move from my gaze to the monitor. "I don't know yet. Hence the meeting."

I roll my eyes, knowing he can't see. I'm pinching my lips together, trying hard to hold back my sneer.

Smartass.

Clearing my throat, I say, "Right. So I'll grab the designs from the office and some notes."

His eyes flick to mine. "Yes. And we need to run through the tunnel staffing. Can you grab the folder for the tunnel project? I want to see if we can move some staff from that project to Park Lane."

"Sure." I stand up and he doesn't say another word. His eyes are back on his computer; he's dismissing me. I exit his office and walk toward Linda.

Pausing at her desk, leaning my forearm on it, I say, "I have to run through a project with Joshua, and then we should be good for a break."

"No worries. Take your time. I'll be here whenever you're ready." She offers me a smile.

I dip my chin and turn, hurrying down to my floor, grabbing the folder and designs before heading back upstairs. I re-enter his office without knocking and take the same seat again. He thrusts out his hand. Clearly, he wants to take the folder and designs.

He snatches them from me. My mouth drops open. *Jerk.*

I was late one time, and now he punishes me with his attitude. This guy is fucking crazy.

He opens the folder for the tunnel, scanning the top of the page. "Let's figure out how many men we can move from this job."

Standing up, I lean over the desk. Feeling my face close to his, my breath catches. But I push past the sparks flying from his closeness and speak. "I have a table with the timeline. It might help you decide." His head jerks back and he stares back at me incredulously with wide eyes.

Where is your attitude now?

"Okay." His voice pitches higher. He lifts his hands off the book and I flick to the page that has the table on it. I ease back and sit back down in my chair and wait for a reaction. He says nothing. My leg bounces.

"I'm going to write a list of men and dates. Could you please inform them of the move? Organize the introduction and I'll call the director of the tunnel and tell them the new plans. And when you finish letting the men know, can you do an updated one of these?"

His posture is unchanged; he's just staring down at the paper as he speaks. But then his flat gaze lands back on mine, waiting for an answer.

"Sure."

Closing the file, he holds it out to me. I am careful not to touch him as I take it from him. He glances down at the designs on his desk. "I'll look over these to see if I can spot anything. But you can have this. Meet you downstairs in the lobby at two-thirty. That will give us time to get there and have a quick chat beforehand."

Inclining my head, I clutch the file to my chest and rise. "Okay. I'll get to sorting this out. See you then."

I exit his office and approach Linda. "I just have to make some urgent calls, then I will be free. How about an hour?"

"Perfect. I will come to your office and then we will grab a bite to eat."

I smile. "See you soon."

Once I'm back at my office, I begin calling some of the workers one by one to help the foreman. I'm on the phone to the last one when Linda walks into the office. I hold up a finger, asking for one more minute.

She dips her head and walks around the office while I talk to the last worker. I hang up. "Sorry about that. I needed to get the calls out before we go. It couldn't wait. I want no more excuses for Joshua to hate me."

Her head jerks back to face me. "Why would he do that? I'm sure he doesn't hate you."

"Pfft. He has hated me since day one." I grab my bag and phone from the drawer and join

Linda at the elevator. I hurry to join her, walking beside her.

"I'm sorry you feel that way, but he couldn't hate a soul. He is the nicest person I have ever met."

My eyes bulge. *No way.*

I'm surprised she speaks so highly of him. It's like we are talking about two different people.

"Today I was accidentally late—I, ah, overslept—and he has been the biggest asshole." I don't want to discuss my reason for oversleeping with someone I just met. Even though I feel comfortable with Linda, I'm just not inclined to share.

We exit the elevator on the ground floor and walk toward the exit.

We step outside and I shiver from the cold air. As I hug myself with my arms, Linda says, "Ohhh, it's cold out here... but getting back to what we were talking about, I really think you have the wrong idea."

At the coffee shop, she opens the door for me and as I enter, my gaze lands on the back corner and my mouth pops open.

He's haunting me. Or following me.

Either way, I inwardly groan. Give me a break.

He is back, with the tall, dark-haired friend I have seen twice before. The first day, that friend called me a vixen, which I kind of like. I dip my head to hide my face and walk to a table closer to the front. I don't need him noticing me here. I want to enjoy my lunch with Linda.

She sits opposite me, thankfully blocking my view of Joshua and his friend. "I don't think so. Maybe I'm the first person he dislikes."

Shaking her head side to side vigorously, she says, "No, he hates two people, but other than that, no. He couldn't."

At her admission, my interest piques, so I ask, "Who?" She leans forward and her hands clasp together in front of her. I lean forward, meeting her in the middle. I can tell she wants to whisper. This must be important.

"His parents."

My eyes widen at the revelation. I take a quick glance over at his table, watching him drink his coffee like the stuck-up prick he is.

"No way," I say.

How can someone hate their parents? I stare down at my hands. I miss mine.

"Yeah, they were neglectful, but as he got older, he tried everything to get them to love him, but they got worse."

I cover my gaping mouth with my hand.

"His parents gifted him the business—which was failing, and in so much debt, it was embarrassing. That poor man may look tough, but under that suit of armor is a soft center. He tries to show this tough, funny guy but inside he is hurt and lonely."

What? I'm at a loss for words. I blink rapidly as I remember my beautiful parents and my loving childhood. Being an only child, I was spoiled with gifts, love, and adoration. I can't comprehend having it any differently. If they were still alive... I know I still would have been the apple of their eyes.

"Ava."

I'm blinking rapidly, remembering where I am. I got lost in the past for a second.

"Sorry, that is awful. I kinda feel bad for him." My gaze returns to hers.

"Yeah, it's not nice, but please don't tell him I told you anything. He keeps everything close to his chest. I don't want him to think I can't be trusted; he has had enough trust broken in his life."

Nodding, I scoop up the menu laying in front of us, wanting to change the subject. "What's good here to eat? I have only had their coffee."

"Well, my personal favorite is the everything bagel."

Reading the large menu, I decide the bagel sounds like a good choice.

"Sounds good. I might get that too."

"I'll grab them. I will be right back." Before I can argue, she has taken off to join the line to order. My heart swells at the generosity. Pouring some water, I drink. I lower the glass and when I look back up, I meet the same assessing eyes as earlier.

"Vixen," his friend says, smirking an appreciative smile.

I laugh out loud. "My name is Ava."

His mouth twists and I peek over. Joshua is stiff as a board, his lips thinned into a flat line. He's clearly pissed off, which makes my smile bigger. Why does he get his knickers in a knot over me? I just don't get it. But it's fun getting under his handsome skin.

The man I'm talking to thrusts his hand out. "James. Nice to properly meet you. Thanks for being a royal pain in the ass to my friend. It's the highlight of my days."

His eyes dance with humor, and that makes me chuckle. "Glad I can bring the entertainment," I respond. I can feel my own eyes sparkling with amusement.

"That you do," James lightly replies.

"Ugh. I'm outta here," Joshua huffs and takes off out of the café.

James watches him exit, then returns to me. "Keep it up. Nice to meet you." And he rushes to follow Joshua.

I laugh to no one and watch through the shop window. James has to walk fast to catch up to Joshua. When he catches up to him, he grabs his shoulder and squeezes it. Joshua shakes his head.

I wonder what they are talking about. Clearly, I'm a hit with his friend... Things don't seem so bad now. I'm still watching Joshua and James cross the road back to the building, they're walking across the road like the powerful men they are. It makes me wonder how Joshua turned the company around. You wouldn't know about the debt by looking at the spectacular glass building. The boys disappear into the building and I just stare at the tower, wondering what secrets it holds.

"I'm back. It won't take long; the service here is quick." Linda cuts into the daydream, making me jump in my seat.

"Thanks. I owe you next time. My treat." I give her a genuine smile. She oozes a momma bear figure and a friend in one.

"Deal," she answers. I'm feeling like the day is turning around. I managed to keep my job, but

I can't let the past get in my way. I may not be so lucky in the future.

CHAPTER 7

JOSHUA

I CURL MY HANDS into fists and walk across the road with James. The prick flirting with Ava in front of me pisses me off. I wish he would have kept his mouth shut and not encouraged her shitty attitude.

"She is hot. Did you see she has a tongue ring? Fuck me; I have been with a chick who gave me head once, and let me tell you, I came so hard."

I wish he would shut the fuck up. I don't want to have visions of Ava on her knees giving me head, but it's too late. Images of her pink, pouty lips wrapped perfectly around my cock, taking me deep into her mouth. The thought of what her tongue and metal would feel like sliding along my dick has me growing hot. But being able to shut her sassy mouth by making it full of my cock has me smiling.

No, get that shit out of your head.

I need to call up a regular hookup and get laid. Clearly I need sexual relief if I'm having dirty thoughts about Ava and lashing out at my friends. Even at my dear friend, James, who has lent me money and believes in me. There is something about Ava that unravels me.

I pull out my phone and text Candice, but I don't reply when she confirms she's free tonight. I just stuff my phone back in my pocket and say, "You're crazy. Remind me why you hired her? Because I'm the one stuck with the smartass, not you."

He smiles and says, "You've seen her résumé. She's perfect for the role, and Thomas is happy with her. Speaking of, how's Lily?"

We enter my building and I say, "Yeah, I think she is fine now. Even so, any accident will shake him up. I'm sure he will be back next week."

"That's good. But it leaves you to run the business and do his work."

I understand James is all about business, but I would have done anything to have parents who wanted to care for me when I was sick or injured. So, when Thomas needs time off for his family, I cannot deny him.

"I don't mind it; it's nice being hands-on. But yes, some of my work is getting neglected. Anyway, I need to go. I'll call you later."

We part ways, and I return to my office and read over the Park Lane designs once more. Afterward, I collect all the designs up and make my way downstairs to meet Ava. I exit the elevator and spot her talking to Maria. I grimace, knowing Maria is under her spell too, and it irks me. Everyone around me is falling for her charms, except me.

She is slouched over the receptionist's desk, with her ass in perfect view. It's one of the best asses I have ever seen and it irritates me that it's turning me on. Needing it out of my face now, I clear my throat loudly. Her head turns in my direction and she pushes off the desk. Her gaze locks on mine and there isn't an ounce of fear there. She thinks she holds the power, which is wrong. I'm in control and yet it feels like a tug-of-war over who is on top.

Maria waves at Ava and then refocuses on her computer.

"You ready?" I grunt out.

"Sure am," she sings back through a smile, not caring how I talk to her.

"Let's go."

We walk out the front and I open the door to my private car for her, but she walks around and climbs in on the other side.

I close my eyes and suck in a breath before slipping inside and slamming the door shut.

"Hi, George," she says to my driver.

"Ava, how are you?"

"George, Park Lane," I interrupt.

Our eyes catch in the rearview mirror, and he nods and says, "Yes, sir."

I settle into the leather seat, neither of us speaking.

The car fills with her scent and I take a peek over at her. My eyes roam over her body, starting at her toes and making my way to the top of her head. And then lower back to her delectable fucking lips. My tongue glides across my bottom lip like I'm parched for water. She really is something else. As if she senses my gaze, her gray eyes meet mine and a jolt of lightning hits my chest.

What the fuck was that?

When the driver pulls the car to a stop, I jerk my gaze back to the front, trying to make sense of the feeling.

I exit the car as if it's on fire and walk to the site, not waiting to see if she follows. I need some space because I can't seem to trust myself with her around; she fucks with my thoughts too much.

The sound of her heels walking across the concrete lets me know she is following. I spot the builder ahead and approach him, saying, "Good afternoon."

We shake hands and I introduce Ava, and then he ushers us into his office. I couldn't find anything wrong with the plans, so I lay the design out on the table and wait for him. He comes over and peers over at the paper and I ask, "Can you show us the issue so we can figure out a new plan and put it together for you?"

He steps back, shaking his head, and says, "We just think there needs to be an add-on to the design, not for whole new designs of the buildings we have started."

My pulse picks up and I turn my body to the side to get a better look at him and ask, "Okay. Where is this new project?"

He points to one building on the paper and says, "There will be a grocery store here."

I rub my chin and ask, "The entire apartment block?"

"No, just on the bottom floor," he answers.

I nod and look over and see Ava is taking notes. I didn't ask her to do it, but I like her initiative. Returning my focus back to the builder, I say, "I'll come up with a design, then get you to approve it as soon as it's drafted. We need to sort it out soon, as it needs to pass approvals and inspections."

"I would appreciate that. Thanks."

I smile, roll up the design, and shake the builder's hand. Ava and I exit the office and walk to the building site to get an idea of where the store will be.

It's just us now, walking to the site. It's strange being near her for long periods of time because she brings out senses I never use. Like the smell of a perfume never bothered me on a woman before, but her gritty, earthy, yet floral smell makes my stomach flip. I wish my body wasn't sensitive to her. It's annoying the fuck out of me, but I don't know how to stop it.

Ava breaks the quiet air by asking, "What are you thinking?"

I don't even think when I am with her. I just speak what's on my mind, like word vomit.

"To be honest, I don't know. Except it's a lot of work. I'll take some pictures and then let's meet up in my meeting room to tackle it."

We will need the space to lay out the plans.

"Good idea," she answers.

CHAPTER 8

AVA

MY MIND IS RACING with images of Joshua from today, starting with his demeanor while we were with the builder. He oozed control, a side I hadn't yet seen, and then the way his gaze trailed over my body seductively in the car sent my brain into overdrive.

We haven't spoken since we left the building site. The car ride back is quiet, both of us lost in our own thoughts. Arriving back at the building, he opens the car door for me and this time, I accept.

We enter the elevator, and I speak. "I will ring all the staff and send the introduction and type up the notes for Thomas. It won't take me more than an hour and then I'll meet you in your office?"

I don't turn his way; I just stare at the back of the elevator doors. My heart gallops and I have to concentrate on my breathing because, in such a small space, his delicious scent fills the air. I try to think of something utterly disgusting so I don't have to let my mind drift to him, but of course my body is traitorous.

"Yes, good idea. I'll prepare the variation until you get upstairs." His voice echoes inside the elevator, vibrating through my body and sending tingles up my spine. I need to get the fuck out of here before I do something stupid.

The elevator doors to my floor open, relief fills my body, and I rush out, calling over my shoulder, "Okay."

I move straight to my desk and begin updating the planner. It doesn't take me long to finish my tasks, and it's just under the hour I said. I trek upstairs to his floor. Linda catches my eye with a smile.

"Joshua said you would come up. He's already in the meeting room." She winks.

I frown.

Why did she wink? That was weird. Please. I don't have many friends; well, I have one, Gracie, and I was hoping Linda would be a work friend. But don't turn out to be here to manipulate me into something with the big boss and then watch when it all goes wrong. I have major trust issues as it is.

I dip my head and say, "Thanks." I hurry out of the room, shaking off the weird exchange.

I stand in Joshua's open doorway, holding myself back for a minute to gaze at him. My eyes soften at the sight of him sitting behind his desk. He really knows how to wear a suit, the way the designer jacket clings to his shoulders and the white shirt complements his tanned skin. Why did I have to have a hot boss? Well, technically, he is the boss's boss, but those fine details don't matter. He is off totally off limits.

And anyway, why did Thomas have to be absent? I wouldn't be standing here having to work closely with Joshua if he were here.

When I finish staring, my mouth is suddenly dry. I swallow and push myself inside, talking to myself.

Be a professional. I can do this.

I straighten my spine and raise my hand to tap the glass.

"Knock knock," I say.

His gaze lifts from the papers he seems to be engrossed in and he says, "Come in."

He stops reading and stands, his hands diving straight inside his pockets, a concentrated look etched on his face.

He drops his chin and explains, "I'm just trying to work out what would work the best with the rest of the buildings."

My body goes rigid, appreciating that he is sharing details of work with me. Thomas does, but I didn't think king dick would, but of course, he is the gift that keeps on giving.

I move toward his desk, noticing there is a catalog in front of him. The colors and designs have me moving closer, so I reach out and grab it. My hand brushes his, causing the hair on my arms to rise, and he hisses. My body grows hot from our touch. I skim through the pages for a distraction.

After a minute of flicking—I'm like a kid in a candy store with all these new goodies—I say, "There are a lot of lights in this. More than Thomas's book downstairs."

"Yeah, it's the latest one available. I wanted to see if we can use new ones; we need to put our best foot forward. I will make a generous profit, so it needs to be perfect," he explains.

As I flick through the book, I bounce from foot to foot and say, "I'm happy to look for the lights, if you want to work out how many you need for each design."

I expect some lashings for bossing around the boss.

He sits down and says, "Good idea."

I glance at him, my mouth falling open. Where is the usual back chat? Now that I'm closer to him, I can see his face clearly. His solid, chiseled jaw has a five o'clock shadow forming, his pink lips are perfect on his handsome face, and I feel my heartbeat pounding inside my body. His gaze turns under my intense stare and his blue eyes lock with mine. The energy in the room shifts and I lean in. I notice the lines forming around his eyes and a sigh leaves his lips. Like the weight of the world is on his shoulders and I wonder what it's like to run an empire. I bet it's exhausting.

Dropping my gaze to refocus on my task, I sit down in the chair as he stands and move over to the whiteboard. Flicking through the pages, I make a note of the few lighting fixtures that would be perfect for a store.

"Have you always wanted to run a business?" I ask.

Linda mentioned his dad handing him the business, but I want to hear more about it from him. He leans back, propping his hand under his chin, looking at me as speaks. "No. I actually never thought I would run my own business. But here I am, and loving every minute. Truthfully, it was the best thing to happen to me. It gave my life a sense of purpose, and I'm still learning the aspects of the job every day." He slowly shakes his head before he asks, "And why did you apply for a position here?"

Darting my gaze away briefly before returning to meet his gaze, I say, "Well, the company I worked for closed down. I drank some wine, applied for a new job, and here I am." I shrug before continuing, "I guess I shouldn't have been honest, but that's the truth. But I will say I am loving every minute."

His mouth opens into a smile. I was expecting a bit of heat for the wine, but he seems relaxed and his eyes are sparkling back at me.

"I'm glad you enjoy it. Thomas is a great guy."

I swallow and say, "That he is."

We stare at each other until he stands and steps over to me. I hold my breath as he asks, "How are you doing there?" He nudges his chin toward the papers.

I blink and say, "Well, I found a few. What do you think of these? These inside the shop, and this one for outside, like a nightlight."

He inches closer and his cedarwood and cardamom scent wafts over, causing me to warm. I cease breathing through my nose and begin open mouth breathing. His scent is causing my sex to tingle.

"They are great!"

"Okay, I will start the list for what we want to show the builder. And then also have the order form ready to go, so as soon as they approve, they are good to go." My voice is husky.

I clear my throat, trying to pretend there is something tickling it when really it's the emotions he is awakening in me. A deep craving... I wonder what would happen if I caved to that desire?

He is a playboy mogul, remember. Focus on your job.

He makes a sound in his throat that I haven't heard before, but it is approval. And it talks directly to my sex.

Fuck.

I'm signing my death certificate here.

"Thank you."

I keep my head down, hiding my face. The heat on my cheeks borders on flamingly painful now.

His phone rings inside his pocket. I tilt my head and watch him pull it out and wince. He hits a button, and a frown forms between his brows as he stuffs it back inside. It rings again, so he has to pull it out, and he hits a button again. I assume it's the hang up or mute button.

Weird.

"Why don't you just answer it? It might be important."

The person called straight back, which must mean it's important. I don't care if he answers his phone during our meeting.

He mutters, "It's not."

The attitude is back. The nice guy only hung around for a second. He gives me whiplash with the amount he changes.

Whatever. I don't give a shit. I refocus on the plans in front of me.

"Do you need to get home?"

I haven't seen the time, but obviously we have been here past five, because his question surprises me.

I turn my head to take him in, a brow rising in question.

"It's dinnertime," he explains.

"Oh, I hadn't realized. I guess it makes up for my lateness," I tease back.

His mouth twists into a grin and he shakes his head and says, "I guess."

A lightness is coming from him again. The earlier dark moment has vanished.

I shrug and say, "I'm happy to stay longer and finish this. It's almost done and then tomorrow morning, we can present it."

Our gazes lock, and he remains still and his mouth drops open before he collects himself and surprises me further.

"At least let me buy us some dinner. I can't treat my staff poorly."

My stomach grumbles as if on cue. I chuckle and say, "I think that would be a good idea."

He pulls his phone out and asks, "Is there anything you feel like in particular?"

"Nope. I eat anything and everything. I'm not picky."

He scrolls through his phone and I return to my work, trying to finish it before the food arrives.

After twenty minutes, his phone chimes and he stands and says, "Food's here. I'll run downstairs to collect it."

"Okay," I call back.

He returns carrying a ridiculous amount of food.

"How many people are you feeding?" I laugh.

He dips his chin down, his gaze fixed on the food and says, "I didn't know what you liked, so I kinda ordered a bit of everything."

The flush and his words make my heart squeeze inside my chest at how sweet he is.

"Clearly. What is it?" I tease.

He places the bag in the middle of the table and says, "Italian."

"I love Italian food," I whisper.

He pulls all the food out of the bag and my stomach flips at the sight. I hadn't realized how late it was.

Spotting the pizza box, I flip it open and grab a cheesy piece and bite, saying, "Mmmm, this is so good." I point. "Where is this from?"

He leans forward and takes a piece too and dips his head. "Guiliano's, the best in town."

"You chose well. I'm sorry I haven't tried it before; you weren't kidding when you said it was the best," I say before taking another huge bite.

He glances at me with a cheeky smirk and says, "Well, that's a first."

I softly shove his arm and say, "Hey. I'm not that bad."

He shakes his head and says, "I don't know about that. You seem to have the opposite opinion to me about...everything."

I shrug and say, "I guess I can't deny that."

We eat in a comfortable silence; I take a few glances every now and then between bites and catch his longing stare. The earlier tension has disappeared, but the electricity still vibrates and being around him in this casual setting is making it harder to push the thought of *what if?* away.

We finish eating and I help clean up, still feeling a battlefield in my stomach. I return to our work and ease back in the chair. I'm done thirty minutes later and I say, "I have finished. Is there something else you need me to do?"

He walks over and peers down at my work. The hairs on the nape of my neck rise from his breath. I close my eyes to recover from the warm rush that hits my sex as he speaks. "No, this is great. We are all set. Let's pack this up and get home."

I can't disagree, after this heavy, carb-loaded delicious food. I feel like I could curl up on the sofa at home and sleep. But also I need the distance between us so I don't cross that professional line. I focus on packing up and I take the files to his office.

"Just pop them on my desk. We will meet here in the morning. You won't be late, will you?" he teases.

Cheeky shit.

I smirk and say, "No, smartass. I'll be here on time."

He smiles and grabs his wallet and keys.

"I have to get my purse and keys from my office."

"Okay, I'll take you down. We can leave together."

I take a step back and rapidly blink, taking in what I just heard and say, "Oh, ahh. Umm, you don't have to. I catch the train."

I cringe at the fact I have to tell him I catch a train, knowing he has a fancy-ass sports car.

Another reason we can't be together; we are worlds apart.

He was on his way to the elevator, but he stops, faces me and asks, "You don't drive? Do you live close?"

"No. It only takes forty-five minutes on the train."

His upper lip curls back and he says, "No, I won't allow it. I will drive you. It's dark and god knows who is out there on the train at this hour."

The way he says it, it's like he is protecting me rather than being his usual bossy self. His kindness tonight is unexpected and my heart rattles inside my chest. Who is this Joshua? Is this the guy that Linda was raving to me about today? This is the first I have seen of him, and I can see why she is being charmed by him. When he isn't rude, he is a caring and humble man.

"The train isn't that bad, but to be honest, dinner has made me tired and relaxed, so I don't want to fall asleep there and end up in an unfamiliar state," I giggle.

Turning his head to the side with his eyes tightly closed, he says, "Don't even joke about that."

I still feel taken aback by him. I don't know what to say back as we enter the elevator, and the surrounding air is tense. The electricity and sparks are flying between us again. And I have to stop my thoughts from going into a no-go zone. *You need this job and money for your future, Ava.* And I need to remind myself how he has spoken and treated me in the past.

You can't trust him.

We arrive at his sports car. I lean forward and grab the handle, but he is quicker.

"Let me get it." His body is only an inch away from mine, making my knees weak. His face is so close to mine and his frame reminds me how big a man's body is and how it feels for arms to be wrapped around me.

He opens the car door and I feel lightheaded, wanting to sit down before my knees buckle. I twist my head and stare into his mesmerizing blue eyes, and my heart falters. The heat and desire match my own buried thoughts and before I have the chance to climb in the car, he captures the back of my neck roughly, slamming his lips to mine, and swallows my "Oh."

The kiss is rough, stirring a new hunger. Most guys I have been with in the past were good, but they weren't passionate. This is setting my mouth on fire with a feral rawness. My lips open and when his tongue touches mine and he feels my piercing with his tongue, he groans loudly and grips my neck tighter, trying to bring me even closer, even though it's impossible. His tongue rubs and teases my metal, which sends a pulse directly to my sex, his appreciation for the metal sending a wave of pleasure running through my body. My hands are gripping his head to keep him in a position that gives me the best angle to kiss. Our tongues are tangling and tasting each other. This raw passion is making me want more than a kiss. A new thrill runs through my body at what he would be like in the bedroom...Rough and dirty.

That's how sex would be with him, and fuck, I want to have sex with him right now. I'm wet and horny for him, not caring I'm in the parking lot at work. As if sensing my thoughts, he pulls back, leaning his forehead against mine as we both heavily pant.

When we catch our breaths, he pecks my lips so softly, it surprises me and they pinch together in response. My raw, swollen lips want more, but he steps back with a heated gaze.

'I better get you home.' His voice strains.

And I know he is struggling to hold back, as I am, but I have to remember he is my boss. To stop from ripping his suit jacket off him, I close my eyes shut for a second, trying to collect myself.

I nod and say, "Good idea."

I sit in the car and close my eyes before re-opening them, thankful his seats are leather. It's helping cool my body down. I relax into the seat and stare out the window and he climbs in beside me.

"Can you direct me or do you want me to enter it into the car?" His voice is deeper than usual.

"I can direct you," I offer.

In the car, the energy between us is still palpable, but I think we are both lost in our thoughts, knowing we crossed a line tonight. My swollen lips are trying to recover from the onslaught.

He reverses and his car roars out of the parking lot. We arrive at my apartment in ten minutes. The entire drive was quiet, but not uncomfortable. My lips kept wanting more, so I rammed them shut. I don't want to offer to come inside and finish what we started. The heat and humidity in this car are like a sauna.

I kept chanting the mantra

He is my boss

He is an asshole

Over and over in my head.

"Just the apartment block on the left," I say, almost forgetting I'm supposed to be telling him where we are going and stop being caught up inside my head.

He pulls in and I unbuckle myself, needing the air and distance between us, because I know if I don't get out, I'll reclaim his lips, and that will lead to him being in my apartment and in my bed.

I push the car door open and say, "Thanks for driving me home."

I want to say more but it would be a ramble, so I just get out of the car and say, "I'll see you in the office tomorrow."

As the words leave my mouth, I realize we royally fucked up. I have to work with him and we crossed a line we can't take back. But for some reason, I'm not mad. His car is still sitting there. I wave to him and walk inside my building. My heart is trying to understand how I feel and what tomorrow will bring.

CHAPTER 9

AVA

I WAKE FEELING HUNGOVER even though I didn't drink at all last night. I tossed and turned with sexual frustration, the memories of the passionate kiss I shared with Joshua replaying over and over in my dreams. My body feels heavy, and I wish I could crawl back under the blankets and doze off again. But two days in a row of me being late would surely get me fired, no matter how hot of a kiss we shared.

I'm sure he kisses women all the time, so I'll be just one of many blips on his radar. I skip breakfast because my stomach is in knots at the prospect of seeing him again. The closer I get to work, the more my stomach twists.

Why was I so stupid?

I bet he sees me as a doormat, or easy, which I'm neither.

Deciding what to wear this morning was a shit show. I pulled everything out of the wardrobe and threw it onto the bed, believing I have nothing to wear. But I know I am acting like a child and I blame him for driving me fucking mad. In the end, I choose a high-waisted skirt and a black turtleneck top with a pair of black boots.

I run my fingers through my hair and decide I want to change up my dark hair, to add a pop of color. I'll need to decide soon, so I can pick up the color before my usual Saturday night with Gracie. I should have called her last night while the kiss was fresh on my mind, but it was too late and it requires a large glass of wine.

I exit the train and enter the building, stopping by Maria's desk to waste time before heading upstairs. I'm here ten minutes earlier than I need to be and the closer I am to him, the more frightened I am. Why the fuck I am frightened... well, it's because I fear I will beg for him to finish what we started last night.

I finish my conversation with Maria and walk to the elevators holding my head up high, pretending to be calm when inside I'm a horny, rattled mess.

I step into my office and look around for Thomas, but there is still no sign of him. I was hoping he would be back today so I don't have to go upstairs to Joshua alone, but if he doesn't show up, I will have no other choice.

I check my emails, but there aren't many, so once I finish responding to the few I have, I suck in a few deep breaths and roll my shoulders back and stroll to the elevator; I can't delay going to his office anymore. Inside the elevator, I feel my pulse pick up speed as it lifts. But I picture my apartment and how much I need this job to continue living there, and that's the perfect distraction.

I walk up to Linda first and say, "Good morning."

She glances up from her computer and says, "Good morning, love. You're here early."

She seems as if she knows everything, not missing a beat, in a way reminding me of my own mom. A twist in my gut at the mention of my mom has me pausing in front of her desk and saying, "Yes, we are going to take a new design to the builder this morning."

"Ah, okay. Which builder... the tunnel?"

I'm surprised she is asking. Would she normally know, or is she pretending she doesn't know?

I shake my head.

Don't be stupid, Ava. You can trust her; don't let insecurities get inside your head. She is kind and maybe Joshua isn't in yet, so he hasn't had time to tell her. Yeah, that's it. It suddenly feels better to say, "Park Lane has added a store on one of the apartment ground floors."

"Ohhh, that's great! More work for Joshua. Which is what he needs."

My brows lift in curiosity at her admission. He seems to need a lot of work and money, and a red flag appears, definitely cooling my libido.

"Anyway, I don't want to be late today."

She laughs, knowing the drama of yesterday.

I walk to his office and it's like he senses me; his gaze locks with mine as soon as I appear in the doorway. My heart jolts at the connection and my pulse beats wildly. He is sitting in his office chair, leaning to one side, and says, "I could tell it was you."

He rubs his freshly shaved jaw and the grin on his lips insinuates he is enjoying the view. I roll my lips and glance down before bringing my gaze back up to meet his again. I need a second to recover before I blush.

"Did my shoes or voice give me away?" I ask.

"Both." His voice is like silk. There seems to be a shift between us and I take a step forward, his gaze shining with delight. I smile, feeling sensual, and the hair on my arms rises.

I'm fucked.

He needs to stop looking at me like he wants to eat me because I can only hold myself back for so long before I'm offering myself up for him to feast on. It's been way too long since I had a guy go down on me and to see Joshua on his knees, devouring me...

Now, fuck, I want to see that. A shudder runs through my body from the electricity between us. I clear my tight throat to ask, "Do you need any help before we go to the meeting?"

That's it, Ava. Talk work so it reminds him that we cannot cross professional boundaries.

His eyes widen and a flash of disappointment flashes on his face for a second before he seems to snap back to boss mode.

"No, I'm ready to go. Let's get it over and done with and then we can grab a coffee afterward."

He picks up the files and papers.

"Okay." I step forward to offer help, to carry a file. He puts the catalogue and list in my hands.

I glance down and scrunch up my face as I return to meet his gaze and ask, "You want me to only carry these two?"

Surely he's pulling my leg?

"Yes. Now, let's go. No arguing with me today."
He pokes my nose.

I roll my eyes. "I can't make any promises."

He doesn't respond. Just walks out of his office, and I follow.

"Linda, I'll be back. I'm going to a meeting. Call me if you need me."

She wears a shit-eating grin and says, "I'll see you whenever you guys get back."

I narrow my eyes at her, trying to understand what she is smiling at. But I can't ask, so I walk past her to catch up to Joshua.

We enter the elevator and I stand on the opposite side, putting as much distance as I can between us, fearful of losing my grip on my desires in this close proximity.

A colleague enters on another floor and I feel my shoulders relax away from my ears as the two of them chat.

We get to the builder's office and discuss the designs we chose. They loved what we came up with last night. And we then choose the final fittings from the catalog. When we finish, Joshua and I leave with the biggest smiles, knowing we had a successful meeting. I feel like I'm really settling in at Ward and finding my place. Thomas and I have a good working relationship, but now that I'm impressing Joshua, it's giving me the security I need to sleep better at night.

"That went well. Thanks for staying late last night. It paid off," he breathes.

I feel my stomach flop. Is this where he talks about the kiss? I need to go back to our normal banter and hate each other. I feel safer there.

"So I made up for being late, then."

"Hm, I wouldn't say that."

Arriving outside our building, we exit the car and wander across the road. He orders our coffees and one for Linda and we are waiting for our order to be called when I ask, "When is Thomas due back?"

"Monday," he says, but he sounds disappointed. Which makes me think this feeling isn't as one-sided as I previously had thought.

I peer down. A part of me is sad that Thomas is coming back, and the other part of me is happy. I want to have Thomas with me as a barrier to stop me from being alone with Joshua. But the other part will miss the time we shared, because it seems to have given us a new peace and understanding around each other, and it's actually nice. He is nice.

"I think the accident shook him up even though it was a bike, not a car. Anyone in his family getting hurt freaks him out."

Thomas has only mentioned the accident briefly in passing, but I don't know a lot about it other than his ex-wife died.

I gaze down at the floor as my eyes become glassy and a heaviness hits my chest and I say, "I love how he cares about his family and drops everything for them."

"Yep. The best dad I have ever known." His tone is sweet but also with a hint of bitterness.

Linda mentioned he and his parents are having issues, and a sadness fills me. The love of a parent is something truly special. My lips perk at thoughts of my own parents and how much they loved me. How can you not love your parents?

I peer at his handsome profile and my fingers twitch as they remember being on his face and the best kiss of my life.

"How long have you been friends for?"

He turns as if sensing me watching him, and a small smile appears on his face as he says, "Since high school. James too."

"Oh, that's the one who hired me," I tease.

A deep chuckle leaves his chest. It's a sexy sound that makes a large smile form on my face.

"Yes, that's him. And he still stands by his decision. You charmed him for sure."

I slap my hand playfully to my chest and say, "Oh, and here I was thinking my résumé and interview were great."

I giggle.

He bites his lip and dips his head to hold back a laugh. Speaking under his breath, he says, "You kill me."

Our order is ready and I'm disappointed we have to break up our fun conversation. We step forward and he beats me to it, grabbing the tray of drinks, and says, "I got it."

I step back and we walk out together, leaving the shop. Outside, he hands me a coffee, causing our fingers to brush, and the bolt of sparks ignites a fire in my belly. I remember his large, rough hands on my neck and I want his hands back on my body.

Get your head out of the gutter, Ava. You're such a dirty bitch who needs to get laid, ASAP.

Thankfully, the chilly winds bring me back to reality. We walk back to the office, and I have my gaze ahead, welcoming the peace, when he speaks. "Do you have friends that have been around forever and support you with everything? Almost like a family?"

His voice sounds like a mix of awe and shattered, and it makes my heart break for him. But as I think of what he said, Gracie comes to mind. She is like family to me, not just my friend. She is my rock, growing up and now.

We met back when I was fifteen, at the temporary housing. I sat down in the only empty chair in the place, clutching my tray with steaming hot soup and warm crusty bread layered with butter. I remember my mouth was watering and my stomach growled with intense hunger. I lowered my tray to the table and the bang made the girl across glance up at me and I remember the pair of empty brown eyes and braided hair matted on her head. But the smile that filled her face made me openly smile back.

"Hey, I'm Gracie," she said, breaking through the surrounding chatter.

"Ava," I whispered back cautiously.

I sat down and ate my dinner while Gracie filled me in on her drug-addicted parents. She didn't feel safe there with the number of people coming and going and believed there was better out there for her. She said she just had to take a chance and run away and never look back.

Her strength was something I always admired, and to this day, she has been strong through our dark times. Her positive outlook and her love are something that I will always treasure. We are more like sisters than two best friends. We bonded over our hard lives and housing days. No one will understand the lives we have had. We trust each other completely and love each other unconditionally.

"Yes, I have a really close friend since fifteen. She is super special to me. More like family than a friend."

Knowing he can relate, I don't mind sharing that snippet of my life with him. I would have laughed if you would have told me I would share pieces of myself when I first started... but times are changing.

I stop walking to pause outside the building. He spins around and a frown settles between his brows, and I know he is wondering why I stopped. I take a sip of my coffee to wet my drying mouth and whisper, "I think we need to talk about what happened last night."

He glances around before he returns to my gaze.

"While it was... nice, it cannot happen again. You are my boss and this job is the best job I have ever had, and I don't want to jeopardize it with an office fling," I say.

His eyebrow raises with a flash of humor across his face.

"It's not funny. I'm serious."

"I know. I'm sorry; you're just cute."

Cute?

No one has called me cute before... And I don't like that.

Aren't I supposed to be hot? Sexy? Not fucking cute. It isn't a word I would use to describe myself.

Feeling like I have just been friend-zoned, irritation bubbles through my veins that he didn't reply to me, calling it an office fling. So clearly, he just saw it as a fling. I knew he was a playboy. I was secretly hoping he wasn't, but I guess I was wrong.

"I'm glad you agree. Let's get back to work. It's freezing out here," I say, wanting to get back to my safe place and well away from him.

"Good idea. The coffees are probably getting cold and Linda will kick my ass if hers has," he jokes.

Arriving back on my floor, I sit and enjoy my coffee and begin working for the rest of the day.

A few hours later, on my way home, I stop by the store and choose a new hair color, deciding on a fire engine red.

I have an extra spring in my step, excited for the fresh look. My life is improving every single day and I know that has to do with loving the job. It's helping fulfill my creative side, which I could never figure out how to pursue, and it's also helping me meet new people and is pushing me out of my comfort zone. I just need to keep away from him; otherwise he could cause my future to come crashing down.

Joshua

Being around Ava after the intense kiss we shared wasn't easy. My hand twitched to grab her neck again and crush my lips back onto hers. I want another taste. Her tongue ring was... interesting. I didn't know what it would feel like, because I haven't kissed a woman with piercings before, but it was a pleasant surprise and now I want more.

I need to get Ava off my brain, so I call up Candice.

"You stood me up the other night," she whines. And I pinch the bridge of my nose, hating that high-pitched sound.

"I know, and I'm so sorry about that, but I had a work emergency. Will you be free tonight?"

I need to take the pressure off and get rid of my blue balls. Candice won't say no. We have a good agreement: casual sex only, with no feelings or relationship expectation.

I just need to remove my thoughts from Ava before I do something stupid.

Chapter 10

Ava

I HAVE JUST FINISHED cleaning the apartment, ready for Gracie to come over, when the phone rings. I smile. *Mom* is flashing across the screen.

"Mom," I answer.

"Hi, darling. How are you?"

I smile to myself. Since my night at her house, she has been checking on me multiple times a day.

"I'm good."

"Are you sure?" she asks.

"Yes, I promise."

I hear a sigh leave her mouth, happy with my response. She says, "I have something for you. Are you home?"

She has my interest piqued. I'm curious to know what she has for me.

"Yes. I just finished cleaning. What do you have?"

"A surprise," she laughs.

"Oh, I hate surprises," I moan, in hopes she will cave and tell me what it is.

"You will love this one, I promise."

I grumble, not believing her, and we hang up. I turn to grab a mug, ready to make hot chocolate and indulge in Netflix until she arrives.

I'm lying on the couch when keys rattle in my door, and I push myself up to welcome Mom.

"Ava, I'm here," Mom's voice calls out.

"Hi. Come in."

I kiss her cheek and follow her into the kitchen, where she puts a bag on top of the counter.

"Is my surprise in there?" I ask.

I rub my palms together, excited by the prospect of food. Mom's cooking is so good, I can't wait to see what's inside.

"I made your favorite chocolate cake. I was hoping you had ice cream. If not, I'll run to the store."

"No, I've got it here. And thank you so much. This smells so good." My mouth drools at the memory of how good her cake tastes. It's a special treat when she cooks this. I must have worried her the other day, which makes me feel guilty. I really didn't mean to do it, and I hate that I worry her.

"I'm heading to the shelter. Did you want to come?" she asks.

My stomach knots. It completely slipped my mind. Bloody Joshua is distracting me and keeping me unfocused on important matters.

"Definitely. Let me get some shoes on."

I grab my phone and send Gracie a text. I need to make sure she doesn't arrive any earlier than dinnertime because I won't be home.

"Ready." I come out in my black leggings, a baggy crew neck, and sneakers. I pull my hair up as I walk to the door, swiping my handbag and tossing my phone inside.

We arrive at the local shelter a few minutes later. Butterflies swarm my belly every time I come because it brings back memories. I get out and the same team is on. The manager's face warms as soon as he sees me. He has been in charge for over twenty years.

"Ava, I swear every time I see you, you become more beautiful. How is that possible?"

I blush at his comment. He is the sweetest and most giving man I have ever met. And he always compliments me, which makes me blush.

"Thanks. Now, enough about me. Where can I help with lunch?" I ask.

I want to get started and help. People will be hungry. It's always busy at lunchtime.

"I have a spot on serving. Is that okay?" he asks softly. He still treats me as if I'm still a young child. No matter how many years I have been coming here, he hasn't changed.

"Of course." I move toward serving, saying hello to the other volunteers.

When the lunch hour is over, I finish helping Mom clean up, ready for the night crew.

I slide back into Mom's car. As she drives me home, I say, "I have missed helping. I need to do it again, but much sooner."

I have a tightness in my chest from the guilt that work has taken me away from the shelter. I'm disappointed with myself and I gaze out the window, lost in my thoughts.

"It's always lovely having you back. But remember: you are working, and that is the biggest compliment. I have plenty of time to help. I'm retired. You need to be at the new job, really concentrate on it. Only help when you can."

I know she is right, but it's just hard not to feel that I could do more. That place gave me a new life, a fresh start, and I'll be forever grateful.

"Yeah, speaking of work. It's so good. I'm learning heaps. And I think losing the job with David and getting this new job in the city is probably the best thing to happen to me. It has pushed me to meet other people."

"Oh darling, I'm so proud of you."

Hearing those words from her makes my eyes well. She is my biggest motivator to become the best version of myself. To keep trying to push and grow and be more than who I was, and don't let the past ruin me or allow it to stop my future from being anything other than amazing. Pain from the past will push me to work harder for a better future. I want to buy a condo on my own and have a secure future.

Arriving home, she drops me off at the door and I rush upstairs and have a quick shower and then sit on the couch, waiting for Gracie.

I must have fallen asleep because the sound of my phone ringing wakes me. I pick it up, seeing the name *Gracie* flashing across the screen.

I sit up in a rush, startled, and answer, saying, "Hi, sorry. I fell asleep. I helped Mom at the shelter today. Are you at the door?"

"Ahh, okay. Mentally wiped. I get that. Yeah, I am."

Gracie doesn't help at the shelter because it's too painful to go back.

I hurry to open the door. She steps inside and we exchange a warm embrace before I've even closed the door. Once we have greeted each other, Gracie follows me to the couch and we sit.

"How's the bar?" I ask, yawning.

"I stayed until three a.m. Some girl passed out in the bathroom with no friends around. So I had to wait until she sobered up, then help her get home."

Shaking my head in a slow, back-and-forth motion, I say in a disbelieving voice, "How do her friends just leave her there?"

Gracie lies back on the couch and rubs her legs and says, "Yeah, some shitty people out there."

Gracie works at the local bar. The owners met her at the homeless shelter and took her into their home and allowed her to work for them. At first, she began restocking and cleaning, and then she worked behind the bar when she was of legal age. She loves it and the locals love her.

Sitting up straight, turning my focus to her and not the TV, I say, "I have some red dye. Can you do my hair tonight please?"

"Of course. I love red on you, so I'm excited for this."

Her excitement gets me even more pumped.

"Let's order some takeout and then we can do it while we wait for it to be delivered," she says.

I rise from the couch and move to the drawer in the kitchen with the menus. I bring the pile over to the coffee table and ask, "What are you thinking?"

She shuffles forward on the couch and moves to look at each menu and says, "Chinese sounds good."

"Excellent choice. I haven't had that in a while."

My pay is higher than David paid me, which is nice. I don't have to scrape money to treat myself to takeout.

I put an order through Uber Eats and begin mixing up the hair dye. I take a seat at the kitchen table and she dyes my hair. The food arrives during the application, so Gracie has to pause to collect it from the door.

She clips my hair up and I grab us forks and we eat while my hair color processes before I step into the shower and then dry off. As I look in the mirror, I smile widely. I love it. Staring at myself and touching the new hair, I cannot help but wonder what Joshua will think of the red. I don't know why I care, but for some reason, I want him to think it's hot.

When I emerge from the bathroom, running my hands through my new locks, Gracie whistles and says, "I love this color on you."

I smile and spin in a circle, modeling the red.

When I stop, I say, "Thanks. Did you want a glass of wine?"

"Yes, please."

I go to the kitchen to get the wine and sense her joining me, sitting on a stool at the counter.

I hand her the glass. She takes it and sips it. "Thanks."

I take a big sip, needing liquid courage. After I swallow, I say, "So, ugh. I kissed Mr. Fancy Pants, or should I say the CEO."

Heat rises from my neck to my cheeks at my admission. I glance down at the counter before looking up to see her reaction.

She spits the wine out, spraying it everywhere. Ahh. I rub the wine off my clothes and laugh. "Are you all right, there?"

"Well, you just said you kissed the CEO, while I was drinking. That's a big fucking deal. You don't kiss anyone. Tell me everything now. I want all the details."

I roll my eyes at her comment; I kiss men. I'm just not as regular as her, so in her eyes, she thinks it's nonexistent.

I walk around the counter and raise my hand to gesture her to follow. I sit on the couch and tuck my legs under my body. Taking a sip of more liquid strength, she sits down beside me, cradling her glass, gazing at me, waiting for me to tell her of all the gory details.

"So we were in the office, both staying late, fixing up a change of a design on a project, and he offered me a lift home. He didn't like the idea of me on the train so late." I shake my head, still shocked at how protective he got.

"Is this the same guy who you said was an asshole?" she asks.

Nodding, I sip some more wine.

"*Wow*. So why the change of mind?"

I'm struggling to understand that, too.

"I don't know, but over the project, we kind of got to relax around each other, and he is actually a nice person. His receptionist mentioned his estranged parents, so I don't know what happened there, but it made me think of him as human."

She laughs at me and says, "He is, silly. What else would he be? Anyway, I want to hear about the kiss; details, please."

I touch my lips as I explain. "Of course you do. So, he opens his passenger door. When I'm about to get in, he kisses me."

Even talking about the kiss makes my body warm.

"Gracie, it was so good. Like... rough and just a really passionate kiss."

I rub my forehead with my spare hand and then rest my head in my hand, my elbow propped up on the couch, to gaze at her.

"You're blushing. I love it. So now what happens?"

A sudden heaviness hits my heart.

"I pulled him aside yesterday for a quick moment, saying this job is important to me and that it can't happen again."

She snorts, which makes me laugh hysterically, and she joins. When we recover, she says, "As if you guys won't go there again. If he can make you squirm...It was a special kiss." Her eyebrows are dancing.

I sip my wine and say nothing, I'm unable to lie: If he kissed me, I would kiss him back. I return my gaze back to the television, my fingers touching my mouth, softly stroking as I flash back to the memory of how his lips felt against mine.

Although I watch our movie, I barely remember any of it. I can't get my mind off Joshua and these new feelings he has ignited. I need to get a grip on my feelings before returning to the office on Monday.

It's Monday and I'm ready, with my new red hair, to work with Thomas. As I enter the office, I can tell he's not here... Again.

Fuck.

I'm so screwed.

I rub my forehead, wishing Thomas would be at his desk and that I wouldn't have to work with Joshua again because I don't know how much restraint I have. Asshole Joshua is a turnoff, but kind and sweet Joshua, who kisses my lips roughly and makes me forget who I am and where I am, is weakening my defenses.

I toss my bag into the drawer and slam it closed, huffing. Yes, I'm totally fucked if I have to work alongside Joshua today.

"Whoa... What did that drawer do to you?"

My gaze lifts and lands on Thomas. I instantly relax, my shoulders dropping away from my ears.

Thank fuck. Who would have thought I would be so happy to see my boss?

"Nothing. It was an accident," I lie, not wanting to explain the real reason for my attitude.

He squints, examining me, but when he realizes I won't be sharing my thoughts, he drops it with a shrug.

"Follow me to my office and give me the rundown on what I have missed. I'm sure there is a lot to fill me in on."

He steps past me and enters his office and I hurry, picking up my notes and following him into the room.

"Also, I like the red. Suits you. Fiery redhead, hey," he says as I enter.

I smile before taking a seat in front of his desk and say, "I'm glad I don't need to explain it."

He leans back into his chair and turns his computer on, asking, "So where are we? Let's start with the tunnel."

I nod and explain to him where each project is and what Joshua and I have been doing while he has been away. Project by project, we talk, and then I fill him in on what the plans are for today. His face smooths; all the tightness disappears as I talk and he realizes he didn't have to catch up on a backlog of work because Joshua and I handled it. I'm sure he's still worried about his home life today and I want to make it easier on him.

"How's Lily?" I ask.

"So much better; such a freak bike accident, but the recovery was hard. She couldn't do a lot and needed help to do everything. Jennifer has been a great help. I wouldn't have been able to come back so quickly without her. I'm sorry I left you here to pick up the pieces in my absence." A sadness hits his gaze, and it makes me uncomfortable.

I thrust my hand out and say, "Don't worry about it. Joshua and I figured it all out."

He chuckles. "Yes, he finally understands how amazing you are. You floored him with the organization, drive, and passion you show for his company."

The sadness is now gone and replaced with a twinkle of what looks like pride.

My eyes bulge and I splutter, "Oh, ah, wow, that's great."

My mind drifts to imagine what their conversation about me would have been like. My heart beats double-time. I already knew Thomas had noticed me, but to affect Joshua, that gives me something to beam about. Truthfully I haven't been able to stop smiling since Thomas returned, knowing I can refocus on work and not the tempting man upstairs making me feel things I have never felt.

We have a meeting planned for midweek, so it will be the only time I bump into Joshua. Otherwise, I am back to solely working with Thomas. I unexpectedly feel all the tension leave, and a sudden lightness enters me. I stand and say, "If there isn't anything else, I'll go get started on emails. Just let me know if you need anything."

"Thanks, Ava."

I nod and walk back to my desk and begin my work for the day.

After a few hours, Thomas calls me into his office. When I walk in, he is hunched over his desk, rummaging through papers with furrowed brows, clearly looking for something. He spots a paper and picks it up with a smile, saying, "Here it is. Okay. We have a meeting with Joshua."

I step back, my mouth opening and closing repeatedly, and stutter, "Now?"

He eyes me critically and asks, "Yes. Is that a problem?"

I shake my head and say, "No, of course not."

When really, deep inside, my stomach flutters and the tension returns. I got too comfortable with the thought of not having to see him, so now, I'm trembling with nerves.

"Can you grab The Marrion project plans?"

I dip my chin and say, "Of course. I'll be one minute."

I take off back to my desk with my heart in my throat, knowing I need to act professionally and not let Thomas pick up on any changes between Joshua and me. I don't want him to work out that Joshua and I kissed.

Thomas stands at the desk as I pull the paper out of the printer and say, "Let's go."

We walk to the elevators, and when we exit on Joshua's floor, Linda's face lights up in welcome.

"Hi, Thomas. How is that beautiful daughter of yours?" she asks.

"Lily is feeling much better. The cast can't come off for six weeks, but for now, Jen is helping her out with homeschooling."

Linda says, with a hand resting on her chest, "Jennifer is a real gem. I hope she's as good a partner to you as she is a role model for those girls."

Thomas smiles with pride and says, "That she is. Well, Joshua is waiting for us. I'll catch up with you soon."

"Yes, he is. Nice to see you back."

"Good morning," I say to her as Thomas walks off.

"Morning, love. Look at your hair. This is my favorite color for you. Your gray eyes really pop."

I smile and drop my chin, feeling my nose tickle at the compliment.

"I best get in."

She nods and sits back in her chair as I hurry into the room. I take a seat and glance around the room, noticing Thomas is up at the front of the room, chatting with Joshua, as more colleagues pile into the room, taking a seat.

I set up my notes and pen before easing back into the chair with nothing else to do. I take a small peek their way. My eyes roam over Joshua's dark gray suit, crisp white shirt, and a pale pink tie. His hair is brown, short, and styled to perfection. He has nothing out of place. Why does he have to look edible and kiss like a pro? It's a mix that is so unfair, and I'm just another woman panting for attention, like a puppy dog wanting to be patted by her owner.

I can't seem to remove my gaze from them. A minute later, Thomas wanders away, back to his seat beside me, and Joshua's gaze lands on mine and his eyes sparkle. My heart beats like a drum in my chest; a small splinter of a smirk appears on his lips. And in that second, I know he likes my hair color. The appreciative look makes my stomach flutter and I look away from his intense glare and look at my notes, desperate for a distraction and not wanting to give him any sign that I'm affected by him.

"Good morning. Thanks, everyone, for joining this meeting about The Marrion." His deep, smooth voice is not very loud, but it commands the room's attention. "We need to look at our number of workers and I need to hire more, but I want to work out exactly how many I need before I set up interviews."

The meeting lasts for half an hour, and during that time, our eyes catch a few times, but one of us breaks the gaze, I don't want to be caught ogling or acting differently by our colleagues. Since we worked together so closely, there seems to be an unspoken shift in respect and attitude between us.

But other than those few glances at the meeting, I barely get noticed. I don't know why I care, but deep down, I do. I wanted him to ask me to stay behind so we could talk more. Ever since the small conversation we had the other night, I know there is more.

The buzz of connection whenever we are in the same room is palpable. But it seems impossible to talk to him because I'm working with Thomas again and there is no reason to talk to him. The only time for us to grab some cheeky glances is at the meetings when we know no one else is looking, like a silent chat for just us inside our minds.

After another week working with Thomas, it's Saturday night, and I promised Gracie I would come to the bar she works at for a drink.

I stand outside the door, running my sweaty palms over my white singlet top and ripped jeans. It's a different version of Ava, still sexy, but totally in a bar style, with an oversized jacket and cream boots to complete the look. I push my way through the crowd of people and approach the long timber bar; the place is full of people, the noise unbearable, and a wave of nausea rolls through my stomach. This might be too much, but just as I am about to spin around and walk out the door I just entered through, Gracie screams out, "Ava. Wine, or do you need vodka?"

I glace up into her gaze and she smiles at me with a look of appreciation. She knows how uncomfortable I am right now.

An awkward laugh slips out, and then I shout, "Vodka!"

"A double coming right up," she says, and I shake my head. But I'm grateful for her right now, reading my mind, knowing I need alcohol to calm the nerves inside me.

Not knowing where to stand, I look around at all the tables, wanting to sit down, but they are all occupied. Looks like standing is my only option tonight. As soon as I have had this drink, I'm out of here, Saturday night or not. I would rather have a quiet night in. A loud cheer rips through the bar crowd and I smile. Football must be on.

Gracie drops a tall glass of vodka and Sprite down in front of me and shouts, "Here you go. I will come find you soon. It's crazy. I can't stop to talk right now."

"Thanks" is all I get out before she slips away to serve more patrons, who are hanging drunkenly off the bar. They all gush at my pretty friend and she loves it because the locals tip her well.

I bring the glass to my mouth and take a big sip, the burn causing me to cough and splutter everywhere. Geez, this shit is strong. She really is trying to get me drunk. My eyes water from the strength. I will need to take it slow with this glass.

"Aren't you gorgeous?" My eyes turn to follow the voice, meeting a pair of heavily drunk eyes. Great. Could this night get any worse? Come on; the guy has to be in his late sixties. Surely I don't have *desperate* written in Sharpie on my forehead. I may be horny, but that is so not happening. No fucking chance.

He is still staring at me, and I cringe. God save me. He sways and falls forward. I take a step back, bumping into the guy behind me. I mouth *sorry* before turning back and mumbling, "Err, thanks, I guess."

"Are you here with any—" he slurs and sways to the side again.

The hairs on my arms prickle.

"There you are. I thought you got lost getting your drink, babe." Joshua's arm snakes around my shoulders and cuddles me into him, his scent and warm body cocooning me. I feel my tension slowly dissipate. Thank fuck. I'm saved by the devil himself.

I mime to the drunk man, "Sorry." He looks like he saw a ghost. A chuckle slips from my mouth. Joshua knows how to scare anybody away. His powerful look and rich clothes in a small town would frighten most. I watch the guy practically run away. I swivel around in

Joshua's arms to face him. He peers down into my gaze and his minty breath tickles my face. I lean into it as a wave of heat hits me, and my gaze roams his face and then stares at his parted lips before making my way up to his alcohol-free eyes.

Lowering my voice, I ask, "What are you doing here?"

His arm is still touching my shoulder, warming my whole body with the simple touch. It feels so natural having his hands on me. I slowly rake my gaze up and down over his casual clothes. I haven't seen him in jeans before, but my tongue darts out and licks my lips at how much they suit him. They hug his thick, muscly thighs and tapered waist. His long black top clings to his torso, showing off every ripple of muscle. My mouth is suddenly dry. I bring my drink to my lips as I stare into his blue eyes. The alcohol is burning my throat but not helping calm the raging hormones that are coursing through my body. I drink like I am drinking him in with every sip.

His hand slips from my shoulder to my hand in the softest of caresses. He scans me from my boots to my face; a heat flickers in his eyes and my mouth pops open in a pant. His other hand reaches out and strokes my hair in a tender touch, making my eyelashes flutter and I have to stop myself from closing my eyes and sinking into his touch.

"I love this color on you." His voice deep rumbles through my body.

I swallow hard, wetting my throat so I can speak.

"Thank you."

I cringe. How stupid. *Is that all you can say, Ava?* Not at all intelligent. It sounds like most women being seduced by a man, and I'm certain he would be used to women falling all over him.

"The casual look suits you. You look like less of an asshole."

That's better. I smile, happy that a bit of me is coming out now.

His head tips back and a chuckle leaves his throat. And why is him doing that so sensual to me? I need to get out of here before I do something stupid. I glance at the exit and before I can get the words out, he tugs my hand.

"Come on; we have a table over here." He drags me behind him with my hand entwined with his. Through the crowd, I brush past many men. I clutch his hand back in a tight grip. It's large, warm, and soft and I have missed the feel of his hand on my body, even if I only had it once briefly on my neck. He has me craving more.

CHAPTER 11

AVA

WE APPROACH THE TABLE; I see his friends sitting around relaxed, cradling beers. I laugh internally; they stand out in my local bar. Three ridiculously good-looking men who ooze success is not something you see often in a small town bar. I notice one person is missing.

I take a seat and Joshua sits right beside me. I ask, "Where is Thomas?"

"He went home to be with Lily," Joshua answers.

I slam my lips shut. What an idiot I am. Of course he is. She is still recovering, and he wouldn't be here drinking or watching sports. It's not Thomas. He is a family man.

"Of course."

I don't want to say anything else stupid, so I say nothing else. All his friends' gazes are on me. I stare back, trying not to show them how nervous I am. My gaze lands on a pair that are familiar: James.

I smile and say, "Hi."

He winks and says, "Hey, vixen. Nice change."

My brows crease, not understanding what he is talking about. And as if he reads my thoughts, he says, "Your hair. You dyed it red?"

Ahhh, of course. Geeze. I have lost my marbles. I can't even blame the alcohol; I only took a few sips.

"Yeah, I always change it up. Too boring to stay the same color."

His eyes twinkle with mischief.

"So, what do you do for work? Other than interviews for Joshua?" I tease.

He chuckles loudly before he answers. "Just helping a friend out there. I own a real estate development company."

My eyebrows rise and I splutter, "Holy shit. That's amazing."

He smirks, taking a gulp of beer before cradling it between his palms again.

"I didn't realize you owned it. I'm surrounded by rich fuckers." The last part slips out unintentionally. I slap my hand over my mouth and my eyes widen in horror.

A roar of laughter erupts from the table, so I don't feel bad about it slipping out. It's not like they don't know they have money. I slowly peel my hand away from my mouth and return it to my lap.

"So how come you are here?" I ask.

They lift their gaze toward the sandy blonde-haired guy, as if looking at him should give me answers, but I don't understand. I don't even know the guy's name.

"I'm Ben, and I had a football game close to here, and a few boys from the club suggested the food and drinks here."

I nod my understanding.

"And how come you are?" James asks, cutting my thoughts off. I know Joshua already knows I live close by, but not the reason I'm here.

Nodding in the bar's direction, I say, "My friend Gracie works here. She begged me to come and have a drink with her."

"I'm ordering the next round of drinks. What's her name? And what does she look like?" he asks me.

Joshua shakes his head next to me and I smirk and say, "I don't think she is looking for a boyfriend."

His eyes gleam, and he says, "That's even better."

I roll my eyes. Oh God. I will not stop him, but I will not help him figure out who she is. That will be part of the fun. I'm sure he will work it out. If not, when she finds me for drinks later, he can meet her then.

I take another sip of the potent drink and grimace. James and Ben stand and James asks, "Another drink?"

I hold up my drink in my hand and say, "Oh, no, thanks. This is a double, courtesy of my friend."

He leans back to scan around the room and across the bar before his gaze lands on mine again, a frown forming between his brows. He asks, "Now I really need to meet her. Come on, vixen, which one is she?"

I shake my head and say, "Not helping you."

Joshua chuckles beside me.

"Fine, then I'll ask around. What about you, Josh? A beer?" James asks.

"No. Thanks," Joshua answers.

And then the boys disappear through the crowd, leaving just Joshua and me. I turn to face him and ask, "You don't drink?"

He isn't drinking a lot for a game day like most men do.

"No. I used to be a huge party boy, but when I got the company, I stopped drinking and sobered up. To be honest, I don't have time for hangovers. I'm working all day, every day." There is a hint of sadness in his tone. I don't know if it's from taking over the business or giving up a playboy life, or if it's because he's working so much. Heck, it could be all three. It all sounds exhausting.

"I don't drink a lot either," I say, hoping to make him feel a little better. His forehead creases at my admission.

"What's your reason?" he asks.

I'm not about to share my miserable life, but I have to give him something, so I say, "Just growing up, I have seen too much drug and alcohol abuse."

He nods and says, "Fair enough." I feel my cheeks heat under his firm stare. I take a sip of my drink, thinking it will help cool me down, but I end up choking on a cough.

He sits up and rubs my back, causing a tremble to run through my body. When I recover and turn to face him and see his concerned expression, I say, "This is so strong."

"Don't drink it then," he responds.

"Alright, smartass."

We sit, staring into each other's eyes. I bite my lip and watch his blue eyes darken; the electricity is pulling me in. And if sensing it, he leans forward and I feel my restraint about to snap. The sparks between us are hard to deny. I want to taste him and have his hands on me again. I need to find out if it was just a one-off or if there is more to this attraction. His gaze drops to my mouth and my tongue skims my lips and he inches closer, watching the movement. Tingles flood my body and his breath is tickling my wet lips. I feel him close in and I can't wait to taste him again. I'm growing wet and achy in between my thighs from anticipation. I'm so fucked, but I don't care. I want it. I want him.

"I don't know which one is your friend, but I'm impressed they only hire desirable women here. We will have to come here more often," Ben says, interrupting our moment.

A heavy sigh leaves my mouth, a mix of annoyance at their interruption and anger that I almost gave in again.

"Please don't. I get enough of you boys in the city to not have you here."

Joshua growls next to me and says, "It won't stop them." His voice tickles my ear, tormenting me. I'm already barely hanging on to my control. I need to get some space before I demand he kiss me, or worse, for me to lose it and kiss him.

I stand abruptly and say, "I just want to check on my friend and let her know I'm sitting here with you and that I haven't done a runner and gone home."

My gaze flicks around to each guy. They nod back and when my gaze lands on Joshua, his lips twist and I can tell he wants to say something, but before he can, I cut him off and say, "I'll be right back." He moves and he drops his head with a laugh.

I weave my way through the crowd and approach the bar. Pushing my way to the front, I lean on the wooden bar and scan for Gracie. Where the fuck is she? I'm in urgent need of some girl conversation and I need her to slap some sense into me. I'm about to push off the bar when I spot her coming out of the back, carrying a box of beer. She dumps it in front of the fridge, ready to restock.

"Gracie," I shout.

Looking over her shoulder, she smiles and steps over to the bar, leaning forward to ask, "Do you need another drink?"

Realizing I left my drink at the table, I shake my head and say, "No way. That drink is way too strong. I can barely sip it."

She moves back and unpacks the beer and I move around to the side of the bar to get closer and talk.

"Joshua and his friends are here. I'm having a hard time sitting next to him," I say.

Her gaze lifts to look at me, her face puzzled, like I have grown a third head and she asks, "Why?"

"Because I want to kiss him again," I explain.

I have barely drunk anything, too scared that if I drink, my sense of control will completely disappear, and I need to keep myself in check.

"You're crazy. Go have some fun. You never have fun; always organized, planned, and guarded. Live a little. You're so young, but you never let yourself act like it."

I stare back at her, absorbing her words. I know she is right, but it doesn't change the fact he is my boss and I need this job. It's my ticket to good money and a stable future.

She puts down two shot glasses, lifts a bottle of tequila, and pours a shot into each glass, then hands me a piece of lime and says, "Cheers to having a little fun." She winks and holds one up, waiting for me to cheer her.

I look at the tequila in the glass. My stomach hardens. But tequila is better than the drink she made me. I pick the glass up and hold the lime piece in the other hand and say, "Cheers." I clink the glass with hers before shooting the alcohol back. It burns down my throat and I want to cough, but when I lift the lime and suck, it helps soothe the ache.

I slam the empty shot glass down and wince. When the burn settles, I say, "I'm sitting at the table over there." I point through at the area past the crowd where I know the table is. "Come join at the end of your shift."

"Okay. Sounds great. Now go have fun. I gotta get back to work." She steps away to finish unpacking.

I push off the bar and walk through the crowd to get to the bathroom. I need a minute before I go have fun with Joshua. As I approach the ladies' door to push it open, I'm yanked by my hand into a hard chest. My heart is in my throat and my pulse is rocketing. My breathing speeds up as I peer into Joshua's dark, heated gaze.

He steps back, taking me into the staff toilet. I watch him close and lock the door. As soon as I hear the click, my restraint snaps. I push him hard up against the back of the door and kiss him with all the passion I had been holding back. He growls into my mouth and kisses me back harder. My heart is thundering inside my chest as my pussy becomes throbbing and wet with desire. I pull away from the kiss to nip at his lip. His mouth opens in surprise and I lick his open mouth. Another growl leaves his chest and I feel the vibration on my breasts, which are pushed up against him and I wonder if he can feel my piercings. My nipples are hard and my body is screaming for more, so I kiss him again, this time deeper, tasting his minty breath. Mixed with my tequila, it's unusual, but isn't that us?

He pulls his mouth away just enough to tug on my bottom lip with his teeth. Oh God, this is totally insane. I have never done anything like this and it's a damn shame. This is so bloody good. The raw need and connection pumping through my veins is captivating. My lip pops out from between his teeth. His heated gaze sends a thrill through my body, causing me to soak my panties even further. I'm so achy that my body is begging for release.

He spins us around and thrusts me hard up against the door.

"Oh" slips from my lips.

His hand dives into my hair and pulls it down. He tilts my body into the perfect angle so he can kiss me deeply with his tongue.

The pinch on my skull from the hair pulling causes me to moan into his mouth. My sex is pulsating with heavy desire and I'm so fucking horny and turned on that I could scream. I want to ride him so hard, but at this moment, he is overpowering me and my body surrenders to his, giving him complete control of my pleasure.

He pulls his lips off slowly, biting my lip and dragging it between his teeth, the pinching pain sending a tingling sensation to my pussy. I'm so wound up right now, I just want him to hurry up and fuck me senseless. I don't even want to remember my name.

He grips my face roughly and turns it to the side, grunting in my ear, "I fucking love this hair on you. It's my favorite color so far. It's made my dick so hard that every time I see you, I have been fantasizing about touching and yanking it between my fingers... Does it match?"

What the fuck?

My mouth drops open, ready to ask what he means, but when he grabs my pussy roughly through my jeans, I get it. But he asks anyway. "Does your pussy match?"

Fuck, his dirty mouth is something I have never experienced before. But in this moment, I fucking love it.

"Ugh no. There is no hair," I choke back.

As he rubs my pussy hard through my jeans with his fingers, the friction on my clit sends me close to an orgasm. If he keeps this up, I'll be coming without him even touching me naked.

His guttural sounds tell me he is barely hanging on too. I lean forward to capture his lips with mine and at the same time, my hands are at the end of his shirt. Pushing it up, he helps me take it off by ripping it over his head. Holy shit!

His body is better than I have imagined, his chiseled chest rising and falling with each breath. I reach out and rub my palms over the smooth warmth. I get to the top of his abs and follow the ripples down to his tapered V. He isn't your normal office boy. No, this man is a fucking businessman ready to destroy me. Here, in the local bar's toilet. What is happening in my life? I'm out of my goddamn mind.

I run my hands back up his abs and chest, then up to his shoulders and down his biceps, taking every inch of him in for my personal memory bank. In case this is a one-off, at least I will have wonderful memories.

I want to say something, but for once, I have no smartass comment. He has left me completely speechless.

My sex throbs, desperate for more. I shrug my jacket to the floor and wait for him to remove my white singlet. I can't wait to see his reaction, so I watch him. His gaze is fixed on my body, as his fingers trace softly over the rose tattoo on my shoulder and down to the end of the design.

He threads his fingers through the straps of my top and pulls it down. "Oh fuckin' hell." I bite my lip, holding back a laugh. The tortured sound makes me feel powerful. Before, I thought it was him who owned me. But now I know the tables have turned. Take that, playboy. Clearly, he hasn't been with someone like me.

His eyes haven't left my nipples; they keep jumping from left nipple to right, like he can't believe what's in front of him. I watch his face with fascination. His tongue slides out over his lip and I feel that between my legs. When his eyes flash to mine and a deep need is there, I know for certain he hasn't been with a woman with piercings.

"Don't be gentle," I warn.

"Fuck me! And here I thought the only metal was on your face. You, babe, are full of surprises." His voice is strained.

He drops his head down to close his mouth around one nipple. And I feel his warm, wet tongue gently play with the barbell and I groan. His powerful tongue moves it around. I slam my eyes shut in intense pleasure and throw my head back against the door and grab the back of his head, his soft brown locks gripped between my fingers. I hold his head against my breast. He smiles around my nipple and then, becoming more daring, he bites the nipple and tugs on the bar. A feral sound leaves my throat, and his lack of experience is not showing right now. He is the master at knowing how to send me flooding into a crippled mess. I'm soaked and panting now, so close to coming. He pops that nipple free from his mouth and trails kisses between my chest to the other nipple. This one is more sensitive and I'm confident I'll come from his rough tongue and teeth.

"I didn't think I could like metal, but you have made me love it. I didn't realize what I was missing and I can smell how close you are. And I want to make you come from my mouth alone."

Fuck me with this guy and his mouth.

"Shut the fuck up and just do it," I groan.

He chuckles but then claims the other nipple and I bang my head on the door, not caring how much pain is radiating through the back of my skull. Because the way he twirls his tongue around my nipple and bites the bar takes away any pain, I only feel intense pleasure building in my body.

I'm done. I can't hang on any longer.

"Fuck, I need to come," I breathe.

He pops off my nipple and my eyes pop open in a *what the fuck do you think you're doing* look.

His sexy smirk sits on his handsome face, but he quickly gets moving to my jeans, snapping the button and unzipping them before stuffing his hand down them. He doesn't go slow; he finds my soaking pussy and thrusts two thick fingers in.

"Oh, shit," I moan.

I close my eyes and enjoy every single quick thrust of his fingers. I'm angry that I have jeans on, but I don't want to stop him just to take them off. I'm way too close to stop him now; I just want to orgasm.

"Looks like you want this as much as me. Does this feel good?" He grunts the question.

I nod frantically up and down, unable to form coherent words as I'm chasing the orgasm.

"I'm close."

He speeds up before slowing to insert another finger. The sting of the stretch feels good. The mix of pain and pleasure is enough to tip me over the edge and I groan as I come hard on his fingers. My eyes shut as I become overwhelmed with pleasure and ride his hand while he groans with me.

My chest racks with heavy pants and I'm waiting to finish coming down from my high. I haven't come this hard ever, so I take a minute to collect myself. I feel his hand slowly slip out and a shudder hits my body from the loss. He zips my jeans and rebuttons them. Hearing the movement and then feeling him near my face, I blink to allow my eyes to focus on him. I bite my lip to hide a sheepish smile; I see a twinkle in his gaze, amused by the state he put me in.

"Feel better?" he asks.

I roll my eyes sarcastically at him and put my hands to his chest and nuzzle him back, feeling his close proximity affecting my thoughts. I force myself to get some distance. What the fuck did we just do?

I can't believe I let this happen. But I wanted it and fuck, it felt so good.

Damn him and how good he made me just feel. His mind and body are consuming me. I didn't even have sex, and I feel this good. Imagine if we had, how good he would have been. Remembering he didn't even get off, my gaze drops to his crotch; the bulge straining his jeans is clear. I bite the inside of my cheek to not offer to fix him or offer sex. I'm mortified I allowed this to happen in the toilet, but also, the other part of me is happy that I should be able to concentrate on work now that I have gotten him out of my system.

He isn't the type of guy who wants to settle down. He and I come from different worlds. Him rich and me poor. He's a playboy, and I cannot be in a casual relationship.

"Are you ready to rejoin the group?" he asks, watching me dress. His gaze flames with desire and he watches me adjust my breasts back into my top.

"Jacket please," I ask him. He snaps out of his stare and scoops up my jacket from the floor. He stands back up and holds it wide open so I can thread my arm in each hole. I step in front of the mirror. Surprisingly, I don't look as fucked as I feel. I just fix my hair, then I spin to meet his gaze and say, "I'm ready."

He holds his hand out toward the door and says, "Lead the way."

I dip my head and open the door slowly, peering out through a crack. With no one walking past, I slip out quickly, not caring if Joshua is behind me or not.

I walk fast through the crowd as if the last ten minutes never happened. When I return to the table James asks, "Have you seen Josh?"

I grab my drink and take a large gulp, forgetting the strength and wincing at the burn. Bile rises instantly, but I swallow it back down and push the glass away. No way will I be having any more of that tonight. "No," I say. "I went to the bathroom."

But just as I say the words, I shiver.

"There you are. Where have you been?" James asks.

I roll my lips, keeping my gaze down, waiting to hear what excuse he will come up with.

"Just buying a round of drinks. It took forever, so I'm not getting the next round," he says in his usual controlled voice.

I flick my gaze up, but he doesn't meet mine. I shuffle down the booth so he can sit down, not wanting to make it awkward. I need to act the same as before he made me come hard with his mouth and fingers.

A shiver runs down my back at the memory. Not the time for a reminder. The table goes back to chitchat and I answer with a nod or a mumble when appropriate. But I do not know what time it is or what they have been talking about. I have just sat there, totally zoned out.

"Hi." Gracie's voice breaks my lost state. I glance up and smile. Thank fuck. I need someone to talk to.

"Is your shift over?" I ask her and touch Joshua's shoulder to allow me up.

He slides out from the table and I follow and say, "Thanks," and he slips back in.

I hear a throat clear, and I can tell it's James wanting introductions, so I turn around and say. "Gracie, this is James, Ben, and Josh. Boys, this is my friend Gracie."

"Nice to meet you..." James asks.

He is not touching her; he is as big of a player, if not more, than Joshua. Gracie doesn't need more instability in her life.

Benjamin offers a quick hi and so does Joshua. I can feel Joshua's glare burning a hole in the side of my face. I refuse to turn. I'm in desperate need to debrief with my girl.

As if sensing my need to flee, she asks, "You ready to go? I'm tired; that was a crazy shift. My feet are aching." She shuffles from foot to foot, trying to ease the pain.

"Definitely. Let's go."

I address the table and say, "Okay, boys. Thanks for a great evening. I'm off with Gracie."

I peer around the table, but when my gaze lands on Joshua, I see humor in his gaze. He clearly knows I want to tell my friend we just made out in the bathroom. I couldn't care less if he knows. I just need to get away from here before I find myself drunk or, worse, in bed with him.

Two mistakes have already happened. I can't let a third slip.

I link my arm through hers and wave at the group, saying, "Bye."

"Bye," they respond.

I take one last look at Joshua, who winks at me, and it makes my stomach somersault.

Gracie tugs on my arm and we exit. I feel like I can finally breathe. I suck in the fresh night air and walk back to her car under the night stars. She is crashing at my apartment tonight.

"Those guys were hotter than hell," Gracie coos.

I giggle and say, "Don't remind me and don't tell them. You are aware they are serial playboys."

"I'm not blind, but I'm up for a good time," she says as she climbs into her car.

"No. Trust me, don't go there… but ah, I kinda made out with Joshua in the bathroom." A loud slap followed by pain on my arm shocks me and I burst out laughing.

She twists to face me. "How the hell did that happen?"

I feel my whole body flush and I say, "He dragged me inside."

She shakes her head. And giggles. "You dirty bitch. I love it."

"So did I," I answer honestly.

We drive home, giggling like schoolkids as I tell her the story.

CHAPTER 12

JOSHUA

I WATCH HER WALK away from the table in those tight jeans. Her hips sway and I can't help but watch them move until she disappears from my vision. I have to hold myself back from getting out of this chair, stalking outside, and demanding she come home with me.

My dick is in so much pain right now, I have to re-arrange it in my pants. I could kick myself. I should have let myself come in my pants like I wanted to in the bathroom, instead of holding myself back. She is making me feel like a teenager who is hooking up for the first time. The feelings she brings to the surface and the intensity of them are all new to me.

Touching her warm, wet pussy was the highlight. She was at my mercy, and feeling her walls clamp tight shut when she was close has me thinking what it would be like to have her tight pussy milking my dick. I rub the back of my neck as I drink some water.

"That vixen sure is fine," James says.

I stare at the exit, hoping she will come back in. But when James speaks, I swivel to face him.

"Isn't she... and so unique," I say under my breath so no one else can hear. They will think I'm crazy. I'm sure I am... but only for her.

James lifts his chin in the direction on the door to ask, "Are you going to tap that?"

I think about it. Will I?

I shouldn't.

I'm her boss. Well, CEO.

But I have little restraint, and after our bathroom encounter...

"I can't," I answer.

"Why not?" Benjamin asks, rubbing his eyebrow.

I turn to him, watching as he sips his beer, and I rub the back of my neck to ease the tension that's building.

"I'm her boss," I say.

"Well, technically, Thomas is. But I must agree that employees are off limits to me," James agrees.

I shake my head, thinking of his new blonde intern, and ask, "Is this a recent decision?"

"We aren't talking about me." He stiffens.

"Calm down and pull the stick out of your ass. I'm clearly stating facts. But back to me, no, I can't have sex with her."

I need to keep saying it out loud as a reminder to myself.

"So one of us can?" Benjamin asks.

"Fuck no."

They both glance at each other, Benjamin whispering under his breath, "He's fucked her already."

"Totally," James snorts.

And they both begin cackling in a fit of laughter.

"Fuck you both. Thanks for having faith in me," I say.

"As if you wouldn't be thinking the same if it was one of us," James says.

I sit back in my chair, arms folded over my body, and let their words sink in. Yeah, I totally would. It's just hard being called out on my shit.

Linda and I are checking the flights for me to join James at a business conference in a few days' time. I'm looking forward to learning new skills and meeting potential investors.

My phone buzzes inside my pocket. I pull it out and stare at the screen. I hit the mute button and shove it into my back pocket.

"Your mom or dad?" Linda asks.

A simple question, but even the thought rattles me. Why does he keep calling? Is he wanting to gloat about his fucking holiday?

I don't care. I don't want to know.

And if my dad hadn't given me this sinking ship of a company, I would still party, drink, and sleep around the city. I guess I should answer and thank him for changing my life, but truthfully, I'm not ready.

Not ready to forgive them for neglecting me or for not giving me their love and attention. I don't even know what it's like to have a parent cuddle you or lay with you when you feel sick. Mom rubbed my hair a few times but mostly just put me to bed and said rest would make me feel better. I look back now and see how bad that was, but growing up, I didn't care. I got to do whatever I wanted and not have any consequences. I had money, girls, and booze. My life was fun until it wasn't anymore.

I want more out of life now, a life rich with people I care about and who care about me. And a better future for myself, so I never need their support. I want to support myself.

I organize paperwork I will need while away and I answer Linda. "Dad."

"Does he call you often?" she asks.

"Recently, yes." I don't expand, just keep my replies short, hoping she gets the hint that I don't want to talk about this.

"Don't you want to find out why?"

"Not really. I guess one part of me does, but the other is so angry at him, I don't want to. Also, I worry it's him gloating about his holiday. I don't think I could hear it without losing my shit."

"Fair enough, love. When you are ready, you can call him or answer one of his calls."

I love how Linda offers parental advice but also respects my feelings. She knows about my life and shit upbringing. She is a good ear when I need a woman's advice, but she doesn't push when I need space.

I feel like I'm one of her adopted children. Her children are lucky to have a mom like her. She is special.

We work to finish so it's all ready before we break for lunch.

Ava

Thomas has told me Joshua has gone away for a few days, so I won't see him until next week. My thoughts return to how I felt when I was with him. Why didn't it feel wrong? Why wasn't I repulsed? I should have... I shouldn't want more. But deep down, I do.

I'm working on a current project when an email hits my inbox. I suck in a breath. It's him. My body warms as I click *open* to read its contents.

To: Ava Johnson
Subject: Park Lane
Message: Good morning Ava,
Hope you're working hard. I just have a question regarding the pantry switches. Is there more than one?
Regards,
Joshua Ward

I smile at his light email; it feels as if his demeanor toward me has changed. He is nicer, but still has a hint of humor.

I sit up straighter and tap my lip, thinking of a cheeky response. My average day is turning brighter just from a simple email.

To: Joshua Ward
Subject: Re: Park Lane
Message: Morning Joshua,
Of course I'm working hard. What else would I
be doing?
I haven't been in any confined spaces with any-
one else, if that's what you're asking.
There is only one switch in each currently. I can
send an amendment over with two in each. Are
you wanting them side by side or on top of each
other?
Ava

I know he didn't ask, but I want to see where
this goes when he isn't in my space. I have fun
with the playful Joshua; it feels easy. I haven't
felt like that with a guy in more than a friend
way in a very long time.

I begin a new invoice for the changes while I
wait for a response from him to see where he
wants the switch placed.

My leg is bouncing up and down. I need to
calm down. I shouldn't be playing because this
won't end well, but when that noise tells me a
new email is in, I feel my adrenaline hit.

I can't click fast enough, reading the reply as
fast as possible with a stupid, lopsided smile on
my face.

To: Ava Johnson
Subject: Re: Park Lane
Message: I'm glad that you haven't been in
any bathrooms with anyone else. I would hope
that's only reserved for me.

And what you could be doing. Now that's a loaded question, and it depends on if we are talking about work? Or something else...
Side by side, please. And send the amendment over when you can.
Regards,
Joshua Ward

I wiggle in the chair, needing to get comfortable and think of a suitable response. I roll my lips and begin typing the amendment form. When I finish the new invoice and adjust the plans, I attach them to the email and begin typing my reply.

To: Joshua Ward
Subject: Re: Park Lane
Message: It's definitely not an activity I do on the regular, if that's what you are asking. And I definitely don't get involved with colleagues. Or something else. What does that mean? You have me intrigued. I want to know more please. Attached to this email is the new invoice and new designs.
Ava

I hit send and feel pretty happy with myself. Feeling a tad hot and irritable from the sexual flirtation, I decide to go have my lunch outside. I'm desperate for some fresh air and time away from the computer.

I pop into Thomas's office and see him hunched over, typing away on his computer, a deep frown set in between his eyebrows.

I giggle and say, "Thomas, I'm going to lunch. Do you want anything?"

His gaze lifts from the screen to meet mine, the frown still set in place. He shakes his head and he says, "No thanks, Ava. I just need to finish this. Enjoy. See you when you get back."

My lips twitch and I push off the frame I was leaning against and say, "Sure thing." I walk off toward the elevator, intending to grab my lunch and sit outside.

I sit in the park near our building. You can see it from our office window. The fresh air and noise are the perfect distraction. My tension disappears just by focusing on what is going on outside rather than reading Joshua's reply. I can't lie. I kind of want to rush back up and see what his response is. But I need to calm myself down and be level-headed about this. I don't want anyone to know what's happened between us, so my reactions to Joshua have to be with me in control of my emotions.

I relax in the sun and eat. When my half hour is up, I wander slowly back up, but as I enter the lobby, my heart jumps at the sight of him. I wasn't expecting him back today. My heart beats wildly inside my chest as his lips twist into a knowing smirk. I roll my eyes and pinch my lips together and stand up tall as I strut past him. He is having a conversation with another stuck-up suit I haven't seen before. But as I pass, his gaze locks onto mine, a heat flaring in his. I secretly love how his focus is on me and not on the conversation.

In the elevator, I lean against the back wall and close my eyes, welcoming the icy metal. My mouth is watering at his black tailored pinstripe suit, perfectly fitted against his desirable body. My fingers tingle at the memory of his soft skin and perfectly toned body under my hands. He makes the naughty side of me come out, and yet he makes me feel powerful and sexy all at the same time. As the elevator stops, I push off and wander back into the office, my mind still in the clouds and as I approach the desk, I know he hasn't responded to my email because he must have been traveling.

"I'm back from lunch." I speak loudly to Thomas, pulling out my chair and sitting down at my desk.

"Okay, Ava," he calls back.

But as I click my computer awake from rest mode, I can see the icon button that highlights a new email. I lean closer and feel myself smile. *Get a grip, Ava. He is your boss, remember. Nothing good will come of this.*

To: Ava Johnson
Subject: Re: Park Lane
Message: Thank you for the attachments.
I'm not your colleague... I'm the boss, and I say so long as you are willing, this is okay. And it's okay for you to change your mind.
So you can't get in trouble... Unless you want to get in trouble? Well then, I could punish you... with my hand on your ass. In particular, me leaving my handprint on your milky white skin.
Regards,
Joshua Ward

What the fuck?

I should be appalled, but I'm not. I'm so turned on right now, I squirm in my chair. My sex clenches at the words and I feel myself become wet. *I want him.*

As I sit staring at his words, I imagine it and now I actually want it. Him in his sexy-as-fuck pinstripe suit, me bent over my desk with my bare ass out, and him spanking me repeatedly and leaving his handprints all over me. A shudder runs through my body.

This is torture.

I shake my head and focus on writing back, tugging my lip between my teeth, knowing I'm about to play dirty.

To: Joshua Ward
Subject: Re: Park Lane
Message: Well, boss, I'm waiting. My ass is twitching to feel your hands on it.
Ava

I smile at the screen and sit back. *Take that, Josh,* I mutter to myself, feeling a sense of victory, but it's mixed with a tad bit of fear. I'm playing with the devil, so I'm bound to get hurt. But my stupid heart doesn't want to listen to my head.

An email arrives less than a minute later and I turn around to check behind me, double-checking Thomas isn't there. He isn't, so I click open the reply.

To: Ava Johnson
Subject: Re: Park Lane
Message: Grand Hotel. Six PM Sharp.

Regards,
Joshua Ward

Oh shit.

A swarm of butterflies enters my stomach and I lean back in my chair and cross my hands over my chest. You wanted this, Ava. Well, now you got it. I sit there and stare at the address. I don't know what to do, so instead of thinking about it, I try to focus on the last few hours of the day.

A few hours later, when I hear Thomas saying goodbye, I realize it's time for me to pack up and make my way down to the hotel. I do not know where it is, but I like the idea of the hotel. Neither of us needs to commit even though I shouldn't even be doing it, but I just can't deny myself. I think if I just fuck his brains out, I will get over him.

I'm a grown-ass woman with needs. Yeah, that's it, I think as I pack up with a new determination. I Google Map the address and walk out of the building. I hurry and follow the directions Siri is spitting out at me through the phone. A few minutes later, I'm out front, looking around before stepping inside the modern building. I realize I don't know what floor he's on, and I don't have his damn phone number. I step inside and see a large reception desk and walk right up.

The receptionist smiles as I approach and asks, "Hi. Can I help you?"

Sweat forms on my back, making my clothes cling to my body.

"I'm looking for Mr. Joshua Ward," I state with a shaky voice.

The neatly dressed check-in lady is in a navy suit, her brunette hair pinned into a neat bun on top of her head. "And you are?" she asks.

"Ava Johnson."

"Okay. Room 1415." She dismisses me, ready to serve the next customer.

I swivel and walk to the elevators. As I get inside and hit the button for fourteen, my legs wobble and I can feel the sweat picking back up.

Why did I flirt?

You play with fire, you're bound to get burned, Ava.

The elevator doors open, and this is it. Showtime.

I step in front of 1415, staring at the door, willing myself to bang. I take a few deep breaths, trying to rein in my nerves. *You can do this.* And with that, I knock on the door.

I shuffle my feet from side to side and hold on to my handbag like a lifeline. Hurry, before I change my mind and bolt out of here.

The door flings wide open and he stands there in his sexy suit. But the tie is no longer there and his shirt has a few buttons undone at the top, showing off some of his bare chest. I rake my eyes seductively over his body. He stands in bare feet, his ankles crossed, one hand on the door and a glass of amber liquid in the other. I know he doesn't drink much, so he must be just as nervous as me to be drinking. Knowing that he is nervous too gives me confidence to follow through with our flirting.

"Hi," I say.

His eyes glide up and down gloriously slowly over me, soaking in every detail before the corner of his lip rises. He takes a sip of his drink and inclines his body in an invitation for me to get inside.

"Come in," he says. His voice is low and laced with the same desire that's racing through me.

I step inside and see a table. Walking over to it, I dump my bag and spin around, turning toward him. I watch as he lowers the glass into the sink, not finishing it.

He turns and stalks toward me. My heart pounds as he gets closer to me. I tip my head back in time for him to claim my mouth roughly. His hands grip the sides of my face and he thrusts his tongue inside my mouth. I match his onslaught with my tongue, tasting and tantalizing every inch of his mouth. But it's not enough. I need more, so, with my hands, I push off his suit jacket. I want him naked and inside me as soon as possible. My feverish body is aching with need.

I no longer care if I appear desperate, because I am. My sex is throbbing in anticipation and my panties were soaking the moment his rough hands and lips hit mine. This pent-up frustration needs to be released, and I know he feels the same. I grab his shirt and undo his buttons one by one until the shirt is hanging open. I pull my mouth from his to stare intensely into his darkened, hooded eyes. His breaths tickle my lips. And I let my fingers trail down his chest between his pecs and hit his rippled abs one by one, down to his pants. He hisses, and the sound speaks directly to my sex. I grab the sides of his shirt and push them off his shoulders. My eyes drop over his delectable body. I slowly blink, thinking I must be dreaming, and lean forward to trace my tongue over his right nipple. He groans when I do it. I smile around it before biting it and standing back up, a smirk on my lips.

"I think I have met my match," he growls.

My eyebrow raises in question.

"A little rough and dirty. Clearly just how you like it, too." He grabs my breast roughly in his hand and squeezes. His finger grazes my nipple through my clothes.

My head tips backward and I choke out, "Ah." His lips find my neck, trailing kisses up and down along my outstretched skin. A shiver runs up my back from the mix of the soft kisses with the rough squeezes. He nips all the way up my neck before trailing up to my mouth and kissing me deeply again.

I feel his hand skim my back, unzipping my black dress. I'm panting in anticipation. How he knew the zip was along my lower back, I don't know. And right now, I don't care. I help him by removing my arms from the sleeves and the dress drapes around my hips. He tears his lips from mine to glance down and help tug the dress over my hips and ass. When it's free, he drops it and it pools at the bottom of my feet. I kick it to the side with my foot. I stand in my black lacy thong and bra. I feel his warm breath on my face. I am watching his eyes sparkle.

"You are so beautiful."

His gaze warms me and his words tell me he likes what he sees. I bite my lip and reach out to undress him. I grab his leather belt and begin unbuckling it and pulling it off. He then takes over to unbutton his pants in a rush, sensing my urgency, and pushes his zipper down. I glide my hands from his chest to his pants to push them down. His briefs are tenting from his massive erection, and I can feel my sex throb. God, he is magnificent.

I can see why he would be a playboy. His charms, good looks, success, and enormous package; he would be the perfect guy. I reach out and squeeze him through his briefs. I can barely get my hand around his thickness and the thought has me swallowing hard.

He is big.

I glance up and his blue eyes stare back at me with heavy desire. I'm feeling on edge like I can barely hold on, he captures my hand in his and drags me by the hand to walk into another room. I follow and when we enter, I see a giant white bed and before I can take in anything else, he sits down and pulls me across his knee. "Oh" comes out of my mouth.

But I pant, thinking I'm getting the spanking I asked for. He pulls my thong down to under my ass cheeks and pushes his fingers from my soaking sex slowly over my back entrance and I slam my eyes shut. No one has gone there before. I can't say I wouldn't want to try it because then I would be lying. But I want sex too much to play with unknown territory tonight.

"Soaked," he growls in appreciation.

I bite the inside of my cheek to prevent myself from saying anything.

He pulls my thong all the way off. Then a loud smack echoes and a sting burns on one ass cheek. I moan and wiggle. He runs his hand over the sting, and I want more, but he caresses the spot and then removes my bra. It falls to the floor. He helps me stand so I'm naked in front of him.

I'm soaked, heavy, and needy.

He runs his tongue across his lips and I watch the movement. This is turning me on, and I am sick of waiting, so I step forward, pushing him to lie down. He collapses on his back, his watching me, and I step toward him and bend forward. I grab his briefs and pull them down his legs and get them all the way off. Then I climb over him, hovering my body over him. He pinches my nipple ring and I moan, briefly closing my eyes, and I have to control myself to not orgasm. I catch his mouth in a deep kiss. When I pull back, he nips my lip. I pull back and ask, "Condom?"

"Wallet; inside my pants," he puffs out.

I nod and jump off him to retrieve it. When I return, he is sitting up, his cock hard and his hand gripping it. It's erotic and the pre-cum that he smears has me gulping down the gush of saliva that forms in my mouth. I want to taste him, but I have no time for that tonight. I want hard and hot sex right now.

I tear the condom packet with my teeth and then roll the condom on with my hands. He sucks in a breath and grabs my waist and tosses me back down on the bed. But I shake my head and say, "I want to ride you."

His eyes bore into me, and he says, "You're killing me." But he rolls onto his back, taking me with him. My hands land on top of his warm, hard body, his chest rising and falling under my palms. I crawl up and hover over him. Leaning forward, I lick his open mouth. And I'm about to pull back, but he grabs the back of my head and tugs my mouth to his. We kiss passionately before I can't handle the ache in my sex anymore. His hands are gripping my waist and I need him inside my hot, wet pussy. I push up with my hands and knees and line him up with my entrance. I slowly lower down, letting my walls adjust. When I'm fully seated, I rise and lower repeatedly until I find a rhythm and angle that works best. My hands sit on his upper abs, which clench under my palms, and I try to keep my eyes on his, battling the need to flutter them closed and soak in the pleasure he is giving me. I love being on top, holding the power over him. I continue to slow my pace until I feel my walls adjust enough and then I ride him harder and faster, moaning out loud from the fullness.

"Fuck, babe. I'm close," he grunts through clenched teeth. His face is taut with concentration.

"Hold on. I'm almost there," I moan.

My eyes slam shut, when I feel him grow inside of my pussy and before I know it, a tingle runs down my spine and I'm screaming, "I'm coming."

"Fuck, babe."

I shatter on his cock, and I feel him jerk, emptying inside. A loud groan leaves his throat. I ride it out for a bit before I roll off and lie next to him, throwing my arm over my face, trying to calm my breathing down to a regular pattern. It was the most intense experience I have ever had; the emotions swirling inside me cause me to shudder in the aftermath.

CHAPTER 13

JOSHUA

I LIE ON THE bed with her hand against my chest, sucking in deep breaths, trying to recover from the mind-blowing sex we just had. She just blew every other sexual experience to smithereens. She is confident and controlling, but not in a fake way, just that she knows what she wants in the bedroom. I love her confidence and her body. Her delicate shoulder tattoo mixed with her piercings offers a combination of sweet but sexy.

"You're incredible," I say.

"Thanks. So were you," she whispers back, sounding as spent as I am.

I push off the bed, naked, and twist to face her.

"Let me get us a bottle of water each and then let's order room service before I drive you home."

The color drains from her face and she says, "I'll be fine." She sounds hurt, but why? I don't understand. We just had the best sex.

I touch the base of my neck and then run my hands through my hair. "No, you will take the ride. You cannot get a train this late at night."

She rolls her eyes at me and says, "So bossy."

I lean over her and tickle her in the ribs; she wiggles underneath me, laughing, her lightness returning. I peck at her lips and say, "I'll be right back."

I grab the bottles of water, the menus, and return to the bed, where she is lying unmoved. I hold out the bottle, which she takes and sits up slowly. She untwists the cap and drinks. I copy and then open the menu and ask, "Is there anything in particular you feel like eating?"

"Burger and chips."

I scan the menu and find a burger and say, "Sounds good. I'll do the same. Do you want anything else?"

She shakes her head, screws the bottle cap back on, and says, "No. That's all."

I call down and place the order. When I turn, I notice she is getting dressed and I ask jokingly, "No round two?"

She giggles, gazing into my eyes, and says, "No chance. I'm tired."

I laugh and say, "Damn it."

But truthfully, I don't know if I could have backed it up so quickly after how hard I just came.

We both dress before room service arrives. A knock arrives at the door shortly after we finish, and I open it. The staff pushes in a trolley with our food and says, "Good evening."

"Evening. Thanks."

I tip him and he leaves.

We sit at the table in the room and eat in silence, her gaze flicking between mine and the food. As I stare in awe at her, I decide to ask. "Tell me more about you."

I stuff a few chips in my mouth and chew. As I watch her sit back, chewing on her chips, I'm expecting her to tell me to mind my own business or some other smartass remark.

"Well, my parents died in a car accident when I was fifteen and I'm an only child and after the death of my parents, I went to live with my aunt and uncle, but they were not interested in raising children, so I ran away. I knew there was a better life out there for me. What about you?"

I halt midchew, swallow, and I just sit back in the chair, staring at her in surprise. Just when I thought I knew everything about her, she drops this bomb. Here I thought I was the only one with a hard upbringing, but clearly I was wrong. No parents at all. That's worse than my situation.

I look deep into her beautiful eyes and say, "I'm sorry about your parents. That must have been hard."

She glances down, picking up a chip and chewing it, and then continues, "It was, but my life changed when I met Anne, who I call Mom. I owe her my life. She helped me when I had nowhere to live; she gave me a roof over my head, and then assisted me to get my last job and then, when it closed down, she believed in me again. And I found your ad." A flush creeps across her cheeks and she says, "Anyway, enough about me. It's your turn."

I lean across the table and put my hand on top of hers, waiting for her to meet my gaze. And when she does, I say with a smile, "Well, I'm an only child, too. So we have something in common."

"One thing in common. Slow down. Don't get ahead of yourself." Her eyes are lit with an inner glow.

I laugh and say, "Always a smartass."

But secretly I love her fire and banter. It's what makes her stand out from other women I have met. And it's not just her unique beauty that has me hooked. It's the mix of her attitude and work ethic.

I lean back in to eat while I allow her turn to ask questions.

"How did you turn the business around? Was it ingrained in you since you were young? To take over the family business?"

The burger I had been chewing gets stuck in my throat and the only way out is to vomit, but I swallow hard and grab the water and chug. Then I clear my throat and lock gazes with her. Her genuine warm smile makes me confess and say, "James had the experience with a successful company, so I called him the day my dad handed it over. He helped me financially, and we researched new areas to make money, and that's how the infrastructure side started. If it weren't for James, I wouldn't be running the business like it is today. But now that I have it, I couldn't have it any other way. It makes me happy and I'm reaching my goals of being successful, proving my family wrong."

I wish the water was alcohol because of the way her eyes turn to beautiful puppy dog eyes; it makes my stomach churn.

I lean forward and poke her nose, to which she scrunches up in the most adorable way and

I say, "Don't look at me like that. You're being way too cute."

I don't normally share my secrets with people I have sex with, but she is different. I don't know why, but she just is. She is more than a simple fuck. But I do nothing other than casual; I just can't commit. I can't trust people easily.

We leave the hotel and I drive her home, parking outside her apartment, and she spins in her seat to face me. She leans forward and pecks my lips, and as she pulls away, she bites my lip with a sexy-as-fuck grin. She is like kryptonite. She tries to push the door open, but I yank her back to kiss her properly. I haven't had enough of her yet. I thrust my tongue inside her mouth and play with her tongue ring. She groans and my dick twitches in my pants; I need to stop this before I fuck her in my car. I pull back, staring at her with a hungry gaze.

Her face flushes before she quickly exits the car and walks inside her building. I chuckle and lay my head back, closing my eyes and taking a deep inhale. She is stirring me up inside and messing with my head. I pull out back into traffic and drive home. Alone.

Ava

Going to work the next few days is easy. I have a fresh spring in my step and by Friday, I have a meeting to look forward to. I like meetings because it means I get to see him. We always catch the other's gaze. Or maybe that is just me, but every time he glances at me and we lock eyes, my heart jumps.

And after our fun night at the hotel, I am craving more. It was supposed to get him out of my system, not make me want more. We haven't talked or seen each other because we have both been busy with work, so today is the first opportunity to see one another.

I choose another jumpsuit, knowing how well the first one captured his attention. And this time, I choose a stunning, tight green one. It makes my hair stand out and my eyes pop. I know it shows off my curves and my best asset to him: my ass.

I strut in on my black heels, making me taller than my frame usually is. I feel sexy and sultry, and as I walk with Thomas into the meeting, Joshua's gaze hits mine and I almost stumble back. He is openly glaring at me, and I feel a tad uncomfortable with the intensity. My gaze shoots down and I take my seat as quickly as possible, feeling my cheeks heat. I keep my head down to recover.

I am organizing the pile of papers for the meeting when I feel his breath on the back of my neck and my breath catches in my throat. My eyes close at the sound and his nearness.

"Hi, Ava." His smooth voice tickles my ear.

I turn to face him and smile shyly. He is way too close compared to anyone else in the room, but he doesn't step back. I stiffen but concentrate on the conversation, not the buzz running through my body from the familiarity of him.

"Hi, Joshua. How are you?" I struggle to keep my voice the same. It has a slight hitch in it.

A knowing grin appears on his lips, and he says, "Good, Ava. Really good." He peers down at my body, then, meeting my gaze, he whispers, "You look fantastic."

My heart is thundering in my chest. What the fuck is he doing? My eyes bulge and I glance around to make sure no one else has focused on us. With no one watching, I offer a small nod in acknowledgement. And then I feel him move behind me and take his place at the front of the room. I close my eyes for a moment, trying to collect myself.

I open my eyes to see him standing, powerful, in the front of the room. It's my turn to check him out. He stands next to the whiteboard in a light gray suit, white shirt, and gray tie. He looks hot. As if feeling my gaze on him, he looks up and my lips lift in an open, smug smile. Yeah, fucker, I'm checking you out too.

No one would know that his father had handed over a crippled company and he transformed it. As you look around, you just think he was born for this.

The meeting goes through all the current projects and staff numbers and who needs to move to where next week. When it's finished, I walk over to Linda. I lean on her desk to hand her a piece of paper she needs for Joshua.

"Meeting all done?" she asks.

"Yeah, it wasn't a long one." Which is a damn shame. I wouldn't mind spending more time looking at him.

I want to talk to him because I haven't had a chance since the night at the hotel; I'm waiting for him to be ready.

"Yeah, he has a busy afternoon," she says.

With that information, my stomach drops in disappointment, and I say to Linda, "Bye," and leave to return to the safety of my office.

CHAPTER 14

AVA

GRACIE IS SITTING ON a stool at my kitchen counter, waiting for me to finish setting up. I'm doing her makeup for her night out. I move to pour us both a glass of wine to sip while I do her face.

"How's work been?" I ask her.

When she works at the bar all weekend, it makes it hard to catch up to talk. And other weekends, she likes to go out with her friends from the bar, leaving only moments like these to tell her things.

"Pretty busy now that football is back on. The bar is full every day. I can't complain, though. The money is good." She has always struggled like me, so anytime she gets extra money, I'm happy for her, sharing in her joy.

"What am I doing with your makeup tonight? What are you wearing?" I ask.

"I'm wearing my long-sleeve black dress with a pair of black heels."

I nod at her answer, knowing I can't put black on her eyes. I peer down at the colors I own and decide to make her hazel eyes pop by using brown with orange hues.

Happy with that decision, I paint and say, "So guess who hooked up with Josh at a hotel?"

She pushes my arm, her eyes wide, and says, "What! No way. You dirty little bitch." But her devilish smile says she is happy for me.

I giggle at her excitement, knowing it's a big deal. I don't hook up with just anyone.

"I don't know why, but I'm so attracted to him. And I was sick of the unknown, so he offered to meet me at a hotel and I thought why not. I need to get him out of my system." I take a sip of courage, knowing what I need to tell her next.

"Because he is hot as fuck. But a hotel seems odd? Not either of your apartments?" she asks.

I had given little thought to that. Why didn't he offer his apartment?

Because he is a playboy.

I shrug and apply eyeshadow on her again. Pretending I'm okay with that, I say, "I don't think he wants anything serious. I think he just likes to mess around."

My heart drops, knowing we aren't on the same page. We both want different things.

"I know, but it's still cold. Do you think he does that with all his hookups?" she asks.

"For sure." I remember he's too familiar with the hotel, it was too easy for him to get a room.

"That's a bummer. Men suck! Now tell me...I have been dying to know. What was the sex like?" She wiggles her brows.

I exchange a knowing look with her and feel my face burning hot, remembering how good he is and how we were together. How well we get along in so many ways. The sex is a bonus. Our chats are even better, like the icing on a cake.

I bite my lip as I remember his rough hands on my body and the teasing but passionate kisses we shared and say, "It was amazing. I don't think I have been with a guy that hot."

"I have, and it's addictive," she warns.

"I don't know why he is in my head. I was happy with my life before him. And he irritates the heck out of me. But he is hot and intelligent, and the sex is too damn good...But it was a one-time thing."

She snorts and says, "I have heard that before."

"I haven't said that before."

I'm very reserved, not as tough and open as my appearance makes me out to be, and I definitely don't do casual sex normally.

"No, but every girl I know has said that before. And it never stays true." Her eyes are still closed as I do her makeup and get lost in my head.

"I'm fucked."

"Yeah, it sounds like his dick has magic powers and is taking over your mind."

I shake my head and say, "You, my love, are crazy."

She is my best friend and the best laugh you will ever have. I finish her makeup and I beam at the result. She goes to the mirror and I follow, watching her gaze at her face from every angle. Inspecting it, she says, "This is amazing. Thank you. I'm going to look so hot tonight." She takes a step and hugs me in a warm embrace. I rub my hand up and down her back before we pull apart.

"You are."

She spins to exit the bathroom, and I follow, moving back to my wine.

She grabs her bag and I trail after her, saying goodbye.

When she leaves, I get to cleaning while sipping my wine. The apartment is silent, so I hurry and pack up. Then, refilling my wine, I go back to sitting on the couch alone, clutching my glass of wine. I wish I enjoyed going out as much as Gracie. Because then I wouldn't be sitting here on the weekend, watching trash television, drinking a glass of wine... alone.

The next day, Mom picks me up and we arrive at the food kitchen. It's already busy because of the rain. Today, I'm on floor duty. I go to assist with the lunchroom, making sure everyone is comfortable.

I pass a young woman around the same age as I was when I arrived, looking every bit as I remember: frightened, lonely, and uncertain. My throat clenches and I feel a pull toward her. I sit down opposite her. Her hair is in a messy bun on top of her head, her clothes are worn, and her eyes are a striking brown—but they are empty. I remember those feelings. Looking at her, they all come flooding back. The backs of my eyes sting with tears, but I push them aside and clear my throat.

"Hi. My name is Ava."

The girl leans back to assess me, but then I see a calm wash over her. And she offers a dip of her chin.

"What is your name?" I ask.

"Sarah." There is no expression on her face, but I remember those days too. She must be very new here.

"Nice to meet you, Sarah. I volunteer here, but I used to be here myself." Her gaze lifts at that. I see a spark and offer a small smile and continue my story of hope.

"I left home at fifteen, going on sixteen. My parents died, and I left a shitty abusive aunt and uncle's house to live on the streets. It was a very hard time. I didn't think I was going to make it, truthfully. It was a hard time...But this place and the people here helped me find my feet. And I got a job and an apartment to rent. I am finding my purpose in life. Hang in there; let them help you. They are the best people with the best intentions."

She gazes down at the table before meeting my eyes. Her eyes are glossy and shiny with unshed tears.

"Thank you," she says. I understand not to push. When you are vulnerable, sometimes being alone is best.

I don't know where life will take her and I may never see her again, but I sure hope I do. I hope she fights for her life and comes out stronger.

"I better finish helping. Let me know if you need anything. Otherwise, it was lovely to meet you, Sarah."

I smile at her before I lift out of the chair and visit the other tables, clearing dishes and wiping tables, offering drinks, helping any way I can. A few hours pass and Mom comes to find me and says, "You ready to go, love?"

I put the last dishes away and say, "Yes. I'm exhausted and hungry."

"What do you feel like for lunch?"

Mulling over her words—What do I feel like?—I shrug and say, "Let's go to a café where there is a decent menu."

"Good idea."

When we are leaving, Sarah gives me a smile in passing, I wave and smile in return.

We walk up the streets and find a café, where we spend a few hours chatting and eating. I tell her about Sarah and how I could see myself in her and how grateful I was that Mom found me. I tell Mom I hope Sarah has the same luck. She promises me she will watch over her, which makes me smile.

Mom drops me home and I run up the stairs to my apartment. Meeting Sarah has motivated me to remember how far I have come and how strong I am. I remember where I want to go with my future and now I have a new drive for life.

I don't need Joshua; I need stability more.

I pull out my phone and open Google and type *design courses*. An entire list of school courses appears. Reading through each, my breath catches at the sight of the prices. They are way too much for me right now; I don't have that amount of money. I need to save for my condo deposit and get a car, but I would rather do a course to further my career. Working at Ward, I have found a new passion and to earn more salary, I need to study further. It will open up new doors and new opportunities for me. I remind myself of what I told Sarah. I smile and now have an additional reason to be motivated at work, one that doesn't involve *him*.

CHAPTER 15

AVA

I STEP THROUGH THE doors at work, feeling tall and ready to move forward.

I can't lie. I envisioned a small glimpse of a future with Joshua, but then, just as quickly as it entered my brain, I pushed it aside. I need to focus on myself, hit my goals, and continue to focus on building my future.

I prepare for the day before Thomas arrives. Because when he comes in, we need to organize our week ahead and it takes a lot of time.

I sit down at the computer and work. Time passes quickly and before I know it, Thomas is whistling as he enters the floor. I glance up from my monitor and say, "Hi, Thomas. How was your weekend?"

He pauses at my desk, staring down at me with a glow on his face, and says, "It was good. Relaxing. Nothing exciting happened, but I just enjoyed being with my family. How was yours? Surely more exciting?" He offers a small smile. I think because I'm young, he thinks I should do something like party, but I much prefer to keep quiet and stay in.

"Sounds perfect to me. It was relatively quiet. I saw my friend and then had lunch with my mom, but otherwise it was quiet."

I haven't told Thomas about my life growing up. It didn't feel right to talk to him about the streets or my parents. Joshua is the first person at work I started opening up to. It was nice because it didn't feel forced; it felt natural at the time to tell him.

"Nice. Well, I better get a start. Give me twenty minutes to get started and answer any emails and then let's go through this week's plans."

I nod and say, "Okay. Sounds good."

He walks off into his office and I swivel around, getting back to my work.

Twenty minutes later, I pause outside his office door and knock on the frame and ask, "Are you ready?"

His gaze whips up from the papers in front of him and he says, "Yeah, come sit."

I step in and take a seat opposite him; we discuss the week we have coming up.

"I can't stay late on Thursday. We need to move that meeting," he says.

"I'll try, but if not, I'll go in your place. I'm sure I can handle it."

He leans back in his office chair, squinting, and he rubs his jaw with his hand, thinking about my offer, then says, "You could totally handle it. I just don't want you overworked."

My brow lifts and I say, "I'm not overworked and I love learning new things and challenging myself. So don't sweat it."

I love that he cares about how I'm feeling, but I want to learn more. It will help me get further in my career and help prepare me for design school when I can afford it.

He sits up and says, "Just send them an email letting them know it will be you. Just in case they would prefer to reschedule it."

My stomach knots. I didn't think of that, but surely they won't mind? All the builders and the workers know me now, so I hope they don't reschedule. I'd love to prove myself to the company.

"On it. I will let you know what they say."

He nods. With nothing left to discuss, I get up and exit. I take a seat back down in front of my computer. I type out an email and as I hit send, a new one hits my inbox and I freeze.

It's him.

Shit.

I close my eyes and take a few calming breaths, trying to calm my twitchy muscles. I open my eyes, click the open button, and begin reading the contents.

To: Ava Johnson
Subject: Meeting
Message: Hi Ava,
Could you please come to my office regarding Thursday's meeting?
Regards,
Joshua Ward

I stare at it, unmoved. It's very professional, with no flirty comments.

Do I reply, or should I just go up there? I decide it would be more professional to send a quick email back, so I drop my head and type back my response.

To: Joshua Ward
Subject: Re: Meeting
Message: I'm just finishing something. I will let Thomas know and then I will be up.
See you soon.
Ava

It's nice and straight to the point with no flirty messages. Just work. It's what I asked for, but now that I have it, I can't deny I miss the flirty banter. It felt good.

I finish up work and then get up and say to Thomas, "I just gotta go upstairs and see Joshua."

"What for?" he asks.

I poke my head into his office; he gazes at me. I purse my lips and say, "I don't know. Something about Thursday's meeting."

"He may want to attend with you."

I blink rapidly. No. Surely not. Being that close to him again could be dangerous, but I can't deny I have missed him. I try to forget and hope it's about something else.

"I will find out. I'll be back soon."

I suck in a breath deep in my lungs and give myself a mental pep talk as I walk to the elevators.

I walk onto his floor and notice Linda isn't at her desk. A heavy sigh leaves my lips and I move past, investigating the office. But she isn't here. Everything looks untouched.

I walk around to his office and see him sitting down, writing on paper splayed in front of him. I move farther into the room. Not bothering with a hello, I ask, "Where is Linda?"

He jerks his gaze up from his desk and says, "Well, hello, Ava. She isn't in today."

That's all he offers. He doesn't expand on why she isn't here.

"Are you okay? Do you need a hand with work in her absence?"

He must need me to help him; he looks a hot mess. His brown hair is usually perfect, but today it's like he has been running his hand through it a million times. And it's a sexy, tousled mess, but it isn't a normal look for him. His tie is loose and the top button on his crisp white shirt is undone.

"No. I'm fine. That's not why I called you here," he says.

He gestures for me to sit down in the empty chair in front of him.

I nod and sit down in front, not in the mood to argue with him. If Linda isn't here, I'm sure he is swamped with work. I don't speak. Instead, I just wait for him to continue.

He scrapes a hand through his hair and says, "I want to go over your notes."

"You don't trust me to cover for Thomas?"

He waves his arms in front of him and says, "No, I'm sure you can handle it. I'm just worried you're new at this and—"

"I'll mess up?"

He shakes his head and his gaze locks on mine, and he says, "No. I don't want anyone to take advantage of your inexperience. I want you to feel supported and confident in the meeting."

"Oh."

My heart flutters at the knowledge, but I try to tell myself it isn't anything and not to read too much into it. We aren't dating; we shared a conversation, kissed, and fucked once. And right now, he is just being kind and supportive of me, so I smile, and I say, "Thanks."

He smiles back, and we spend the next half an hour running over the job and the potential questions I may get asked. Afterward, he rubs his forehead before leaning forward with his hands under his chin, letting out a deep sigh.

"I want to explain myself. Because I want..."

"Son," a deep voice calls from behind me and from the look on Joshua's face, he isn't happy. He looks murderous. Oh shit. This isn't good.

I swivel around in my chair, knowing it's his father. I want to see what the man looks like.

In the doorway is a little old man. He is shorter and slimmer than Joshua. But I see some similarities. Joshua has his nose, face shape, and blue eyes. But the lips and height must be from his mom. His dad is handsome and I can see where Joshua gets some of his looks, but I bet his mom is beautiful.

It's such a shame they weren't the loving and kind type of parents. No one should do that to their son.

My heart can't help but break for Joshua.

CHAPTER 16

JOSHUA

I MOMENTARILY FREEZE BEFORE I flick my gaze between my dad and Ava.

I must look like I have seen a ghost because the pain and concern etched on Ava's face make her look frightened, like I might break. She moves her gaze between my dad and me. I told her about how he left me with a shit company completely in debt, so I know she understands the enormity of him standing in my office space.

My hands are curled into balls beside my hips and I'm breathing hard and fast. I close my eyes, trying to rein in my brewing temper, and figure out what the fuck he wants. I haven't answered any of his calls for a damn reason. I don't want to speak to him or Mom. I'm still fucking fuming from the way they handled handing over the business. I don't need him showing up and being in my space right now, a space I built without his help.

I don't want to have a showdown in front of Ava. I was in the middle of trying to explain Candice to her when he showed up, but it will have to wait because I need to talk to him first.

He needs to stop blowing up my phone and now he needs to be told to not come to my office unannounced.

Using a carefully controlled tone of voice, I look into Ava's wide gaze and say, "Ava, I'm sorry, but we will have to reschedule."

She nods vehemently and says, "Of course. Take your time." She takes one last longing look as if to ask if I'm okay. I nod and offer her a small false smile, then watch her sexy ass exit my office.

Once she is out of view, I drag my glare back to his, the only similarity we share. His hair is gray and short, but he still wears a suit. However, just because he wears one doesn't mean he is successful. I straighten my spine, tip my chin up, and wait for his excuses to come pouring out of his mouth.

I won't kick him out unless absolutely necessary because I want him to look at this place, and if I am honest with myself, I want him to be proud of me. Even when you have parents who neglect you, you still require approval and are desperate to make them proud. Fuck knows why, but I do—and I hate myself for it.

He steps forward and I jerk back, but he merely drags out a chair and sits down. I don't offer him a drink because I don't want him to get comfortable. I stare and stay strong. Even if my bones shake inside, I need to know why he's here.

I lean forward. He blinks repeatedly as a glossy sheen covers his eyes, and he says in a flat voice, "Your mom is sick."

Sick?

"What do you mean, sick?"

My dull stare looks into his glossy one as I scratch my temple, trying to understand his words.

In a tearful voice, he says, "They have diagnosed her with colon cancer. The doctors have only given her a couple of months at best."

I sit there with an empty stare as his chin trembles and he leans to one side of the chair and digs inside his pocket, pulling out some tissues and tapping his eyes and blowing his nose.

Colon cancer.

I sit there taking shaky breaths, needing a moment to process the information. Even though there is a heavy feeling in my stomach, I just can't believe this. It can't be true.

"It's why we had to cut our trip short," he says.

Of course, your trip. Always about you two. You couldn't even afford the trip, but of course no one knows how broke you really are. I'm at a loss for words right now. I scratch my jaw, trying to find words, but the words keep replaying in my head. A couple of months... colon cancer.

My body feels numb and nausea rolls in my stomach at the thought of losing my mother. I had wished for this at certain stages growing up, when I was so angry, but now that it's actually happening, I realize I don't want it.

I become restless and turn away from him and peer over at Ava's email sitting there on the screen and mutter a bunch of curses under my breath. I wish she was here even though that's selfish when I'm not ready to commit, but I can't control this feeling that I need her here. I want her support; she makes me feel less alone. I can't call her back with him in the room. He will see me as weak, and I'm not weak. I'm Joshua Ward, CEO of Ward Electrical and Infrastructure.

"Where is she?" I stutter, trying to find the right words.

He leans forward, balancing his elbows on his knees, his head in his hands, talking through a breaking voice.

"At home, but eventually she will need to be in palliative care for pain and sedation."

I suddenly feel cold so I fold an arm over my stomach as time seems to slow down.

"That's a lot to take in right now," I say. Nothing will change how he feels toward me, so I may as well be honest.

"I know. I'm sorry. I tried to call. But you ignored my calls," he says with a glare that's supposed to make me shrink in my chair.

It doesn't work.

"I was busy fixing up the broken company you gave me with kindness so you could retire and travel. It's impressive, don't you think?" I say back.

How does he expect me to answer his calls after that?

My dad's jaw tics and I know I'm pissing him off, but if he wants to come here and poke the bear, then he can deal with the consequences.

"The building looks great, really great," he says.

His gaze leaves mine to roam around my large office. I bet it was hard to give me a compliment. But I'm dancing inside at it.

I offer a curt nod and say, "Now, I have a meeting to get back to. Keep me in the loop with Mom." I twist to type a new email to Ava. I need her now after having him around.

But as I'm about to hit send, heavy steps move along the tiles in my office. I sag in my chair a little at the sight of James. He seriously knows the best time to come and save me. I owe him once again for saving my butt from my parents.

"You will answer my calls?" my father asks sarcastically. My gaze moves from James to him and I turn back to stone.

"Regarding Mom? Of course."

My dad twists his head and his face falls when he spots James standing inside the office. He moves out of the chair and says, "I better let you get back to the meeting."

"Yes," I answer.

"James," Dad says.

James offers a dip of his chin but nothing else. His frame towers over the space, making my dad flee.

"What did he want?" James asks as he enters, taking a seat in the chair my dad was sitting in. Unlike my imposter father, James is powerful.

I swallow past the gravel forming in my throat and say, "Mom's sick. She has colon cancer and has a couple of months to live."

"Fuck that's shit. I'm sorry."

I suck a good breath in and answer, "Yeah, my head feels a bit messed up, to be honest."

"I bet that's some heavy shit. I came by to hand you paperwork for another apartment building. They need upgrading, so you can enter the bidding process."

I take the paperwork from his hand and lay it down on the desk. I try to focus on the paper, but I can't focus. I feel the walls are closing in on me, so I ask, "Do you want to go for a walk? I think some fresh air, coffee, and food might help. I don't think I can look at work right now."

I pick up the papers and stack them neatly in a pile and grab my wallet and phone.

"Deal, and then I can fill you in on the little minx working for me. Sent to fuck with me." He runs a hand through his hair with a perplexed expression.

Chuckling loudly, I say, "This I have to hear. Plus, I might need to meet her if she is ruffling your feathers."

He stands and says, "You will do no such thing."

We walk out to the elevators.

I'm intrigued to see who is keeping James' attention. He usually is a multiple-woman man. No one makes him look twice.

Ava

A few days have passed and I haven't heard Thomas mention anything about Joshua or his dad. I want to know why his dad was there and if Joshua is okay. I don't know why, but I care about him and after seeing his face and how deeply upset he was about his father being there, I'm curious and desperate for answers.

It's finally Thursday, which means I will get to see him alone after the meeting and find out more. We have shared a few small bits of our past, so asking about his dad won't seem out of the blue. I finish up work and send Joshua a quick email to see if they are ready for me.

> **To:** Joshua Ward
> **Subject:** Ready?
> **Message:** Josh,
> I have finished my work. On my way to the meeting. Are they ready?
> Ava

leave my inbox open and begin tidying up the office.

A few minutes later, with nothing else to do, I return to the computer.

> **To:** Ava Johnson
> **Subject:** Re: Ready?
> **Message:** Evening Ava,
> Yes, whenever you are ready.
> See you soon.
> Regards,
> Joshua Ward

As I close the screen and power down my computer, butterflies swarm my stomach. I run my hands smoothly down my black dress and open my purse to touch up my lipstick. Before I toss my bag over my shoulder, I hold the paperwork to my chest and walk to the elevator. Ready or not, here I come.

Chapter 17

Ava

THE MEETING WENT BETTER than I expected. I'm so proud of myself. I was well prepared thanks to Joshua, and we wrapped up quicker than we had scheduled for. Joshua watched from beside me, and he smiled up at me the whole time, silently encouraging me like my own personal cheerleader.

After we said goodbye to everyone who attended, Joshua asked me to grab another building's plans from my office. Now, I stand with my back against the elevator, riding it up to his floor, and think about the questions to ask. His dad was in his office the other day and all I can think about is how his face filled with tortured pain, and it won't stop haunting me until I find out. I know some of the story, but it is not enough; I want to know more.

When the doors open and I walk through the office, it's eerily quiet. The bright lights are replaced with softly lit warm lights that leave a glow. I walk across the tiles into his office, pausing at the door to watch him work, his gaze focused on the computer, and my stomach, which only fluttered before, is now a twisting mess. The pull that happens when we are both in the same room zaps his gaze to mine. My breath catches in my throat and I swallow hard, unable to move.

I can feel my heart beating loudly inside my chest as I keep my gaze glued to his fierce blues.

The room is intoxicating, his sexy scent filling my nostrils, and I can't get away from it. It stirs something deep inside of me. I am so turned on in one second from the memories which cause me to shiver even though his office is hot now that we are in an intense eye-fuck.

A twisted, knowing smirk appears on his lips. His face is handsome under the glow of the lights and I feel it in my core. I bite down hard on my tongue ring, rolling it along my teeth, trying to cause pain to take away the heaviness between my thighs.

Both of us are unmoving and I mentally slap myself for acting like a teenager and push myself forward. I clear my throat and walk toward his desk with my head held high. He slowly rises and I watch his every move. My breathing is shallow, as if I'm expecting him to pounce on me, or was that me secretly hoping?

He clears his throat, I'm sure feeling the same thick sexual tension in the air. Knowing I affect him as much as he affects me makes me feel lighter. I grin at the minor victory.

"Are those the plans?" he says.

His strained voice has me biting down hard on the metal. His voice did not help dampen the desire coursing through my body.

I forgot about the plans, which I had been clutching to my chest, until he mentioned them. I thrust them at him as if they are going to stop him from kissing me.

He softly takes them from my hands, and I break my stare and watch as he lays them down on his desk. He holds either side of the paper to prevent them from curling in on themselves. His broad chest leans over the plans and his white shirt pulls taut across his muscled back. My gaze rakes over his body, taking in every inch. Each time I see him, the pull becomes stronger. I want to run my fingernails down his back and leave marks on his body.

I gaze at his back and he must feel the heat because he lifts up and raises a brow and I wince at being caught.

"This complex is taking a little longer, and they are behind schedule. I think we should mix up the staff, see if it helps. Can you tell Thomas tomorrow and get the workers moving and give them a new deadline?" he says but doesn't acknowledge the desire swirling between us. My throat is dry, so I don't want to speak, nodding my understanding instead. The sexual magnetism is still floating in the air, but I push all my dirty thoughts from my brain and keep my eyes on the plan. He continues on with the meeting and I see an agenda sheet. I smile to myself because he is now using all these organization tools. I know how they help keep me focused and stay on track, and I am glad he feels they are useful to him.

When the meeting is over and it's quiet, I take a deep breath and ask, "How come your dad was here the other day?"

His empty gaze captures mine before he lowers it again, making my heart crack. He looks like a little lost boy. I just want to go up to his side of the desk and wrap my arms around him and tell him everything is okay, but we aren't a couple.

He lets out a shaky breath and says, "I had been ignoring his calls, so he came here to face me. My mom is sick with colon cancer."

My eyes bulge and my mouth drops open, but I can't seem to form words. They are stuck in my throat and I'm trying to find the right ones anyway when ultimately there is nothing to take his pain away. Losing your parents isn't easy; even losing one is hard. I know. I have lost both my parents and so I say what is in my heart and is sincere. "I'm sorry."

I blink the sting from my eyes, not from pity, but from sadness that only people who have lost a parent would understand.

He offers me a small smile and says, "Thanks. I don't know how to feel, to be honest. My parents weren't there for me growing up, and now I am stunned by this information. It's not like I have time to process it. She doesn't have a lot of time."

He thrusts his hands through his hair, his fingers tugging his brown locks as he gazes at the ceiling, frustration rolling off his body in waves.

"Do what is right for you. Live with no regrets. If you want to see her before she goes, that's okay. It doesn't make you weak."

He stares at me, blinking rapidly. I can see the wheels turning in his head, trying to work it out.

How do I know that? How do I understand so much for a young woman?

I stare into his sad gaze, trying to get him to talk to me.

I cross my arms over my chest to hug myself, waiting for him to share more when he is ready. Already, I'm surprised by how much we have shared about our lives.

"Even though my parents didn't give me the love or attention I deserve, it's tearing me to pieces. She won't be here much longer. The person who raised me will be... gone."

He says the last word in a choke, and it almost breaks me.

I ask in a gentle voice, "How long does she have?" I'm feeling the fragility surround us. We're both on the verge of a breakdown.

He may be tough, but losing your parents is soul-crushing. I know. In one moment, my life changed. And now I'm scared someone will take my new life from me. The fear runs through my body.

"Only a few months," he whispers.

My breath hitches and a rush of tears floods my eyes. Tears sit on my lower lashes, ready to fall, but I'm sure once they fall, they won't stop.

His gaze flicks to mine, and his eyes also have unshed tears.

We have a connection on such a deep level, it scares me. He takes a big step around the desk and I copy. The movements are slow, but we both follow the other until we are standing an inch apart, gazing at each other. A few warm tears trickle down my cheeks. He reaches out and dusts his thumbs across my cheeks, swatting the tears away. I can hear his deep breaths. The lust is undeniable. His hands are holding my head at an angle, his gaze flicking from my lips to my eyes. My lips are begging to be kissed; they are parted and needy.

My heart is hammering inside my chest, waiting for him to kiss me legless. But I feel wrong for wanting a kiss while he is in pain.

My mind ceases all thoughts when his soft, full lips hit mine. I gasp into his lips, the feather-light kiss so different from anything we have shared before, sending shock waves through my entire body. It's surprisingly soft and thoughtful and my eyes flutter closed, unable to stay open with the raw emotions pumping through my veins.

The many feelings make me light-headed, as if I'm on a rollercoaster I can't and don't want to get off.

I push my hands into his hair and dust them down over his neck. I try to pull him closer, gripping him roughly. I want to bring the unhinged version of him back. The normal rough makes me feel comfortable, but this softness is hitting my heart in an unusual and unnerving way.

He walks me backward until I hit the wall behind me. I lazily open my eyes under heavy lids to see one of his muscled forearms above my head and his other on the other side of my face, caging me in the most intimate way. I breathe lightly between my slightly parted lips, his eager eyes staring at them. I try to recover by taking deep breaths.

His mouth then swoops down to capture mine, our tongues massaging and tasting. I am trying to enjoy every firm thrust of his tongue against mine. He hits my metal and a hiss leaves his chest. It encourages me to toy with his tongue. The intimate kissing is replaced with rough again, making us both feel more comfortable.

When we are out of breath from kissing, he pulls back, pecks me, and stares into my eyes, looking deeply for something. My brain is turning to mush and my core is pulsating. I want to feel relief soon. I'm stroking his soft hair with my fingers and then softly along his jaw. Unable to hold back any longer, my restraint snaps.

"Let's get out of here and go to my place."

He lifts his eyebrows and his mouth curves into a devilishly handsome grin, and he whispers, "Are you sure?" His breath tickles my face.

Breathing him in, I nod vehemently and say, "Yes, definitely. Let's go."

He pecks me one last time before peeling himself back, giving me air I didn't realize I desperately needed. His cologne is still in the air, but at least he isn't suffocating me with it. His gaze roams my face before he looks away.

He wanders over to his desk and turns off his computer, packing up his desk and grabbing his phone and wallet. I'm unable to move and feel hypnotized watching him. He comes to stand next to me and grabs my hand; I look down at our joined hands in amazement. My hand twitches at the surprising feeling he has on me. We walk out of his office, holding hands. His soft, warm, large hand feels easy. It doesn't feel uncomfortable, as I had imagined. I had this mapped out as being worse than it turned out to be. I'm safe with his hand in mine and knowing he will be at my place. I already feel less alone, and I can't remember the last guy's hand I held.

We arrive at his car and climb in. As soon as we settle in and he drives off, he captures my hand again, resting our joined hands on my lap. There is barely any traffic, the silence in the car is comfortable, and the music in the background is relaxing. Twenty minutes later, he pulls up near my apartment complex.

My heart beats faster from the adrenaline that has just hit, knowing he is going to be in my apartment.

I hope he doesn't mind my small, simple apartment. I can only imagine his place. With no time to dwell on our lifestyle differences, I exit the car and walk upstairs on shaky legs. He follows behind me and I'm surprised, given the way he seems to always be checking out my ass, that he doesn't try to touch it. And the quiet now hits me. I tingle. Opening my door, I push it all the way open, allowing him to step in. He walks inside and takes it all in. I close the door behind him, then move to put my bag down. He hasn't moved, still staring and taking everything in. I don't know what he is thinking until he says, "This is cute. Very you."

I giggle and say, "I hope that's a compliment."

He steps toward the kitchen counter and says, "It is."

"Drink?" I ask, trying to keep myself busy before I freak out.

"Water please."

He slides up onto a stool and, shit, he looks hot sitting in my kitchen. I can imagine him in the morning with bed hair and no shirt and my mouth dries, reminding me I was getting us a drink. I need the cold liquid to calm my heated body. I twist and grab him a bottle from the fridge and hand him one and grab me one. After a few gulps, my body feels so much better. I twist the cap on and pull out the drawer with menus.

"What did you feel like eating?" I ask.

He chuckles at the number of menus I pull out.

"Anything."

"Pizza?" I feel like it's a food everyone loves.

"Sounds good. Just order whatever you eat and I'll eat that."

I eye him suspiciously. I don't know if he is just trying to be nice or if he really doesn't care. But fuck it, I'm too hungry to care.

I pull out my phone and order the pizza and peer at him, still happily sitting in my apartment. A small smile lifts the corner of his mouth. He looks so natural and at ease in my space.

"Come. Let's go chill and watch something until the food arrives."

He slides off the stool and follows me to the couch. We both sit. I leave enough room for a person to sit in between us. But I don't trust myself to keep my hands to myself. I kick my shoes off and tuck my legs up next to me and he reclines back and tugs on my arm to cuddle next to him. There goes me keeping to myself. I glance around, trying to decide what to do.

Fuck it.

I shuffle in closer to him and lower my head into the crook of his arm and chest. His warm body against my cheek and the thrum of his beating heart make me smile. The fast tune matches mine, which makes me happy. He is just as nervous as me.

He hugs my shoulders and I snuggle in. The closeness and ease of us surprises me, but I allow myself to indulge, even if it's just for tonight. I'm sick of being alone every night. Having my body tingle from his contact makes me feel alive; I'm sick of just being and existing, feeling nothing. He brings out a need, a tenderness I haven't felt with a man before. It's a foreign feeling but I want to explore it further.

I put the television on and flick the channel to sports, knowing I won't be paying any attention to anything that's on anyway. My thoughts and focus are on the man I'm snuggled against. I feel my heart rattling inside my chest the longer I'm cocooned beside him, my hands becoming sweaty. I don't know why he makes me nervous. Maybe it's because back at the office, the vulnerability he showed scared me. It showed me the real Joshua, a man I could easily fall for, and that scares me. And it gets me thinking, so before I stop and overthink, I ask, "Have you ever been in love before?"

His body tenses underneath me, but his soft voice soothes me and he says, "No. I spent too much time drunk to make any genuine relationships. Most are casual flings."

A little thought pops into my head. He must see me as a casual fling. Not wanting to get ahead of myself, I push it aside and say, "That's sad. Don't you ever want to settle down? Marriage? Kids? House?"

He's in his thirties and has never been in love. That's a little concerning.

"I do, but not just with anyone."

His tone and body language are telling me he feels uncomfortable but he is being polite.

I get that. It's exactly how I feel. The doorbell chimes, breaking up the conversation, and I welcome the pause. I push off him and go to the door, pay, and carry the pizza back in.

We eat and watch football in comfortable silence. After we finish, he pulls me back to his lap and the comfort mixed with exhaustion makes it difficult for me to keep my eyes open. It's not uncomfortable; it's a peaceful silence. He pulls me back to the previous position and my heavy eyelids struggle to stay open.

"I should get going," he whispers into my ear, stroking my hair.

The soft strokes are calming and I don't want him to go. My body tenses at the thought of being alone.

"Please stay."

"We have work tomorrow," he protests, but his gaze is tender and I know I have him.

"So? You're the boss."

He chuckles and says, "Touché, Miss Johnson." The lightness in him makes me content. I lean forward and press my lips hard into his, trying to coax him, with my mouth, to stay. I know it's a weakness for him. He returns my kiss but slows the pace down so we are back where we are in that unknown territory, that intimate zone I haven't been in before.

I push him back on the couch and he wiggles so he is in a seated position and I can climb on top. I have a feeling he likes me on top, and I can't complain. I'm able to set the pace and take the power. Maybe he recognizes how important that is to me, how alive I feel when I'm in charge. It makes me feel sexy and confident. I wrap my legs on either side of his and sit on his lap, his hard length poking my skin. Only our layers of clothes are between us. My arousal starts and my thighs quiver, feeling how hard I have made him. I lean forward and claim his mouth in a consuming kiss. His palms run up and down my legs, bunching my dress at the top of my thighs. I slowly rock my pelvis up and down, torturously slowly, along his hard length. He lets out a loud growl, and that sexy sound makes me break out in a cheeky grin. I'm enjoying myself a little too much when I open my eyes to see him pleased and sedated. His hands move up and down over my outer thighs in a rhythm to my movements. So when I stop, he stops. I continue the slow grind up and down, and he hisses at the friction. The tension on my clit is sending me wild. I need more: our clothes off and to feel him inside of me.

I sit back and begin unbuckling his belt and then his pants. His eyes open and the hunger swirling in them makes me giddy. I try to free his cock, but it's stuck. I try to shuffle his pants down, but without his help, it's useless. So he lifts me up with his pelvis and pulls his pants over his ass so they are around his upper thighs. He frees his cock from his briefs and fuck if it isn't perfect, thick and ready. The bit of pre-cum leaking makes me fist him and smear my thumb roughly over the tip. He sucks in a sharp breath and briefly closes his eyes before pulling out his wallet and tearing a condom and rolling it on; I watch in awe. He is perfect.

My pussy throbs and I lift my dress in anticipation. I tear my undies off and a deep chuckle vibrates from his chest. But I don't get long to enjoy it because he is lined up and ready. I rise on my knees and slowly lower myself down, stopping every little bit, allowing my walls to adjust to his thick cock. I groan and grind my teeth, staring into his face. His head tilts back and his eyes roll back inside his head in pure ecstasy. I watch him come undone and it's one of the biggest turn-ons. It urges me on, so I push down all the way in one swift motion. The fullness has me gasping. I squeeze my eyes shut. Once I adjust to him, I ride him up and down in a rhythm. I pick up the pace, feeling my walls already clamping down around him with every stroke. His large hands are on my thighs, digging in. I like how he doesn't handle me like I'm his perfect silverware. Instead, he's treating me with such passion I have never experienced before, evoking new feelings.

I rock harder and faster, up and down, until I say, "I'm coming."

As my sex clamps down hard, he says, "Ohhh, fuck."

He thrusts forward, helping me finish, and I feel him follow me, his cock jerking inside, emptying completely. I collapse down on his damp chest and his arms wrap around me in a cuddle, his chest rising and falling from his hard and fast breaths.

The sex we just shared was intense, and I suddenly feel exhausted. My mind and body feel heavy and I want to lie down. When I have caught my breath, I shuffle off him and stand. I turn to face him and his eyes spring open and his head tilts. He's staring up at me. I bend over to grab his hand and help him up. He reaches out to catch his pants, which are falling. I let his hand go so he can button himself back up. But I leave him shirtless and I drag him into my bedroom. I push him onto the bed, where he straightens himself out, and then I climb on and cuddle him. But he rolls me over so he can spoon me. His even breaths tickle my hair and ear. His heart beats on my back, helping me easily drift off into a state of bliss.

CHAPTER 18

AVA

WHEN MY ALARM WAKES me the next morning, I stretch and turn it off. I roll back over, rising on my elbow to balance, expecting Joshua's muscular body to be next to me, but my heart feels like it's shrinking. He isn't there; I glance around for any clothing or evidence he is still here, but a heavy sigh slips out of me and I collapse back onto the bed and cover my face with my hands.

He left.

I get up and inspect the apartment, thinking maybe he left a note somewhere. But after a walk around, checking every room, I come up empty. A clenching in my stomach sets off a roll of nausea, so I set off to get ready for work, skipping breakfast.

Over the next few hours, as I ride into work, my thoughts change and I have a new fire in my belly. I'm pissed off that the fucker left in the middle of the night. It's such an asshole thing to do. I'm so done with playboys, Joshua included. They suck, they hurt, and I'm done... so fucking done.

Even if he knows how to destroy my body with his hands, tongue, and cock, I need to stay strong. I can't handle the casualness. He can find that elsewhere, not from me. He doesn't deserve my time; he fooled me into thinking we had something special, but in his eyes, we just fucked again. When I asked him to stay by cuddling with him after sex, I expected him to be here in the morning, not ghost me. If he wasn't up for it, why didn't he have the courtesy or the balls to say no and leave straight after sex? Not cuddle me and sneak off in the middle of the night when I'm sleeping.

To say I'm pissed would be the understatement of the century.

I get to work and plaster on a fake smile, as if inside I'm not a raging mess. Thank fuck it's Friday. It's the easiest day of the working week because I won't have to see him, and I will avoid him at all costs.

I walk into the office. Thomas eyes me suspiciously, looking me up and down, a deep frown forming between his brows. I know he wants to ask me why I'm so dressed up for work, but he has women at home, so I'm sure he understands when not to ask questions. My mood today is clear: I'm not in a chatty one. At least he is smart enough to sense it, and right now I appreciate it because I'm worried I won't be able to hold my tongue about his shithead friend and what a douchebag player he is.

I power up the calendar and I see there are no on-site meetings scheduled, so at least I only have to get through today, and then I need to debrief Gracie.

The day goes quickly and I pack up my office, ready to get home. I close my programs and see a new email has come through. It's from him.

To: Ava Johnson
Subject: Meeting
Message: Hi Ava,
Are you free before you go home to come upstairs for a chat?
Regards,
Joshua Ward

I stare at the words on the screen, a storm brewing in me. No fucking chance, asshole. I'm not at your beck and call and I definitely don't want to hear your shitty, pathetic excuses. I'm not interested. No thanks. Bye.

I power down my computer and hear Thomas say, "Bye, Ava. See you Monday."

"See you next week. Have a good weekend," I say back as he exits the office before me.

I half expected Joshua to come down here because I didn't answer his email, but he didn't and I'm pleased. I need space to clear my head. I'm still way too wound up to deal with him.

I leave the office and it's the best feeling: two whole days ahead of me with no Joshua. I'm humming tunes because life is bliss.

Until it isn't.

Arriving home, I grab my mail and I still. The sender's address on the letter is familiar, and it brings up memories I don't want to remember. My breathing catches and I force myself to get inside and grab a glass of cold water and then sit on the couch to watch something that will take my mind off the letter.

I haven't opened it. I just threw it on the counter like it would burn me. I'm not ready to read the contents.

Not tonight. Not after the sex from last night and the emotional turmoil running through my body tonight has me exhausted. I can barely keep my eyes open. I curl up on the couch with a blanket and, after a while, it isn't long before my head is dropping to one side, jerking me awake. I force myself to crawl into bed. I'm asleep as soon as my head hits the pillow.

In the morning, I wake and avoid going near the counter with the letter.

What could they want?

I wander back to my room to text Gracie to come over. I'll get her to help me read it. Otherwise, I won't do it by myself, but they wouldn't send me mail unless it was important. I haven't heard a word from them in years. So, I need to read the contents. It must be important.

My phone pings with a response from Gracie. She agrees to come over in a few hours. I let out a huge breath and the tension slowly releases. To keep myself distracted, I get on with my weekend chores and it isn't long until I hear a knock at the door.

I practically run to the door, yanking it open.

"Whoa. What happened? What's going on?" Gracie asks as I hug her, needing the comfort of her arms.

She hugs me back, her hand running up and down my back in a soothing motion.

Whispering into her ear, I say, "I got a letter." And then pull back.

Her brows knit and she asks, "A letter?"

"Yes." I nod and say, "From my aunt and uncle."

Gracie slaps her hands over her mouth, smothering a squeal, and her eyes grow wide, knowing the big deal this is and how I'm feeling. She breathes, "Oh shit. What the hell do they want?"

If only I knew. To fuck with my head more? Like really, why can't they just leave me the fuck alone? They have given me enough mental scarring that I don't need to be harassed. I'm finally moving on with my life peacefully.

It's as if the universe has told them that, so they then have to come and shit on my parade.

I point to where I threw it last night, and I say, "I don't know. I can't bring myself to open it. It's there, hence why I asked for you to come here."

She steps forward to the counter, taking the letter in her hand and lifting it between us, asking, "Do you want me to tear it up or read it?"

Nausea rolls in my guts. I move closer to her, gripping the counter tight for support, and say, "I don't know. Why do they have to send me a letter? Like leave me the fuck alone."

I'm on the verge of crying. My eyes prick with tears, and that pisses me off. I'm sick of the emotional shit of Joshua and now the letter. I want to feel alive again in this moment, so I say to her, "Let's dye my fringe blonde."

Gracie's mouth pops open and she says, "You get a letter from your aunt and uncle and you want to get your hair done instead?" She rubs the middle of her forehead.

I shrug, not understanding why she can't see why I want a few more minutes. I'll do anything to not read it.

She makes a *hm* noise in her throat and says, "Fine. Let's hurry; it's only your fringe." I walk off to the bathroom, my shoulders dropping away from my ears, I'm excited to put distance between the letter and me.

She touches up my red, and then carefully adds the touch of blonde. I know Joshua loves the red, so I won't get rid of it just now. I want to piss him off, make him see what he won't be getting anymore. My lips twitch, knowing I'm going to pick another week of wicked clothes to show off the body I know he loves.

Both colors are in and we need to wait about half an hour.

She rubs her hands together and walks back to the kitchen.

"Just wait until after my shower," I say.

My chest is tight and I try to slow my breaths back down.

She turns around and looks at me and says, "You are really worried about what's in there, aren't you?" It's not a question; it's a statement.

"Why, after these many years, do they need to contact me?" I whisper.

I drop my gaze down, thinking of the envelope on the counter. I wish I knew its contents. How bad is this blow going to be?

"I don't know," Gracie says, "That's why we need to open it. But let's make tea and then, after your shower, we will sit and do it together."

I nod, liking the sound of that, and walk out to the kitchen. She finishes making the tea. I take it from her and fill her in about Joshua.

I grip the hot mug tighter, watching the steam rise, and say, "So I should tell you something."

She wiggles her eyebrows as she blows the steam off her tea to take a sip and asks, "Oh, is it about Josh?"

Trust her to guess it straightaway. I bite the inside of my cheek and nod. I flick my gaze up from my mug to her eyes and feel my cheeks flush.

Just spit it out.

"He came here after work last night and we had sex."

She claps loudly and I chuckle with a roll of my eyes before cutting it off. "But...he left at some stage... like, during the night. I fell asleep with him spooning me. But then woke in the morning to a cold bed. No note or anything."

She is staring back at me, and I can tell she is puzzled by the story. It's exactly how I feel inside about it. Why?

"Why wouldn't he just stay?" I ask.

I trust her with my life. Growing up in the shelter with Gracie allows me to trust her wholeheartedly. She doesn't judge and understands my reservations in life. She just tries to help, so I tell her everything, knowing she has my best interests in life.

"He said some shit about work before we hooked up, but I joked about him being the boss. Do you think it's possible he's worried because of work? Like he is having regrets?"

She sips her tea and says, "Huge possibility—if he is new to the position. But then he still shouldn't sneak off. That's just rude."

Exactly. I'm the one already struggling with the whole *we can't do this because you're my boss.* I need this job. I need a roof over my head and I want a condo for my future.

He kissed me.

He started it. Yes, I should stop him, but I'm weak for him. I love how driven and smart he is in his role. I love his smart mouth and how he gets under my skin. He makes me stop and feel when I have felt nothing for so long. I have been so numb, so alone. I'm tired and I just want someone to lean on.

When my timer goes off, I move, wanting the shower to wash away my Joshua thoughts and get my head back in the game, ready to deal with the letter.

"I'll be back soon."

I walk to the bathroom to wash my hair. I'll have to add toner to it, so I'll be in the bathroom for a while. Gracie is fine to entertain herself. She is pretty much family. She may not be blood, but close enough.

A little while later, I came out with freshly colored hair. I dried and styled it. It's gorgeous. I'm totally loving the highlights.

"Whoa…You look amazing. I love the strips. Great idea."

She wanders over to touch my hair.

"Thanks." I smile bashfully and say, "Now, let's open this letter."

I walk to the kitchen and she trails behind me. I slide it from the counter and hand it to her. No way I'm opening it. She will take the blow for me first and see if I need to know its contents.

We both lock eyes and take a deep breath in. She looks down and I follow. The tear of the letter is the only noise in the apartment beside slight mumbles from the TV, but the letter is loud in comparison.

She pulls it out and her eyes widen. My heart is skipping wildly in my chest. I ask, "What is it?"

Her face drops and it makes me want to know what happened. Why, after this many years, do they care? And how did they find me? My stomach churns at the thought. I'm going to have to be more careful when I walk out of this apartment.

Her eyes widen and she says, "They're dead."

I gasp, covering my mouth and shaking my head in denial. I say, "But that's her writing." My voice is disbelieving, pointing at the letter, trying to understand.

She hands it to me and says, "Read it."

I take it from her with trembling hands and read it. The light chest pain returns as I read it. It says that if I'm reading this, then both my aunt and uncle are dead and they are sorry for everything. It's a simple letter with not much in terms of a personal note, just a sorry, and the way it reads, it isn't convincing.

Then it is more legal stuff about the house, cars, and money all moving to my name.

I glance up at Gracie with teary eyes, feeling a mix of emotions, one part of me happy and another sad.

A sense of dread washes over me as I realize something.

"I'm not going into that house. I haven't been there in years. And I don't have any good memories. I just want it all sold," I explain.

I put the paper on the counter as if it's going to hurt me and cross my arms over each other. I hug myself like it's going to protect me.

"I totally get that. I would feel the same."

She steps over, tilting her head, and she rubs her hand up and down my upper arm.

"I might call Mom. I want to get some advice. I'll ask her for dinner. Did you want to stay too?" I ask.

I know my mom will offer neutral advice. She knows what I went through and knows what I can handle. She may offer advice that will help me figure out what to do next.

"I can have an early dinner, but then I gotta go to work," she says as she sips her tea.

"Fair enough. I'll just give Mom a quick call. I'll be right back." I sip my tea, but it's gone cold. Yuck. I lower it to the counter and walk away.

"I'll make us some fresh hot tea."

I smile, loving how she just knows what I need.

"Thanks," I call over my shoulder and call Mom.

Mom is lost for words on the phone but agrees to come for dinner. We hang up and plan to discuss it properly when she is here.

She arrives a little while later and I relay the letter and hand it to her. She scans it and I can see concentration lines on her face and I love how hard she cares for me. We debrief on how

I feel, and she stays for dinner and way past Gracie's leaving. I think she is worried that if I'm alone, I'll break down and no one will be here to help. But truthfully, I'm mentally tired, so I'm able to fall asleep easily tonight. But unfortunately, during the night, a nightmare appears. It's the time I lived with my aunt and uncle. I see it so vividly: the cold, dark attic, dirty blanket, and hunger. I had just lost my parents and I'm alone. No one visits. No one offers comfort. I'm in a new town.

I wake in a pool of sweat. But it reminds me that I need to concentrate on my future and bettering myself.

Joshua

Lying beside her was something I haven't experienced before. The emotions swirling inside me make my heart swell. Her brain and body are my kryptonite. So why am I standing at the bedroom door watching her sleep like a creep, instead of spooning her until the morning? Because I can't do more than casual.

I can't let myself be vulnerable to anyone ever again. To feel pain and hurt from the people you love and who are supposed to love you is something I'm still trying to recover from.

I turn around and don't take another glance back at her sleeping body. I just tiptoe to the door and leave her apartment.

I drive home and crawl into my cold and lonely bed. I close my eyes, but I can't sleep, punishment clearly from leaving the goddess in the night and going back to my cold, empty apartment. It looks nothing like Ava's. Hers is warm, cozy, and lived in, the opposite of my simple, and sterile place. I can afford nice things, but I can't get the warm feeling that Ava's apartment gives, or maybe it's her. The hard exterior is a front but what's underneath is a caring, sweet, and loving side that you wouldn't know unless you peel back her layers, that's hiding, it's a front to make others think she is a hard bitch. Her spitfire attitude, it would scare most. I smirk, thinking of her and her tongue-in-cheek comments. Sick of tossing and turning, I get up and hit the gym earlier than usual and then get in to work, figuring I will get a head start, as it's a Friday and I can plan next week.

As I sit in my office, images of me boxing her in against that wall next to me enter my brain. The sexy little pants that leave her lips when she is aroused and her sexy-as-sin body are the perfect fit for me.

I swallow past a hard lump, regret filling me. How will she be with me because I never stayed or said goodbye? I just snuck out without giving her a thought. I'm a selfish dick.

Have I ruined it? Our friendship? But I just can't commit to a relationship. Is that something she would want? Because I wouldn't want a committed relationship ever. I know how un-fair that is, but it's how I feel. The thoughts inside my head are bringing on a headache. I rub my neck and decide to venture across the road and grab a coffee.

It's the weekend. The usual offers of parties and football pop up, but I ignore them all. I want to focus on work. I have only started see-ing huge progress, so no time to slow down now. Being lost in work allows me to not focus on my life.

The sound of my phone tears me from the monitor. I glance down at a text from Dad, letting me know Mom is in the hospital and which floor.

I stare down at the details. Rubbing the back of my neck, I try to figure out what I should do; I stop myself from worrying about how I will be perceived by them. Do I want to follow what I should do or what I want to do?

Ava's words remind me to do what I want to do. Bad luck if that means I look weak to him. I'm proving with the business that I'm somebody worth loving. And I'm worth it. Deep down inside, I'm still a kid who wants to be loved by his parents. So be it, because hidden inside, I need their approval, even now, at thir-ty-four.

I want to see her. I wouldn't forgive myself if I let my stubborn head choose to not see her because she never cuddled me or loved me the way I wanted her to. I had a roof over my head, which is more than some people. Surely that's something.

I walk to the hospital with heavy, slow steps. I push myself and enter the hospital. Perspiration hits my forehead and I swipe it away with the back of my hand. I have never felt so nauseated before, but today I'm about to visit my sick mom, a person I value and love.

As I take the elevator, I feel so small. I reach the floor and search the ward for her. I take a breath outside the room and knock with a trembling hand, the door firm against my knuckles. The sound echoes inside the room and I stand still, waiting for her to call out so I can enter. I feel the pulse in my neck increasing.

"Come in," her soft, posh voice calls out. It's quieter than usual.

I take a few steps in and as her sunken eyes meet mine, tears spring up. She wears a hospital gown. It's loose all around her and her collarbone is prominent. She was always elegant and slim, but now she has thin hair and zero makeup on. Her signature ruby lipstick is nowhere in sight, the blue from the gown showing off her pale skin. There are piles of blankets on her to keep her warm, and it's the first time I realize that soon, she will no longer be here.

I wonder how long I will have before she will be gone forever. I thought when my parents died, I would feel relief, but I'm surprised by my choked-up state. It's tearing me up inside.

I'm waiting for her to say something because words are stuck in my throat and I'm unable to speak. I'm speechless at her appearance; she really is sick. Her radiance is gone and in its place is a sickened body. I feel my heart beating hard inside my chest.

"Mom," I say.

She half smiles at me and it breaks my heart. I don't know what else to say. I will myself to move forward. She taps the side of the bed, urging me to come closer. I follow the command and I pull out the chair beside the bed and sit. She reaches out and I take the offering without a second thought, surprised how cold her hand is. I envelope it with mine to help warm it up.

I sit in silence, not knowing what to speak about. We have a strained relationship; I don't know what her interests are and she wouldn't know any of mine.

"It's okay, son. This is no one's fault. Unfortunately, it's my time."

Her breathlessness worries me, but as I open my mouth, she cuts me off by saying, "Your father tells me you have made quite an impressive company for yourself."

I didn't know what to say, so I stare down at our joined hands, squeezing them and brushing my thumb across the top. My lips turn up and I say, "Thank you. James helped me."

"I'm sure it wasn't all James. Don't discredit all your hard work."

My ears thud, disbelief filling me. If I was choked up before, now I'm borderline going to pass out. I feel myself breathing hard and fast. My eyes sting and she tugs my hand. It's a simple *look at me* request. But her eyes are full of tears sitting on her lashes, waiting to be shed. My own eyes sting at the fragility of it.

"I'm proud of you."

Tears now fill my eyes and I'm struggling to find my breath. Who would have thought hearing those words could split open my heart, but here I am, holding back tears, not wanting to cry at those loving words.

It's all I ever wanted to hear.

CHAPTER 19

AVA

I'M BACK AT WORK on Monday and I don't waste any time getting back into it. I left the letter and my inheritance in the back of my mind to just focus on doing my job. I'm passionate about this job and my future here, so I need to focus on it and not on the letter or Joshua.

I'm yawning from my restless weekend. I haven't been able to sleep well. Too much is on my mind.

"Did you want to go for a coffee?" Thomas asks.

I peer over my shoulder at him. He is walking toward my desk, his eyebrows raised, waiting for my answer.

"I don't know. I have property to sort through."

His brows pinch together and he says, "What do you mean?"

I have the screen up, showing me property prices and agents, so I point to it and explain. "I can't find an agent to sell a house."

"Your apartment?" he asks.

I blow my cheeks out and say, "Well, I just inherited a house and I need to sell it."

"James is an agent. He rarely does suburban houses unless it's for friends, but for you, he'll make the exception. You seem to have him as part of your cheer squad."

That makes me laugh out loud, something I haven't done genuinely in a while. It feels good.

"How come?"

He smirks and says, "You are a smartass and give Josh a lot of shit. And it clearly annoys the shit out of him."

I return to the computer and escape the page and grab my purse and say to Thomas, "I'll come for coffee, but only if it's your treat. And I can grab James' phone number."

"Deal."

We leave and grab a coffee before returning to work. When we return, my walk falters and I suck in a sharp breath. Joshua is standing by my office window with his hands stuffed into his pants pockets, looking like the handsome man that he is. His navy suit defines his taut ass. I know he is a fan of my ass, but I'm becoming a fan of his. I raise my gaze up to his broad, powerful back. He screams power, the way he stands. Anger rolls off him and I pinch my lips together, knowing it was probably me who pissed him off.

He is obviously here to talk to me because I avoided his last email on Friday, but I don't care. He can't just leave my apartment in the middle of the night like a jerk. He does what he wants? Well, I'll do what I want, and my stubborn ass is back and my body is not for him. Well, not anymore.

Thomas walks in, rubbing his brow, and says, "Hey, bud, what are you doing? We just grabbed a coffee. I didn't think I should have called you."

I'm glad you didn't, I say to myself. That kind of distraction is something I don't need right now.

Joshua turns to face us but his gaze is set on Thomas, his jaw tight and anger rolling off him. It's obvious now that he is facing us.

"Hi, Tom. Hi, Ava," he says in a sharp tone.

"Hello, Mr. Ward," I say with light sarcasm, but add no more conversation.

"Could you grab The Marrion file?" Joshua asks.

"I'm still on a break and I need to make an important call. The file for The Marrion is in the cabinet there." I point to the filing cabinet.

His jaw clenches and he mutters, "Fine."

He storms to the cabinet, scanning for the file, and I set my stuff down on top of my desk. I hear him stomp behind me, and it makes me smirk. I sit and get back to work, ignoring him, and dial the number Thomas gave me for James. It rings a few times before his deep, smooth voice enters my ear.

"Hello. James speaking."

"Ah, hi, James. It's Ava. Thomas's assistant."

"Well, hello, vixen. What do I owe this pleasure." His tone is lighter, with a hint of a purr. It's the funniest because in the small amount of time I have known James, I know he is a funny guy, not just super intelligent, but also a great time. I have overheard Thomas mention some girl at the airport, but he doesn't have a girlfriend. They laugh at the idea that a girl would have to be special to stop James from his playboy ways because he is the guy you find buying sex or having threesomes. The complete opposite to Joshua, who is standing behind me, the electricity between us pulling me in and reminding me how good he felt inside me on Thursday. A shudder runs down my back with pleasure, but I shake my head.

Focus, you dirty cow.

I carry on talking and ignore Joshua; I hear his footsteps and feel him pass me, following Thomas into his office to chat about business. I can't hear much because they are too far away, so I return to the phone call with James.

"Thomas gave me your number. I hope that's okay?" He isn't my friend, so I want to make sure he is okay with helping me. I don't want to force this on him. Surely he could refer me to someone if he can't.

"Of course it's fine. Now tell me what's up?" His voice soothes my worries away.

I take a breath and say, "So I have recently inherited a house from my now deceased aunt and uncle. We were—" I pause, looking for the right words before I continue, "estranged."

"Hmm," he mumbles so I know he is listening, and encourages me to continue.

"I don't want to go back to the house and I also don't want it. I want it sold as soon as possible," I say firmly, keeping my voice neutral even though I feel anything but. Inside, I feel my stomach clench, having to explain this.

I'm slumped over, tapping my fingernail on the desk. My other hand clutches the phone, waiting for his answer.

"I don't normally do residential work, but I can sense some family issues. And I help my friends." He emphasizes the word *friends*.

I smile, even though I know he can't see it, and say, "Thanks, James. I'm happy to pay you."

"Nonsense. Just pay the marketing fees, but the rest is on me. Just keep driving Josh crazy. That's enough payment." He snickers through the phone and I giggle. He is an evil but good friend.

"That I can do," I smugly say, knowing that is my intention.

"Okay, well, can you send me an email with all the details you have and I'll get started on it."

I sit back in my chair and let out a huge breath. One less item to deal with.

"Sure. Give me your email and I'll get started on it now."

He tells me his email address, which I scribble down and then hang up. I'm typing the email when I hear Joshua's deep voice get louder. As he finishes his conversation with Thomas, I can hear him approach me and he pauses.

The hairs on my body rise from having him so close, but I bite my lip and concentrate on the email. He clears his throat so I tilt my face up in the noise's direction. I glare at him while I wait for him to talk. His face flashes with annoyance and I have to bite back a laugh. After a beat, he finally says, "Come upstairs. I want to talk to you." It's firm and not negotiable.

It's loud enough so only I can hear. He doesn't want Thomas to know about us, and neither he nor I will say anything.

"No," I say in a simple, sharp tone.

"Why?" He's frustrated, but there is a plea this time. I take a quick look to see if Thomas is paying any attention. When I see him glued to his monitor, typing away, I focus back on Joshua.

"I'm not interested in hearing why you left. You want to be casual. That's fine. I get it. And I want nothing." I turn around and begin typing again, dismissing him. It's not completely true, but opening myself up to be in a relationship and allowing someone to hurt me freaks me the fuck out. To be vulnerable again is risky. He is simply too risky. He already showed me he will let me down and I don't want to give him another chance. Everyone I love or care about ends up leaving, so it's safer to protect myself.

"Fuck," he mutters under his breath and stomps off. I roll my eyes at his dramatics. He thinks everyone should speak to him whenever he wants them to. Obviously, if it was work-related, I would be there in a heartbeat, but the fact he was careful about Thomas, making sure he didn't know what was going on, meant it was personal, and I'm not losing sight of my career.

Joshua

"Grrr." I thrust my hands through my hair and lock the fingers of both hands behind my head and let out a gutteral scream. The emotions that woman brings out of me are too much. I shake my head, even more frustrated as I realize a headache is forming. How can I want to kiss the shit out of her in one second and argue with her the next? She gives me a serious case of whiplash.

This is why I stay casual. I don't get involved with the same person regularly.

I'm pissed off that Ava won't let me apologize for leaving her apartment the other day. She acted like it didn't bother her, throwing *I want nothing* in my face. I just wanted to make sure it did not hurt her because we need to work together, and I really should have left a note or stayed. But staying would involve opening up and letting someone in, and letting someone in scares me. I can't do that.

When I stood at her desk, I was sure she would cave, but she didn't, and my heart dropped. I really wanted to say sorry, and I never apologize. If you ask my friends, they will confirm.

But I can't deny the chemistry I feel with Ava; there is a truckload of it. Whenever she is in the room, I am drawn to her. I want to shove her against any surface and have my way with her; her gritty, earthy, yet floral scent is addictive. Half of me wants to be around her to just talk to her. The qualities she shows are rare. She is caring and thoughtful, but I just can't have someone let me down again. It's better to cut it off now before any deep feelings are involved.

I pace around my office, deciding I need to move on if she wants nothing, so I pull my phone out of my pocket and bring up a fling's name. My lips press together in a slight grimace as I agonize over calling her. My chest tightens and I exit the screen, throwing the phone on my desk.

I can't fucking do it.

CHAPTER 20

AVA

IT'S BEEN A COUPLE of weeks and I'm getting dressed for work when my phone rings.

"Hello, James," I say while fumbling with my phone between my head and my shoulder, trying to get dressed in time to grab the train. I zip my pants, but the zipper busts open. I glance down at the broken zipper, closing my eyes, and curse. *Fuck my life*. I take a breath and open my eyes and push the pants down my legs as I listen to him.

"Ava, good morning. Sorry to call you so early."

I kick the pants off and grab some new ones from my drawer and say, "It's okay. How can I help you?" I'm puffing as I put my legs through the new pants and pull them up and zip them. And thank god these don't break. I hold the phone to my ear and walk around the apartment, picking up what I need.

"I have some good news. Well, splendid news, actually. I have sold the house with the furniture for four hundred and ninety-five thousand dollars with a thirty-day settlement."

My ears ring and my heart picks up speed. Surely he didn't say four hundred and ninety-five thousand dollars.

My mouth dries, but I ask, "Sorry. How much?"

I need him to repeat it. I hold the phone painfully against my ear.

"Four hundred and ninety-five thousand dollars."

I stop moving and say, "Fuckin' hell. Are you sure?"

A roar of laughter leaves James' mouth before he says, "Yes, deadly. Now, let's meet on your break to sign the contract. Let's meet at the café across the street at, say, noon."

It's not a question; it's him telling me that's when he is free. He is a boss man for sure. He secretly scares the hell out of me. His height and intelligence are a scary mix.

"Okay, sure. Thank you, James." I choke on his name. I'm still trying to process what this means for my future.

I hang up and drop my head in my hands, taking deep breaths. I try to not freak out and just concentrate on taking breaths. When I feel relaxed, I continue moving and finish getting ready for work.

I get off the train a stop early because I want to walk through the city, I think about how I can afford the design courses and the apartment, and become a city girl. It's a lot to think about when I have been comfortable in my town, and I'm always scared about more people and new things. But a new apartment would be closer to work, which would mean I wouldn't have the forty-five-minute commute every day. Even if I become a city girl, I don't have to go out. I can still stay in my bubble. I'll just miss Gracie and Mom, which makes my stomach twist. I rely on them so much. So many thoughts are entering my mind and I can't talk about it all right now. It's too much, so I push them aside for the moment and decide I need to slow down and take one day at a time.

Joshua

I'm knee-deep in paperwork. My office is a mess and I'm trying to figure out the projects we have. If *she* were in here, I can imagine her face: horror. Pure horror at the disarray that is going on here.

Ava is back to avoiding me or being a total smartass—which, don't get me wrong, I miss.

I miss her smart mouth.

But I miss her sweet mouth even more.

Her unique beauty causes me to want something I haven't before. She is metal, tattoo, and colorful, coming here and turning my life upside down.

I have tried getting her to come here and talk to me. But as usual, she is fighting with me.

Normally, that would turn me on, but the fact I can't explain my issues is killing me. She has me all wrong, but I can't seem to get her to listen.

"Hi, Josh." Candice's voice sends my stomach twisting.

My gaze flicks to hers, not interested in why she is here.

But why is she here?

Our agreement involves sex at the hotel, not office visits like a couple. The only person I want in this office right now is Ava. Papers are littered everywhere, and now that Candice is invading my space, I can't think clearly.

"What are you doing here?" I say in a sharp tone.

My gaze moves to Linda to see if she is paying any attention. I don't know why I'm checking, knowing she will drill me with questions when Candice leaves. She is team Ava, so my flings coming here won't go down well.

"We need to talk." She crosses her arms over her chest.

I can't deny Candice is beautiful. She is, but it does nothing for me. There is no warmth flowing through my body or cravings to be touched by her. I look at Candice, and I feel nothing. We don't share a connection; it's just a need that she's fulfilling.

I move my hands around the papers and say, "Take a seat and make it quick. I need to get back to work, as you can see. In the future, text or call me first. We are not anything more than casual. I don't need the building knowing we fuck."

I'm trying to not be too angry at her, but when did she think it was okay to drop in? I have always explained we are casual. I'm not serious with anyone ever, and if anyone was to change my mind, there would only be one person.

Ava.

She gasps and there's a new tightness around her eyes, but then she walks forward and takes a seat, sitting up tall with her chest popped up. She crosses one long, slim leg over the other. I don't like the twirl of her lips. Something feels off. I glare at her and watch her mouth twitch into a cheerful smile.

Clearing her throat, she says, "Looks like I'm pregnant."

My mouth falls open. Fuck off. She is lying; there is no way. I'm careful. I turn away from her to gather my thoughts, my gut swirling, and the nausea that's swirling has me looking down my nose at her.

"You are on the pill, and I always wear a condom. So it can't be mine," I say confidently with a raised voice.

She leans forward and says, "The pill isn't one hundred percent, and neither are condoms."

I shake my head vigorously, her attitude pissing me off. I pinch the bridge of my nose and retort, "No. I'm careful. Always sober now and careful."

She sits staring at me, wide-eyed like I just slapped her for thinking the baby isn't mine. Bile rises at the back of my throat and threatens to come out; it has me hunching over. I feel a sense of dread washing over me, but I still don't believe it. Please. No. Raising my palms in front of me, challenging her, I say, "It can't be mine. No. You need to get a paternity test."

I'm not ready for this. I cannot be a father. I wouldn't know how. The role model I had was awful. I never want kids, and definitely not with a woman I don't love. I barely like the girl. I tolerate her for my much-needed relief. Fuck. This seriously can't be happening right now. I close my eyes like it will help block out all the noise, and then when I reopen them, it will be a figment of my imagination.

"Why? But the baby is yours—"

"It isn't."

She stutters back. Her eyes are glassy and she presses a hand flat over her chest and says. "We can be a family...Don't put our baby through a paternity test."

I lower my gaze to my hands. A lump forms in my throat at what she wants. What the fuck is happening to me? Why does everyone want a relationship with me? I close my hands and glance back up, finding the strength to say, "No. We will not be a family, not now, not ever."

I can't lie. She needs to hear that no matter the outcome, she will not change my mind on this.

She flinches before she lashes out and says, "It is yours. I'm not doing it."

"Bad luck. You want to come here and tell me I'm a father when I don't think that's true, then you need to prove it. Then and only then, I'll care for you and the baby. But until then, you need to leave me alone." My blood boils. Surely I didn't fuck up this badly.

She smiles and her eyes sparkle and she says, "Fine, but you're wasting our time and putting the baby at risk."

Her smugness pisses me off. I grind my teeth, trying not to lose my shit. My life is an utter mess right now. Mom is in the hospital, Ava is blocking me out, and now Candice is accusing me of fathering her unborn child. Fuck. Can life get much worse? I need a drink, stat.

I won't disown my own child. I would always be there for him, provide for him. I hope to love him. Shit, what if he's a she? I'm so fucked. I scrub my brow and close my eyes, needing to collect my thoughts.

I'm fine. I just need to work, to take my mind off everything.

I reopen my eyes with determination and fight and say, "I need you to leave before I call security. I have work to get back to."

I need to sort this chaos out.

"You will pay." She stands, twisting and stomping off in her loud heels. I watch her exit my office and vow to stop putting my dick in women who are batshit crazy. My life was just turning for the better. I won't let her ruin it. I refuse to believe that the baby is mine until I get confirmation.

I rub my hand down my face, then put my hands on my hips and scan the mess. Having had enough, I decide I need help.

"Linda, are you free?"

I peek up at her as she takes in the office floor, littered with papers.

"Sorry," I say. "I can't concentrate in such a mess."

She steps forward, picking up papers and reading them, and says with a chuckle, "Looks like chaos, not mess."

I groan, not feeling the laughter that she clearly feels, and say, "I know, and I can't get any work done."

She frowns and says, "I heard."

Of course she did.

"It isn't mine."

I hope.

"I don't believe her. She is a gold digger who wants a better life; you can't blame her. This place screams money. But she knows nothing about you. You don't allow anyone to get through that wall you built around your heart." Her voice is low and her approach gentle.

"I know. I can't."

"You can. There are some outstanding women, and I know one in particular, who is special." She winks and I dart my gaze to one paper, and I swallow past the lump that's formed in my throat. I'm unable to answer, so I just nod.

Ava is special, but that doesn't mean I'm ready to let the walls down.

I clear my throat. Needing distraction, I ask, "Can you help sort the projects into different piles?"

She offers me a kind smile and says, "Always."

Linda gets me. I can be myself, and she will always be there to support me.

CHAPTER 21

AVA

A FEW DAYS LATER, I'm hanging out with Gracie at home. We just finished the latest episode of *Outer Banks*.

"I need to go to work now," Gracie says. She sighs heavily as she rises off the couch, looking back at me, and says, "Why did we have to start this? I need to know what happens."

I sit up and pause the TV and say, "I promise I won't watch any without you. I wish you didn't have to leave me."

I stand up and we walk slowly to my door.

"I know, but work's too busy not to turn up."

We stop before my door; I open my arms and we hug.

"It's fine. Go have a good shift and get some good tips."

She crosses her fingers and says, "Yes, I'm hoping for another good weekend."

I open the door and say, "Bye."

I wave and close the door after her. I pick up my phone and walk back to the couch and scroll through social media. A thought enters my mind. Should I search for him online? I haven't done it before, but I decide to search for some gossip about him. I hit Instagram with no results. Damn it. Next I hit Facebook and after a good browse, I find him. I hover my finger over his profile. *Go for it, chicken. You have come this far.* I hit it and slam my eyes shut before slowly peeling one eye open to see if it's private. But it's not. My eyes widen and I sit up straighter, shuffling to get comfortable. His profile pic is him standing alone in his signature navy suit, with a matching tie and a crisp white shirt. His brown finger-length hair has been swept to perfection and his wicked panty-dropping smile is proudly on display.

I laugh loudly. Trust him to have a picture like that. Having a company to run, he needs to look the part. But when I click the image to make it bigger, I hiss a breath. God damn it, he is gorgeous. My whole body ignites with a flush and I'm sure I am beetroot red. His lips are soft and full and it reminds me of what they felt like on me. A shiver rocks me and my inner core is pulsating. I'm getting all hot and bothered by a damn profile picture. What is happening to me? Men don't do this to me. I never needed company and sex, but now I'm craving his touch and affection.

Why do I have to be attracted to him? A glimpse of what if...What if he was available and I could trust him?

But I get little time to think because my phone starts lighting up in my hand. It's James. I wonder why he is calling me on the weekend. I don't think any more about it; I just quickly hit the answer button and say, "Hi, James." My voice wavers from being caught drooling over his friend online. My cheeks are hot and I'm glad he can't see me right now.

"Ava, how are you?"

"I'm good... you?" I trail off, trying to understand the reason for the call.

"I have found a condo for you to look at. It hasn't gone to market yet. I asked them to hold off until you have seen it."

A fluttery feeling hits my belly. I can't believe how nice he is. He barely knows me. I pinch my lips together. I'm going to look at a condo that I will be purchasing. My body lights up at the thought. My dreams are coming true. I'm so close, I can almost taste it.

"You there?"

Oh, shit. "Yeah, yeah. I'm here. Sorry," I breathe out.

He chuckles loudly, and he says, "Okay, so do you want to view the condo or not?"

"Yes. Definitely. Thank you."

"Okay, I will arrange it for next weekend. I will send you a text with the details."

"Sounds good."

A few days later, I almost skip into work, feeling high as a kite. Life is giving me everything I could need right now.

I sing inside the office, knowing Thomas won't be here yet. But I feel him before I see him. The hairs all rise on the nape of my neck.

"Nice, ahh, singing." Joshua's eyes twinkle with joy. And it ruffles my feathers, his teasing me while I'm in a cheerful mood. It makes me snap and say, "What are you doing here?"

I see from the corner of my eye he is approaching my desk. I look at him, surprised his eyes are sparkling with humor, and he says, "I wanted to hear your tune. Why don't you keep going?"

"Go away, Joshua." My tone isn't angry now; it's just tired. I can't with the whiplash. I want to go back to my happy bubble. I prepare for my day, trying to ignore him.

"Awww, are we touchy today?"

I stare daggers at him. Back the fuck off. Don't go there.

"Bugger off; I'm trying to work. Speaking of, shouldn't you be running the company? Surely you have actual work to do. Work that doesn't involve annoying your employees."

And his smug grin appears. I close my eyes and suck in a deep breath through my nose and out through my mouth, trying to calm my now tense body. Trust him to ruin a moment.

"I do, but I need my star employee to work with me."

I groan. "Really, why?" I ask before mumbling under my breath, "In your dreams."

"Trust me, babe. You star in my dreams." He winks and steps closer.

I step back, feeling weak from his closeness. The back of my legs hit my desk and I reach out and grasp the edge to support myself. He steps closer, closing the distance, his cologne hitting me like a truck. I tuck my hair behind my ear, not dropping my gaze from his. My mouth hangs open at his words and I just stand there with an arched back, staring back at him. The electricity and sparks in the room are undeniable. He clearly won't budge and leave me alone, so I just will stay still and try to resist him.

As I sit on the edge of the desk, I take him in. He looks different today. His hair is shorter and his light gray suit complements his blue eyes. We stare at each other in some kind of showdown. I'm trying to be patient about why he so desperately needs to chat, but he is getting on my nerves, standing there but not saying anything. He just stares like he wants to eat me. I watch his tongue skim his lower lip as his eyes darken, gazing seductively over my body. An ache begins in my sex at the intensity, but the sexual tension between us annoys me. I don't want to desire him anymore. Why doesn't my body understand? I cross my arms tightly over my chest, about to lose it in frustration, when he begins.

"Thomas will need some more time off. Lily's cast is off, but unfortunately it hasn't healed correctly."

My breath catches. Oh no, poor Lily. And Thomas will be beside himself if she has surgery at her age.

But then the next thought enters my mind. I have to work with him again, and last time, it led to our first kiss. My body warms with the memory of the all-consuming, toe-curling kiss. But since we work for the same company, I will have to suck it up. I will have many moments when we need to work together, and I will need to act professionally.

"Sure. Do we know when yet?" I ask, secretly hoping I have some time to get my head together before having to work with him.

"Not yet. He is waiting to sort out a date with the surgeon's office."

I push off the desk, putting my face in his. My breath catches; we are so close. He doesn't take a step back, which means I brush him to get back to my work. Touching him causes pleasure to flood my body. Cursing under my breath at my stupid, traitorous body, I grab the mouse to check the planner and a thought pops into my head.

Turning my face to him with a blank look, I ask, "Where is Thomas today? He could have told me himself."

He's standing relaxed, feet wide apart and hands stuffed in his pockets. "That he could have, babe."

I do a double take. What did he just say?

"I'm not your babe. We are not together."

His face softens, and the sexy smirk on his face has my inner core waking up and dancing, thinking it will get some action again, but it will be sadly mistaken.

"I need to get upstairs for a meeting, but I'll check in with you later."

"To save you the trip, I will tell you now. I'm fine."

His smile bursts wider and he shakes his head.

"I will talk to you later," he says in a firm tone.

I watch him turn and walk to the elevator. I can't stop myself from watching him, torturing myself as I stare. I'm a sucker for punishment.

I scratch my head and push myself to get on with the day. I dump my bag in its drawer and go for a walk. I need to take a minute before starting work, too rattled to begin right away.

Stepping back into the office, it's too quiet without Thomas. I prefer to work alongside someone in this big office. I lower my cup to the desk and work on the tasks and emails I can do. The tasks or emails I'm unable to do, I email Thomas and CC Joshua so one of them can do it.

My stomach grumbles and I glance down at the clock on my computer screen. It's coming up to lunchtime and I haven't told Linda about the condo, so I email her a quick invite. She agrees and I'm excited to share my good news over lunch.

I enter the top floor and see her jumping up and down like a rabbit, and I giggle loudly.

She turns her head at the sound of my voice and she says, "Ava, hi. I need to finish filling in this form once I get a folder down, and then I'll be ready to go."

There is no way she will reach the file. She is less than five feet tall and whoever filled these cupboards didn't think of how she was going to get folders down.

Moving toward her, I say, "Let me help you."

"Thanks, love."

I reach up to grab the folder she needs and as I bring it down and hand it to her, I freeze on the spot. Joshua is standing there, his hands in his pockets, staring at me. I watch his Adam's apple bob up and down. The heat in his gaze is a direct line to my sex. He's staring fixedly at my

middle and I frown, unsure of what has transfixed him. I glance down and realize my navel
ring is sparkling under the office lights. I forgot
the top I'm wearing can easily ride up. I don't
pull it back down; instead I leave it bunched up
higher, showing my sparkle off. Torturing him
is way more fun.

"Joshua, you would have been handy five
minutes ago," Linda jokes, pulling him from his
daze.

"Who put these files up there? Poor Linda has
no chance of getting them down," I say.

His gaze keeps darting down and then back
up, then he says, "I'll move the files to somewhere more suited." His voice is strained, and
he's shaking his head. He walks past us, saying,
"Now I've got two women bossing me around.
I'm screwed."

I laugh internally. Yes, Joshua, you are!

Linda and I go to lunch, and when I return,
I see there is an email from Joshua. I click the
email and skim its contents.

To: Ava Johnson
Subject: Problem
Message: Ava,
Are you trying to kill me? My hand is twitching
up here. I can't get the vision of your body and
outfit out of my head.
Regards,
Joshua

I bite my lip. A rush of excitement rolls
through me. I'm getting under his skin. When
he talks about his hand twitching, I can vividly

imagine the spanking he would give me across his knee. Hard and sharp. Something in my core pulsates, and if I wasn't so stubborn, I would probably be upstairs begging for him to do it.

But I remember how I felt when I woke up alone, and I'm not allowing that to happen again.

I type out a smart reply, laughing to myself, thinking how crazy it is that I'm flirting with the boss.

To: Joshua Ward
Subject: Re: Problem
Message: To Joshua,
It wasn't on purpose, but I'm glad you enjoyed the show... because that's all you will get.
Ava

I hit send before I change my mind; I don't want to think about it anymore. I continue on with my work and it isn't long before he has responded.

I open it and read.

To: Ava Johnson
Subject: Re: Problem
Message: Please, would you meet me at the hotel?
Same room? Tonight?
Hand twitching Boss
Joshua

An angry huff escapes my lips. I am not going to his hotel room. Does he think I'm his plaything? I'm not a casual fling; I don't do that.

For a smart guy, he is really thick.

I type out a reply.

To: Joshua Ward
Subject: Re: Problem
Message: Joshua,
No!
I'm busy both after work and at work. If you don't mind, I have work to do. Which I'm sure you do too.
Ava

I close the application. He can send emails but I'm not reading them anymore. I will not be a casual fuck. Not now and not ever, no matter how good the sex is.

I spend the rest of the afternoon working and when I go to see if there is a response, I see there is, so I delete it without reading it. I figure why would I bother? It's about sex, not work. And I told him my answer even if my body is pissed that it won't get relief.

CHAPTER 22

AVA

THE NEXT DAY, I walk into my office and rub my eyes, thinking I must be seeing things.

Thomas is sitting behind his desk, even though he wasn't due back for a few days. However, I could skip with joy, having missed him.

I quicken my pace and when I get closer, I spot Joshua reclined in a chair across from Thomas. The hairs on the back of my neck rise and I stumble, almost falling flat on my face. I'm sure I look like a Bambi on ice trying to stop myself from toppling over.

He looks like a sculpture, his ankle draped across the other knee, his thickly muscled thighs straining inside his gray pinstripe suit. His jacket is opened and his toned, broad chest is hidden under a white shirt and gray tie. He hasn't noticed me yet, his head held up by his long fingers and palm. God, those hands are sexy and does he know the right way to use them on the female body. They are rough and perfect.

Jesus, Ava, they are just hands. Get a fucking grip.

I suck in a deep breath and roll my shoulders back. I try to muster up some courage and not call him out in front of Thomas.

I give him credit for trying hard to talk to me. But I'm also annoyed. Why isn't he listening?

Fucking persistent fucker.

I dump my bag on my desk and step over to the doorway. "Thomas, you're back."

I keep my eyes on him and do not allow my gaze to drift to the man opposite him. I can feel Joshua's gaze burning a hole in the side of my face, but I can't look because I can't think straight around him.

"Ava. Yes, I sure am. Jennifer is looking after Lily for me." There is a twinkle in his eye and he keeps looking between Joshua and me.

"That's nice of her. So last-minute surgery went well and Lily is okay now?" I ask.

"Yeah, surgery was scary for me, but she was a superstar. And now she has a few more weeks of recovery, but overall she is good, thanks," he answers.

I open my mouth to speak.

"Hi, Ava," Joshua says.

I turn to face him, and now his hands are in his lap and he's wearing a sexy smirk. Suddenly, I have the urge to sit on his lap and rub myself over him.

What am I becoming? A dog in heat? For fuck's sake. What is wrong with me...That's right, because you have had him underneath you before, you dirty whore.

The memory of him and me at my apartment, where I rubbed myself along his hard length, sends a shiver running up my spine and I feel my heart thud. I need to get out of here.

"Joshua," I say. That's all I say back, worried that if we talk long enough, Thomas will know we have slept together. So I swivel and walk back to my desk, running my sweaty hands down the front of my clothes.

A little while later, I hear rustling at Thomas's doorway and the boys exit the room. Side by side, like a pair of handsome gods.

I roll my eyes and refocus on the paperwork in front of me.

"Ava, come have a coffee with us. James is meeting us," Thomas says.

I peer up into a pair of pleading blue eyes and fuck, my heart hammers.

No chance.

I move my gaze to the safety of Thomas and shake my head vigorously. I say, "No, I'm meeting Linda." It's a lie, but I will email her as soon as they leave.

Joshua eyes me suspiciously, knowing I'm lying, but he can't prove it. I sit back and pop a brow, as if to say, what are you going to do about it? Then I turn my back on him.

"Okay, I'll see you when I get back," Thomas calls out.

I watch the boys from the corner of my eye, then email Linda, asking her for a coffee. She responds with a yes so I grab my purse and make my way to her.

"Linda, are you ready?" I call. Her desk is empty, but she pops up from the floor. I put my hand on my chest and say, "Shit. Linda, you scared the crap out of me."

Linda giggles and says, "Sorry, love. Just dropped a paper." She places it down and then walks around the desk. "Let's go."

We walk across the road and my body temperature jumps with each step, knowing the boys could be behind the coffee shop door. And an idea comes to me.

"Linda, would you mind if we didn't sit near the boys? I just wanted to chat with you alone."

She gives me a perplexed look, but she nods and says, "Of course that's okay. Is this about Joshua?"

And I suck in a breath. How the fuck does she know? I bite down on the inside of my cheek, not wanting to say a word until I'm safely inside.

We walk through the doors and the boys are in the back corner, deep in conversation, so they don't notice us. I veer toward a table at the front and say, "My treat. Cappuccino?"

She takes a seat and I wait for her to respond.

"Yes, please," she says.

"Okay, I'll be right back."

I make my way to the line and try to stay hidden behind people without it looking obvious. But I feel a breath tickle my face and cardamom overwhelming my space. My nostrils flare at the invasion and I try to inhale more of the pleasant smell.

"Ava, are you avoiding me?" he whispers and his breath tickles my cheek.

I go to spin around but I feel his large hand on my waist, gripping me, and I fall still on the spot. I enjoy his demand, and I know he doesn't want me to turn. But when he steps closer, I feel him poke my back. I close my eyes shut before reopening them, willing my balls back.

"What do you want, Joshua?"

"You under me. And in my bed." He whispers it into my ear so only I can hear. I almost moan. My legs are shaky and my inner core is burning up. I'm internally begging for his hand to move from my waist to the inside of my pants. My panties are wet just from his firm hand and brash words. He knows how to get to me.

"In your dreams," I grind out between a clenched jaw. I'm barely hanging on. The line moves. Thank fuck. He has to let me go, and I swear I hear him groan. His groaning is probably the sexiest sound I have heard, and the line moves again, which puts more distance between us but also allows me to feel how wet he got me in just a few seconds. Damn him. Now I'm walking around with wet panties. It makes me feel even dirtier and I can't lie; it's hot.

It's the weekend and I'm walking around a new condo in awe. It seems surreal. Surely this isn't my life? Here I am in the city, a block away from work, shopping for an apartment. Like, what is my life? For all the hell I have been through, I finally feel like I'm finding my feet.

"Oh darling, look at the bedroom closet." I follow my mom's voice.

I enter the walk-in closet, and my mouth goes slack at the size of it. I say in a whisper, "Wow."

"Impressive, isn't it?"

I have no words. This is a huge, organized closet. My little organized life would love this condo. The all white, floor to ceiling racks, shelves, and drawers are something out of a movie. This is like a real-life dream.

How far have I come that I am looking at buying a house like this?

Is this real?

Am I worthy?

It's one-point-two million, so more than double that of my aunt and uncle's house that I sold, but instead of paying rent, I'll be paying a mortgage, and this will be all mine. No more stressing about being unstable anymore.

"What do you think?" Mom asks in a whisper, not wanting James to hear. He is on the phone. I swear it's glued to his ear or hand; I haven't seen him without it.

I bite down on my lip, then say, "I think it's perfect. What do you think?"

Mom nods and says, "I'm worried it might be too much. With you moving away from me, and the added expense. But I agree it would be the perfect condo for you. It's in a safe area, close to work, and there is a lot to do. Maybe you'll meet Mr. Right?"

Oh god.

I roll my eyes. I know she wants me to settle down. I think she worries about me spending so much time alone, but I don't mind it. Heck, I don't love it, but I don't have many choices. Here in the city, I'll have options to go out.

"I know it will be a big change, but this is the right step for me. I know it. I need to follow my gut and put an offer down."

I walk to the floor-length window in the bedroom. It overlooks an extensive park and my heart swells; this is it. This entire apartment makes me smile, and it's perfect. Nothing else will compare.

We walk out of the master bedroom, and I join James, who is still deeply absorbed in his phone.

He turns at the sound of our approach. A wicked smile breaks out on his face. I internally roll my eyes. *Charming fucker.*

"And what do we think?" he asks.

"Let's put an offer in," I say happily.

I know he is showing me property because he classes me as one of his friends, and I appreciate the time and help. My chest suddenly feels tight, but I hold it back.

"Excellent choice. Now let's fill in the paperwork so I can show the sellers. Take a seat."

He gestures for Mom and me to sit.

He hands me forms to complete and when I'm finished, I hand them back. I rub my palms together. Even though it's not cold in here, my nerves are making me fidget.

I hope they take the offer. It's as far as I can go. I can't afford more than that, but I want this badly.

"Thanks. I'll have an answer to give to you soon. The client wants a quick sell. Break up." He shrugs as if that explains it. He really doesn't like relationships, not that I can blame him. There is no way I could be in one either. I can't trust anyone, and the one person who I can't get out of my head, a.k.a. his friend, doesn't do commitment.

We leave the condo and head to the homeless shelter to volunteer. By the time I stagger up to my apartment, I'm totally wiped, emotionally and physically. I just want to chill out on the couch and pass out. On the car ride home, James had said that it looked like they won't accept the offer, and it was like it punched me in the gut

I envisioned myself in that condo, and I had a feeling it was mine. So the call was a shock.

He is going to keep working on the condo for me, as he was sure they would accept below the asking price.

So right now, on top of passing out, I want to eat ice cream and watch trash TV.

Gracie is at work again and I wish she wasn't, but I don't want to be begging her to quit work tonight and be around my moody ass. Plus, I will probably end up asleep early, so it would have been pointless. I wish I had someone to live with.

Joshua on the couch and me dry humping him flashes in front of my eyes and I wince. I need a new apartment stat because I am seeing him everywhere and it's driving me insane.

CHAPTER 23

JOSHUA

I RUB MY TEMPLES as I read the emails coming through. The thump in my skull worsens. I spend entirely too much time checking my email, waiting for paternity test results. Since Candice came into my office with the news, I have barely slept, waking up in a pool of sweat, the same dream on replay of her telling me about the baby, and then there is a baby who is the spitting image of me. I'm such an idiot. What did I think would happen?

I shake my head to clear it. There are a lot of emotions running through me. My mom is dying in the hospital, I can't stand my father, a baby... And a woman who drives me fucking crazy. Maybe if one thing were off my plate, I could sleep at night.

The temptation to drink more than I allow myself has been proving hard. I so badly want to go to a party and drink until I pass out, but with the business and reputation I'm making for myself, I simply can't. The emotions I am experiencing, I have to face, even if they are scaring the fuck out of me. I'm not used to it and I don't like it one bit.

I stare at the monitor, unable to concentrate even after many attempts, so I run my hand through my hair down to my neck, which I squeeze. There are still no emails, so I stand and grab my wallet and phone from my drawer and call James. I need fresh air and a coffee to clear my head.

It rings in my ear. As he picks up, I say, "Are you free for coffee across the road?"

"Are you still on your period? Clearly, Ava is still driving you mad." James' sarcastic voice speaks dryly into my ear.

"Are you coming or not?" I ask. I'm angry he can read me so well.

I hear his chuckle before he answers, "Fine. I know you need me."

I roll my eyes. *Dickhead.*

"See you soon." I hang up and stuff my phone into my suit pocket.

James is always saving people. In our group of friends, he is the dad. The helper, the support, and the leader. But yes, I need my friends. My head and heart are freaking out. I can't be a father. I just started my life. And to a casual fling and not someone I...No, I can't go down that thought process. Having my friends to lean on when I'm freaking out inside is required.

Speaking of, I will see if Thomas wants one. As I pass Linda, I say, "I will bring you a coffee back."

"Thanks, love," she answers and continues typing.

I step into the elevator and arrive at Thomas' office. My brows crease as I walk closer into the room and see there is no sign of Ava.

A sadness sweeps over me. I wanted to hear her smart mouth or simply catch a glimpse of her beautiful face. I crave familiarity, the way things were before I was told Candice is pregnant and my mom got cancer.

Her backtalk and snarky attitude is fun and I love her *don't take shit*, feisty attitude. Speaking of feisty, my mind flashes back to the way her eyes glow with desire. Her body underneath me, giving in to pleasure. Her taste, her whimpers, her soft skin. That and my body wrapped around her while she slept would help me sleep and stop the nightmares.

I stare at her desk. It's perfectly in order and completely untouched.

Where is she?

"If you're looking for Ava, she won't be in today." My gaze moves toward Thomas' voice. I'm so transparent, it annoys me.

He is standing just outside his door, his arms folded over his chest.

"I'm not looking for her. I'm just not liking her attitude. She hasn't been at the company long and she is already taking time off? Not a good look." I stuff my hands in my pockets and stand a little taller.

Thomas raises an eyebrow and says, "Linda has taken a day off, so don't be a hypocrite. Are you sure that's the only reason?"

"Yes. Why, do you think it's professional? Seriously?"

"No, but—"

I shove my hand out to stop him from continuing. "There is my answer. I think I'll have to give her a warning. She will be lucky I don't fire her ass."

I know I won't be able to fire her because she is good at her job. And this stupid crush I have on her makes me selfish and to not want to let her go. Yet I can't have her.

It's fucked.

I'm fucked.

"You will do no such thing. I haven't been here long, and I have needed time off. You didn't give me a warning. If you want to know, she is at the bank, trying to get money for an apartment in the city. I told her to go, or should I say *begged*. Didn't you know her aunt and uncle died?"

Well, fuck.

No, I didn't.

I turn my head and lower my gaze, repeatedly swallowing the gravel that's formed in my throat. I'm such an ass.

"Feeling bad now?" Thomas asks, as if reading my thoughts.

I scratch my forehead and nod. Do I ever...I feel like the biggest prick. She lost her family and here I want to fire her.

"Don't stress. I understand you are the boss and you want to keep it professional. But I also know you like her," he says.

"Get out of here. You. Thomas. Are. Seeing. Things."

"Keep lying to yourself; it's not my life. I'm busy with my girls. I don't need your shit. But I just want to say, Ava is seriously awesome. She would be the perfect woman for you: loyal, kind, and fun. Also, the banter you two have is pure chemistry."

His words are like a sledgehammer, hitting me hard in the chest. I'm already getting enough shit from Linda, but now my friends are on her side. I'm surrounded by her cheer squad. But no matter what they say, I can't commit. I can't even trust myself, let alone someone else.

"I'm not indulging you in this conversation. I came here to ask if you want to grab a coffee with me and James across the road. Not to discuss Ava."

Even saying her name has my heart jolting. But I need to tell them about Candice.

He returns to his office and says over his shoulder, "Sure; I'll grab my stuff. Hang on."

I wait less than a minute and he walks back. "Let's go."

We walk to the elevator down to the ground floor. I spot James' large frame standing outside, facing the traffic. His phone is glued to his ear and his other hand is stuffed inside his coat. He seems coy and always hiding something at the moment.

"Boys," he says as he hangs up.

"James," I say as he approaches us. We all shake hands.

"What's happening?" He nods to me and Thomas.

"Not much," Thomas says. "Lily is getting better; sassy as ever. She almost walked in on me and Jennifer the other night. I'm going to need to buy locks for my bedroom door. It mortified poor Jen, hiding behind the door naked while

Lily stood there asking why I have so much hair around my doodle."

James and I crack up in hysterics. I feel my eyes prick with tears and I rub them with my knuckles. Lily is so damn honest and full of funny one-liners. She is going to be such a handful as a teenager. Jennifer and Thomas will need all the luck they can get.

We are crossing the road, and James' brows are drawn together and he asks, "Josh, you look like shit. What's up?"

A heavy sigh slips out of my mouth. He can read me like an open book. "Well, Candice thinks I'm the father of her unborn child."

James stills midwalk and says, "Sorry. What the fuck did you just say?"

I laugh, trying to lighten the situation, not wanting to tell anyone how scared I am of having a child. How I have been waking up covered in sweat after nightmares. Not just having a kid, but to Candice. I didn't want kids, but as my life has thrown me this and I have had more time to think, my new answer to this question is *one day, but not with someone I don't love.* I want to be a better parent than what I had. The pain and disappointment are not something I want another child to feel. I rub my neck roughly.

"It's not mine. I'm careful."

"You know condoms aren't one hundred percent," Thomas says.

"Don't I know it. But it's not mine. I know it." I know I sound crazy, but it's the goddamn truth.

"I hope you're right," James says.

We continue walking to the café and enter and as I walk inside, the memory of my first interaction with Ava hits me. Man, was I taken aback at how beautiful she is. Her brown hair with the blonde showed off her stunning gray eyes. Pain from hot coffee was all over me and I was so angry. Pissed at how attracted to her I was, but also pissed I was a mess so early in the day.

Her smart mouth asking me to pay for her coffee was alluring. I haven't had a woman stand up for herself. They usually just want to please me. Boring. But not Ava. No, she wouldn't put up with my shit. Or anyone's shit.

"What are you having? Hello."

I blink rapidly at movement in front of my eyes. James is waving his hands in my face, trying to get my attention. I wonder how long I was out, daydreaming.

I shake my head and say, "Sorry. The usual. I'll grab us a table."

Thomas chuckles behind me and says, "Thinking about Ava again." He follows me to the usual table in back.

"Shut up," I say.

"Come on, bud. You like her. I don't know what the big deal is."

Of course he doesn't. He's stuck in his little love bubble with Jennifer.

"I fuck. No strings attached. My head is way too fucked up for that," I say.

"You aren't. You just don't let yourself settle down. You keep it casual so there are no expectations." He takes a breath, runs his hand through his hair, then continues, "But you and Ava are perfect. She's smart and she doesn't take your shit."

"That little vixen is hot. I can't believe you haven't talked about that." I didn't hear James approach the table. Fucking Hell. Thomas telling me Ava is good is one thing, but James as well? Fuck my life.

I take the coffee and drink, the scalding hot coffee burning my throat. For fuck's sake. Can today get any worse?

"Enough about me. What have you been up to? You are shady about your phone lately. Is there some lucky lady?" I ask James.

He laughs, a deep belly laugh, and says, "As if. I like variety too much. No one could be that hot and like my dirty mouth. That would be a miracle."

I throw my head back and let out a roar of laughter.

"One day you'll change your mind. Josh here is just in denial," Thomas says.

"Hey! I am not, dickhead."

"Okay, let's get off this topic and leave Thomas in his land of love. Did you watch the game?" James asks.

"Yeah, our Benny boy killed it. We need to go to his next home game," I say, happy we are away from the Ava topic.

We finish our coffees and as we exit, she enters. My pulse rises and my mouth drops open. She is ravishing. My dick comes to life at the sight of her and it reminds me of how much I have missed her. I just stand there openly staring, my mouth opening and closing.

"Oh, hi," she says.

"Vixen, what a pleasure it is to see you. We were just talking about you," James says.

I turn my head to glare at him. I'm going to murder him. Why did he say that?

"I hope all good things," she says. Her gaze catches mine before flicking to the other boys.

"Always. I'll see you back in the office," Thomas says.

She nods and walks off without a second glance and I feel like a kicked puppy. Where have my balls gone? Why couldn't I speak? Not even utter the word *Hi*. I push the door hard and don't say another word. The boys are discussing the game while I have arguments in my own head. I forgot Linda's coffee in all that, which means I have to go back.

"Shit, I forgot to grab Linda a coffee. I'll speak to you later."

"Sure, that's the reason," Thomas says.

"Keep kidding yourself. But you ain't fooling us," James says.

I glare at them and mime *Fuck you both* and then turn around to cross the road and go back to the shop. When I rub my palms together, they are perspiring.

Be nice and talk to her this time, idiot.

I push open the door and see her waiting for her coffee, scrolling on her phone, her back to me. Her delicious body wears tight black pants, a black shirt, and black heels. Her sexy red hair stands out in the sea of people. I walk up to her and her gaze lifts up and her eyebrow raises. She probably thinks I'm going to grab her again. But I'm restraining myself right now by keeping my hands stuffed into my pockets, even though my hand is twitching to touch her skin.

"I forgot Linda's coffee," I explain.

"Oh, okay." She sounds disappointed. Or am I hearing things? Why is my brain mush around this girl?

"Sorry about your aunt and uncle."

She glances down and then back up. A small smile appears on her lips and she says, "Thanks, Josh. I guess I should be lucky you didn't fire my ass."

"Oh trust me, I wanted to, but Thomas told me they died and that you went to the bank because he told you to...but before that, I was totally losing my shit."

Her plump lips widen, showing off her teeth. It's nice to see her beautiful smile again. My heart is beating like a drum inside my chest at being near her. I so badly want to touch her. Her neck arches as she gazes up at me. I would love to bend down and leave a trail of kisses over that exposed skin as she whimpers under me.

She chuckles, breaking me from my thoughts to say, "I can imagine. But I wouldn't have let you. I would have fought you on it."

"No doubt you would have. Even Thomas would have had my balls. I don't know why, but he has a soft spot for you."

"Because I am awesome," she says.

That you are. But I don't say that out loud. I keep that to myself. She is so easy to talk to, and the banter is fun. She gives as good as she gets. I miss her.

"If you think so."

"I know so."

Being with her here alone makes me forget all about the Candice drama. I just want to tell her...

"Order for Ava," the barista calls.

Damn it. I want more time with her, but it's gone.

"I better order. See you back at the office."

"Sure thing."

And I watch her ass swing from side to side as she walks up to the counter.

Taking a big breath, I shake my head and line up to order.

When I get back, Linda is typing away on her keyboard. I walk up to her desk; she pauses and smiles and I hand over her coffee.

"Thanks, Joshua."

I nod and say, "Linda, did you know Ava's aunt and uncle died?"

The horror on her face answers me.

"I guess not."

"I will call her."

"Yeah, good idea. I sent her flowers from the company on my phone on the way back here and had them delivered to her apartment."

Her eyes go wide. I know it must shock her that I had done it, but I don't know how else to help.

"Very sweet, Joshua. And the right thing to do."

I feel my cheeks heat and I say shyly, "Thanks. I'll be in my office if you need anything."

I don't enjoy compliments and I didn't do it to be sweet. I just did it because I wanted to make Ava smile.

I sit back in my leather chair and rub my chin. I feel the prickle of stubble on my fingers. My thoughts are about Ava and maybe I am way too hard. I think about the boys' words. I have had no one twisting me up like this. Are they right?

But if I try, that means allowing someone into my world completely and letting those walls around my heart down. I take a deep breath and open the computer.

Fuck. It's here.

My stomach knots, knowing the answer to the question if I am going to be a father is here.

My heart picks up speed, my finger hovering over the click of the mouse. I want to open it, but I can't. I'm frozen in my spot. *Come on, Joshua. Use those heavy things hanging between your legs. Open the goddamn email, you chickenshit.*

I click. Suck in a breath, and hold it.

CHAPTER 24

AVA

I AM BACK IN the office after getting back from the bank to get pre-approved for a higher mortgage. I hold up a compact mirror to touch up my smudged makeup with a wet wipe and then add some powder to cover my splotchy skin. When I finish, I close the mirror, putting it back in my bag with a sigh.

The damn sellers rejected the offer I first submitted, so I tried to borrow more money from the bank, but I can't get a higher loan because I haven't been working with Ward long enough. The stability I worked hard toward has now slipped through my fingers, and that condo is now gone. I had a good feeling about it when I walked through it with Mom. Now I have to find another that I like and can afford.

I need a distraction, so I get stuck in correspondence emails and read through all the project updates before Thomas arrives.

"Ava. You're back," he says.

I raise my gaze and stare into his wide-set brown eyes. I smile and his face mirrors mine. I need a friend right now.

He comes over to my desk and asks, "How did it go with the bank?"

My ribs grow tight, restricting my breath as I quietly say, "Unfortunately, they won't lend me the amount I need."

A stony expression flashes on his face and he whispers, "I'm sorry to hear that. That sucks...But maybe there will something even better out there for you."

"You sound like my mom. She always tells me things happen for a reason."

"She must be a really awesome person, then." He winks.

I sit up and smile, feeling grateful to have found a friendship with Thomas. He is the nicest guy and colleague. Nothing would ever happen between us. There is no sparkle or fire in my belly, like what happens with Joshua.

I love talking to him about his girls and his girlfriend, Jennifer. Their love story makes me wish I had that. But I don't think anyone has sparked my interest to fall in love... well, maybe except *him*.

"She is. Also, thanks for the flowers." I say.

Thomas tugs at his ear and gives me a puzzled look. I don't understand, but his office phone rings, so he pushes off my desk to answer it and I shake my head in confusion.

I return to work but Thomas calls out, "Ava, can you come here, please?"

I hop out of my seat and head into his office and ask, "Yeah?"

He is holding the phone to his ear and covering the mouthpiece to speak to me. "Can you please take this file to Joshua?"

"Sure," I say smoothly even though my pulse has now picked up. I take the file and turn around and make my way upstairs. I take slow, steady breaths knowing I'm about to see someone my body vibrates for.

The elevator doors open and I wander over to Linda and say, "Hey."

She peers up and says, "Oh, hi, love. I heard about your aunt and uncle. I'm so sorry. Are you okay?"

"I'm okay, thanks. It was unexpected, but I wasn't close with them," I say, feeling comfortable sharing that truth with her.

"Did you get the flowers Joshua sent?"

What?

I blink. Surely I didn't hear correctly. He sent the work flowers? Not Thomas? Every time I think I know him, he pulls the rug out from under me and keeps surprising me.

The feelings for him come in waves, but I feel like I'm liking him. I keep pushing him away to keep my freedom and independence. But I'm sick of being lonely, and the passion we share fuels me. I want more excitement; I'm so sick of holding myself back.

"Yes, thank you. They were beautiful. Is he in?"

She smiles and says, "Yeah, just go in. He had a meeting; that's why the glass is frosted, but he is in there."

"Thanks." I push off her desk and walk in, still clutching the file.

I knock on the glass and say, "Josh."

His gaze lifts off the papers that are sprawled out on the desk. A grin appears on his lips and his eyes are dark, desire swirling through them. I feel my own body heat from the stare and I suddenly feel self-conscious. I smooth one hand down my soft shirt. Yep, my clothes are still in place. It's like I am naked, standing here in front of him. The way his tongue glides over his lip and his eyes slowly rake over my body, fueling the fire, I feel like I'm about to combust. I bite the inside of my cheek, waiting for him to talk.

"Ava, hi. How are you?"

Right now, horny and uncomfortable. But I don't say that. Instead, I say, "I'm okay. I have the file for you."

I don't tell him the seller declined my offer and the bank won't let me borrow any more money. I'm too embarrassed. I step over and hand him the file. He takes it from me, purposely touching my hand. That causes my whole body to tingle.

A knowing, sexy smirk appears, and he says, "Thanks. Come take a seat."

He slides in and leans on his elbows. A loud sigh slips through his soft, full lips.

I keep my gaze on him as I take a seat. I can't get enough of him in a suit. It is designer and fits his broad shoulders perfectly. A slight five o'clock shadow is starting, but his hair, messy from his fingers running through it, is the thing that has me shuffling in my seat, trying to ease the ache that's started between my thighs.

He flicks through the file tiredly, but his slumped posture and circles under his eyes have me saying, "Are you okay? You seem exhausted."

His eyes flick to mine, and my chest tightens at the emptiness filling them. "My mom is deteriorating."

I gasp, covering my mouth with my hands, before saying, "Oh, Josh. Shit, I'm so sorry."

He drags a hand through his hair and says, "Thanks. Truthfully, the hardest part is that I seem to have forgotten how badly she treated me. I just caved and forgave her, forgetting the neglect and the lack of love they gave me growing up...When I visited her in the hospital, she said sorry." He pauses, glancing down at the desk, then meeting my eyes again and asks, "What do I do with that?"

My heart breaks for this man. He looks like a broken little boy, dying to be loved by his parents. I miss my parents, but at least they loved me. I just lost them young and had to live with my horrible aunt and uncle, but it's not like they were my parents.

Joshua's parents should have provided love and care, but they didn't, and that's a tough pill to swallow. The relationship they share is evidently fractured.

"I'm all fucked up. I just hope I'm doing the right thing."

He runs his hands over his face before returning them to the desk. It's quiet for a moment, both of us lost in the heaviness and honesty the conversation has resulted in. Our gaze locks and sincerity is pouring out of his. He is completely baring his soul. It's only fair if I let him in, too.

"I don't know what to say. Other than life is short and do what you think is right. I love my mom. But the truth is, she isn't my real mom. My parents died in a car accident when I was young and..."

My eyes prickle, but I hold back the tears threatening to leak. Talking about this is hard. It carries a lot of emotion, hence why I don't tell anyone about my life. I keep all my cards close to my chest; it involves me being vulnerable and opening up. But I feel like on a deeper level, we are connecting and this Joshua is the one I like.

A knock from behind on the glass frightens me. My heart is in my throat from all the emotion and information we are sharing, and to be interrupted and reminded of where we are brings me back to reality. I gulp and close my eyes as I hear a unfamiliar voice.

"Am I interrupting?" a soft woman's voice calls.

I turn and watch her walk in, her hand on her stomach, and my gaze moves from her to him. My eyes are wide and my mouth has dropped open.

Get the fuck out of here.

This can't be true. I close my eyes for a second, trying to calm my raging emotions. All the warm thoughts I had about Joshua evaporate in a split second. I will not think about him in that way again. Is he about to be a father because if he is, I will not impede that. I'm not a home-wrecker. And I'm sure it's just the great sex and warm body I miss. Surely.

I can't believe I thought we could be more. Of course it would be one-sided. I just thought a minute ago we were heading somewhere. Bile rises in the back of my throat and I swallow hard to keep my stomach contents in place.

I look at Joshua, who is glaring at her with murderous eyes. I don't know what the fuck is going on between them, but I feel out of place. Then her gaze moves to me, and the bitch is glaring at me with an arched brow. Like she owns the place. Fuck you. I stand in a huff. He is about to speak, but I cut him off. Not giving a fuck.

"Bye, Mr. Ward," I say and spin around and walk out, not looking back or waiting for his goodbye.

"Candice, what are you doing here?" he barks at her, and I have to bite my lip not to laugh at her. Good luck to them. Passing Linda's empty desk, I strut toward the elevator, my head held high.

CHAPTER 25

JOSHUA

I GLARE AT CANDICE, wondering why she is here. Damn her and her stupid timing.

"Why are you here? I'm in a meeting. You can't barge into my office." Where the fuck was Linda? Candice interrupted me and Ava having a heart to heart. We were talking and I don't talk openly to people about my personal life. But with her, she is different. She makes me want to open up so she can understand me.

"She wasn't at her desk, so I helped myself." She shrugs as if it's no big deal.

"Of course you did." I pinch the bridge of my nose and ask, "What are you doing here?"

She takes the seat Ava just vacated and sits down, and it irks me further. I want Ava back and Candice to go back to where she came from. Ava had more to tell me. I know it. I feel it; we were connecting and baring our pasts, and I wanted to ask her out on a proper date before Candice walked in.

"The paternity test, obviously," she says.

I frown and glance down, needing a second to control my anger. When it simmers down to a comfortable level, I say, "I'm not the father. So, again I will ask, why are you here?"

"I don't know who the father is and I can't bring this baby up alone. Do you think you can pretend it's yours?" she pleads.

My mouth drops open. The audacity of this woman. She is truly delusional. "Hell fucking no. You need to find the father. He deserves to know, and I'm not ready to be one, especially to someone I don't love."

She winces, and I feel bad for being so brash, but I need to be honest, and I don't want to lead her on. There will never be an *us*. The way Ava makes me feel cements those thoughts. I want Ava; I need Ava.

Her eyes well and tears hit her cheeks. But it won't make me change my mind. Crying to me won't help her. My heart isn't in this room. It's with Ava. I return to my work, dismissing her, and from the corner of my eye, I see her stand and exit my office. Once I'm safely alone, I sit back and blow out an exasperated sigh, then link my arms behind my head, leaning back in my chair, closing my eyes, and trying to calm my racing heart.

I hear Linda before I see her. My lips turn up and I say, "You want to know why she was here, don't you?"

"Of course. I went to the bathroom, so she must have snuck in."

I open my eyes and sit up to see Linda taking a seat directly across from me.

"Just like Candice, who had been trying to tell me I was the father of her baby. Which thankfully I am not. The paternity results came through and confirmed what I already knew."

I lean on the desk and watch her shoulders sag in relief, and I can't help but chuckle. It's the same reaction I felt when I first found out.

"She asked me to pretend to be the baby's father."

She shakes her head and says, "That's some cheek of her. Ava left, upset. Did she know the baby isn't yours?"

My heart shrinks, hating that the woman I care for is hurting because of me. I wish she didn't have to deal with my past and my mistakes. I need to talk to Ava; I don't want this to cause us to go backward to her hating me and for that special moment to become a blip in the past.

"No. She left before Candice and I spoke."

The rest of the day, I try to focus on my work. It's taking me a lot longer than usual, but I finish and wander down to Ava's desk. I have rehearsed what I want to say, but when I arrive, I see she isn't there. She must have finished up for the day because Thomas's office is also empty. A tightness forms in my chest and disappointment runs through me. I walk to the car. What should I do?

Deciding to drive down to her apartment and talk to her on the way, I call James.

After a few rings, he answers.

"You leaving work already?" he asks teasingly.

"Yes. I need to talk to Ava. You won't believe it. We were in the middle of a conversation when Candice walked in and ruined the moment. Ava and I were having a, I don't know..."

How do I explain it to him? He doesn't get women, so I'm sure I'm wasting my breath.

He chuckles. "You got the love bug too."

"I'm not in love with Ava." I don't know why I lie because it's useless. James will totally call me out on my lie.

"But you like her."

"Whatever," I say, not wanting to confirm my feelings to him. I change the subject and say, "Also, while I have you on the phone, did you get my email about the condo?"

"Yes, I was just completing the contract. And you say you're not in love."

"Just tell me where to send the money, dick-head," I say.

"Okay, I'll send you an email soon."

"Bye." I hang up and continue to drive with a stupid, lopsided grin on my face.

I stare at her apartment door and raise my fist and bang on the door. I wait for her to answer, feeling my heart beating harder with every second I stand here. The door opens and the scowl on her face has me smiling.

"What are you doing here?" She glances behind me as if checking to be sure no one else is with me. Once she realizes no one is there, her gaze returns to mine.

"Come on; it's freezing out here. Can I come in and talk to you?" I plead.

"Where is baby momma?"

She is obviously still upset about Candice being in my office. Or maybe she is a little jealous? Which I can't help but feel a mix of sorry and happy over.

Maybe she wants more, too.

"It's not mine," I say firmly.

She rolls her eyes but steps back and opens the door wider.

She is trying to keep her wall up, to keep people out, but I plan on knocking it down, starting right now.

As I pass her in the entry, I pause and gaze down into her eyes. I watch her suck in a breath and her eyes widen at our closeness. A wicked smile plays on my lips at the obvious attraction. I feel the pull and electricity. I so badly want to throw her up against the wall and have my way with her, but I know we should talk first.

But when her gaze drops to my lips and she licks hers, I snap, unable to hold back another second. I kick the door shut and I grab her jaw. My mouth captures her whimper. I taste her fresh breath and I lick across her lips. Instinctively, she parts them, allowing me full access.

I let go of her jaw and back her up against the wall; I pull back an inch. My breath is tickling her lips, my gaze is boring into hers, challenging her to stop me from fucking her right now, against her entry wall. Her eyes glow under the light, heavy with desire. I don't even know if I could stop, but I don't have to think about it. She grabs my head with force, smashing her luscious, full lips to mine. Our lips move together in a frenzy, her tongue seeking entry. I open my mouth and she shoves her tongue inside, her tongue ring touching my tongue, the metal sending me crazy. We kiss passionately for a while, then I pull away, nipping her lip and then along her jaw to her neck and up to her ear. My heavy pants fill her ear. I whisper, "I want you."

A soft moan escapes her lips as she arches her back, and I smirk. I nip her ear and ask her, "Do you want me?"

"Yeahhh," she stammers. Her arousal is not helping me slow down and I rip off her sweater. I can't wait. I need her right now, her warm body under mine, tangled in her sheets. She raises her arms and I realize at this moment that I'm falling... This girl won't slip through my fingers ever again. She is mine and I will show her exactly how I feel about her with my body.

I'm staring down at her chest, her torso covered in a t-shirt. I squeeze her breast and feel her soft, plush skin. No bra. My cock jerks with appreciation and I rub my thumb over her bud and her metal. This woman is killing me. No one has driven me as crazy as she does. I'm so desperate and horny right now. She rips her shirt over her head, tossing it to the floor in one swift movement. Her rosy pink nipples are hard and standing at attention, her metal sparkling in the night light coming through.

I lean down and take a bud in my mouth, worshipping the breast and nipple, her moans urging me on. Her hands are on the back of my head, pulling my hair, her body responding to my mouth. I finish lapping one and move onto the second breast, then I kneel, pulling on the strings of her sweats until they untie. I tug her pants down over her hips, taking them off each foot and throwing them, leaving her standing in her red panties. I tilt back and gaze into her bright gray eyes. The air swirling around us is thick and full of our desire. I grab her panties and pull them down, leaving her naked and me fully dressed.

I lean forward, gripping her soft, fleshy hips, and inhale her scent before kissing the top of her apex.

The sweet scent stirs me crazy inside. I move one hand to her opening and rub my hand over her pussy.

"Josh," she says in a breathy moan.

"Open your legs wider," I ask.

She follows my instruction and I bring my fingers to her clit and rub them in hard circles.

"I have missed you," I say.

She moans and I move my fingers across her opening, back to the clit. I'm teasing her and not giving her my fingers, which I know she desperately wants.

Her hands move into my hair and she pulls tight, urging me to enter her with my fingers. I smirk, knowing she wants more, but I won't give in. I want to tease her until she begs for my mouth.

I continue the slow, torturous up and down pattern. Her slick juices coat my hands, helping me glide through her sex.

"Beautiful."

And she snaps, "Josh. Fuck. I need you, god-dammit."

Gotcha, babe.

I cover her with my mouth, rub my tongue along the nub, and enter two fingers. I groan at her warm pussy and taste; she is the best I've ever had. Her sweetness is compelling.

"Your body is addictive and all mine. You. Are. All. Mine."

Her body shivers under me and I continue licking and pumping her in and out with my fingers until I feel her walls clench down, her moans getting louder the closer she climbs to orgasm. I increase my pace and graze her clit with my teeth, and it unravels her. She comes on my tongue and fingers, so I lick it all up and when her shudders stop taking over her body, I slowly remove my fingers and pull my mouth away. Tilting my head back, I take in her sedated, post-orgasm state. I slowly stand. Her body is flushed and beautiful and I can't help but lay a kiss on her mouth. Her eyes slowly blink open and her bright eyes meet mine. I kiss her again and I feel her hands on my pants, undoing my belt. I unbutton my shirt, but her gravelly voice interrupts and she says, "Let me."

I drop my hands from the button. Even though I want to control it, I know she needs it as much as me.

She finishes undoing my pants and they drop to the floor, then she continues unbuttoning my shirt and slides it off my shoulders until it's falling at our feet. She drops to her knees, and it makes my heart pound like a jackhammer. I know exactly what she is implying.

"You don't have to," I say, reaching out and stroking her face.

"I want to."

Fucking hell, this woman is perfect.

Well, I can't say I haven't thought about this, probably a little more than I should.

She pushes my briefs down and I step out of them. She rubs her hand along my thighs and then grabs my cock. Her warm, soft hand feels so good wrapped around me but when her lips wrap around the head of my cock, I almost come in her mouth, so I have to hold back with everything I have. I take slow, deep breaths to calm myself. But when she takes my cock deep inside her mouth and then pulls it out so she can lick down my length, her tongue flat so I can feel her ring, I shout, "Fuck, babe. I'm going to come. You need to stop."

She keeps sucking up and down in a slow rhythm that sends me feral. There is something about that ring that is on another level intense. It's warm and fuck, I say, "I'm coming."

I try to pull away, but she grasps my thighs tightly and swallows me. This woman is going to ruin me.

I feel like a boy who has never had sex before, unable to hold back. She is sinful.

She stands and I shake my head, trying to recover.

"What?" she asks with a cheeky grin.

"You know what...You little sex goddess."

She pokes her tongue out and I capture her mouth with my own and slam her back against the wall. She instinctively wraps her legs around me and sags into my arms. Our mouths are still attached in a seductive kiss. I pull away to grab a condom and tear it, covering me and then line myself up to her opening and thrust into her in one swift move. A small gasp leaves her mouth, but I swallow it. Once I'm all the way inside her, I begin to move in and out in a steady rhythm. Her hot, tight walls clench around me, causing me to say, "Babe, you feel too good."

I continue to thrust inside her, picking up the pace until I feel my balls tighten. I break the kiss to see her eyes closed and her lips slightly parted. She is gorgeous in my arms.

"Come," I say, needing her to come before me.

A few more hard thrusts and she says, "Josh, I'm coming." She moans.

I then feel my own release coming and I empty inside her. When I finish, I just hold her tightly, not wanting to let her go. Her head drops into the crook of my neck as we catch our breath.

When we recover, she slowly drops her legs and we pull away from each other, picking up our clothes off the floor and we both dress.

"Come have a drink. Tea? Coffee? Water? Beer?" she asks.

"Water please."

We walk through the apartment and I take it in, remembering its warm, homey feeling. On the hall stand, I see a picture of a couple with a daughter. A lightning sensation hits me and I smile and pick it up. Clutching it in both hands, I ask, "Are these your parents?"

I hold up the frame, turning it to show her.

She offers me a warm smile back and says, "Yes. It's the only picture I have of them."

Looking at the picture again, I say, "You look like your mom."

She grins and says, "I think that too. She was beautiful."

"Just like you," I say.

Her eyes lock with mine and a soft blush creeps into her cheeks, and she bites down on her bottom lip.

I love how shy she gets with compliments; it makes me want to kiss her and give her more. I put the frame back where I found it and then say, "This is a nice apartment. How come you want to move?"

I watch her move around the kitchen, grabbing us a bottle of water before she gestures to the other room.

I take a seat in the living room next to her and turn to her. She gazes at me as she speaks.

"Well, I was trying to tell you back in your office."

Her voice clips with anger and I wince, hating how hurt she sounds, so I say, "You don't need to worry about Candice. She is part of my past."

Her gaze assesses me and I think she wants to say something about Candice, but she doesn't. Instead, she says, "So, like I said, my parents died when I was young. I went to live with my aunt and uncle, but they made me sleep in their cold, dark attic, with a basic bed, dirty sheets, minimal food because they didn't want me eating theirs. Basically, they didn't want me, so I ran away to the streets."

My eyes bulge and my breath catches in my throat. What? This stunning woman went through all that? How could they mistreat her? How dare they do that to a child? To my woman? My body vibrates with anger and I grind down hard on my teeth, wanting her to finish.

She glances down at her hands before returning her gaze to meet mine to explain. "Then I met Anne. She found me on the street, took me to the homeless shelter she worked at, but then we got talking and we clicked, so she offered to let me live with her. I will be forever grateful to her for giving me a new start."

My brows crease as I try to understand who that is. So I ask, "Who?"

"My mom... well, that's what I've called her since she took me into her home."

"Oh, okay. Sorry; just trying to make sure I understand."

"She pretty much adopted me. I was so lucky to have met her. She saved my life. I don't know what I would have done without her or you. I got a corporate job, even with my piercings, but even more than that, I found my self-worth. People paid attention, *you*, Thomas, Linda all paid attention. You and Thomas offer me more than what a typical assistant does because you believe in me, and know that I am capable of more."

I'm rendered silent. My mouth opens and closes as I try to find the right words. I was not expecting her to share such intimate details, but I'm glad she has. I'm also surprised we share a similar neglected past. It makes us able to connect on a level most people won't understand. What it feels like to have family do that to you.

My phone rings so I pull my phone out of my pocket, about to hit decline, when I see my dad's phone number flash across the screen. I clutch the phone tighter in my hand and my stomach clenches.

"Sorry. I better grab this; it's my dad," I say, feeling like I have to explain it to her. I don't want her to think it's Candice.

"Of course."

"Dad," I answer.

"Your mom is unconscious."

I stand in a hurry and run my hand through my hair and say, "I'm on my way."

CHAPTER 26

AVA

I GLANCE OVER AT Joshua, who looks as if he has seen a ghost. His face is as white as paper. I frown, wanting to know what's happened. As he hangs up the phone, he stuffs it back into his pocket.

He rubs his forehead with his hand. My stomach drops, knowing something is off.

"He said Mom is unconscious."

I cover my mouth with my hand and step closer to him, wanting to take his pain away. "Are you okay?"

His gaze meets mine. A bewildered look is on his face as he says, "I don't know."

My heart burns for him. This is awful. I step even closer and wrap my arms around him; he hugs me tightly back. The warmth, love, and tenderness right now are laying our wounds out in the open. But it's also bringing us closer with no words being spoken.

The room is silent; I hear just our breathing.

We stay embraced for a while until I hear his heart beating under my ear. I ask, "Did you want me to drive you?"

He shakes his head. "No. Thank you. I will be okay. But ah..."

Squinting, I lift my head off his chest and wait for him to continue.

"Can I come back here later? I don't want to be alone. I need you."

My heart squeezes for this man, laying his heart out and being completely honest with me. He says he needs me, but I need him too.

I nod with a small smile and say, "Of course. My door is open when you're ready."

We kiss tenderly and I'm in a cloud of lust. I have never felt like this before, and by the unsure way he acts with me, I think he feels the same.

He whispers against my lips to say, "I better go."

I nod. And we hold hands until we get to the door, where he spins to face me and reaches out and tucks a strand of hair behind my ear.

"Thank you." He pecks me and says, "I'll see you soon?"

I smile and watch him pull the door open and leave.

I hope nothing bad happens to his mom, but also know I'm expecting the worst.

A few hours later, a knock on the door frightens me awake. I was half watching the TV, but fatigue had me napping. I swing my legs off the couch and walk to the door; I check the peephole to see it's him. I run my hands through my hair, smoothing down the wild state it's in. I take a breath and open the door. His gaze meets mine, red-rimmed and glossy. My hand lays flat against my chest as I stare at him. I'm at a loss for words, and my eyes fill with tears.

Seeing his face, I open my arms wide, knowing he needs the support right now. He steps into them and buries his head in the crook of my neck. We hug tightly and stay connected, breathing into each other's skin. The longer we stay here, the tighter my chest feels. I wish I could say the right words, but I know there isn't anything anybody can say to make it feel better. I let him just find comfort in my arms. His enormous arms feel easy, comforting, and his scent reminds me of home. I would never have thought this until he pulls away and the cold air hits, sending goosebumps rising on my skin.

I close the door and turn. His pained expression crushes me. I step closer and reach for his face, one hand on each cheek. I lean up on my tiptoes and kiss him softly on his lips. His eyes flutter closed when I do and I linger on his lips, and when I pull away, I hear him expel an audible breath to explain, "She's gone."

My heart hurts and I want to console him and find out more. I skim my palms down his face and grab his hands, dragging him to the living room, his shuffled steps behind me. He sits down next to me, our knees touching, his eyes staring into mine, and I see tears on his lashes, making it hard for me to breathe. I can't take his pain away, but right now I wish I could.

"What happened?"

He clears his throat and says, "When I got to the hospital, she was unconscious. I sat and held her hand. And within a few hours, she passed."

Hearing him struggle to speak, I feel my tears slip down my cheeks.

"Your dad. Was he there too?" My voice cracks as I ask.

His hand lifts to brush my tears away, even though I'm the one who is supposed to be comforting him.

"My dad held her hand too, on the other side of the bed. He was a mess. It was hard to watch, truthfully. I even hugged the fucker. I felt that sorry for him."

"You are so kind and pure. To give your father a hug, even after the hurt I know he caused, speaks volumes about the man you are," I say as I lean my forehead to his, breathing in the same air.

I pull back and stroke his face, watching as his eyes fill with new tears.

He kisses me tenderly, and he says, "You have no idea how much you mean to me. I hope you know that you pushed through a wall I had built up around my heart. You make me feel so deeply inside. I have never wanted to be around or talk to someone all the time and heck, even to settle down and to have a future. But you make me want to. Fuck, the way you are right now. You make it hard not to fall. Please...just don't break my heart."

I half choke on a sob. Is he kidding? He is beyond beautiful, baring his inner self to me like this.

I sob and say, "There is no way. I swear I'm all in too."

He leans forward and kisses the tears that are streaming down my face before whispering, "Are you ready for bed? I want to wrap you in my arms until we fall asleep."

I nod and say, "Yes."

I grab his hand and pull him into my bedroom, stopping to turn the TV off. Wiping the tears from my face, I wish his control was back, but losing someone you love will break you. I just wish I knew how to piece his splintered heart back together.

In my bedroom, I feel more butterflies, not knowing if he wants me to be naked or in clothes. My mind is ticking, and he isn't helping me. I stand by the bed and watch him peel off his suit jacket, pants, and suit, leaving him just in his briefs. He slides into my bed. Well, I guess that answers that. I love how he just doesn't want to be alone. And he just simply wants me to comfort him. But little does he know he is filling a void in me, a piece of me that was missing, and having him here makes me feel whole.

I gaze over at him. My lips lift in a small smile. He looks perfect in my bed, his naked, toned torso on show and just my sheet covering his bottom half. He is a sexy man and I'm happy to have him here, wrapping his body around me, even if the circumstances are sad.

I change into my shorts and t-shirt, ready for bed, and then slide in beside him, careful not to disturb him, but when my head hits the pillow, he wraps his arms around me and spoons me and drags me flush into him and it's the most perfect feeling. I'm on cloud nine. I feel at home in his arms. My eyelids feel heavy, and I'm surrounded by his intoxicating smell and his labored breathing. He is already asleep, with him filling all my senses in the best way. It doesn't take long and I drift off.

In the morning, I stretch out and feel the cold empty bed beside me. I groan. Not again. I feel like this is déjà vu, him slipping out in the middle of the night, trying to avoid heavy conversations, and we still haven't had a proper chat about Candice. I know now isn't the time, but I need to understand why that bitch looks at him as if he is her next meal. Not knowing what time he slipped out, I get up and go to the bathroom before walking to the kitchen for coffee. I stop dead in my tracks when I see him moving about in my kitchen, cooking breakfast practically naked. Holy Fuck. I could get used to this.

"Oh. Er, hi. I thought you left," I say.

His gaze lifts at the sound of my voice and he says, "Hi, babe. Nope, still here."

I walk closer to him and wrap my arms around his middle and gaze up. His lips meet with mine in an all too brief kiss.

It's so nice to have him in my space. I have a smile permanently plastered on my face now. I love not being alone anymore but I'm not really understanding if this means we are together.

And after how raw the conversation was last night, I decide to be honest, to not beat around the bush anymore and say, "I like it. This...You and me."

I need answers. I will not be a casual fling. He needs to know we are a couple or nothing. I have a dream job, money for a condo and design school, giving me the stability I crave. The icing on the cake would be to have a life partner to share this all with, and not just anyone. I want Joshua.

I can picture coming home from work to have dinner with him and then watching trash TV and falling asleep in each other's arms. The electricity and heat we share are undeniable. We still have more to learn about each other, but this would be the step I want to take. But ultimately, he needs to take the next step too. He has to want a girlfriend, want to let someone in. I can't do it for him. I know he implied that this is what he wants, but I just need confirmation.

He stirs the eggs in the pan before turning back to me and says, "Oh, really?" He pokes my nose with his finger playfully before kissing it.

"I want this... us."

My heart skips a beat. These words mean so much to me and I didn't even know I wanted to hear them until right now.

"Me too."

I smile and step forward and kiss him. It's a passionate kiss, and it feels as if we are sealing our feelings. We pull out of the kiss, and I feel like I'm floating.

"I'll have breakfast with you and then I want to go home and shower grab some fresh clothes," he says.

At the mention of his condo, curiosity gets the best of me, so I ask, "Where do you live?"

He wiggles his eyebrows and says, "You are dying to know."

I laugh and slap his chest playfully, saying, "No, I'm just asking. You never talk about your place."

"Sure, babe," he teases, then continues, "Well, it's in the city...would—"

And he doesn't continue, so I ask, "Would what?"

I look up at him. His gaze turns away before meeting mine again.

"Did you want to meet me at mine tonight? Have takeout and I don't know. Hang out?" The last few words hang in the air.

I feel a blush coming on. What is this guy doing to me?

He is making me soft. But I love it.

"Yes."

He grins and says, "I'll dish up. Let's eat before I need to leave."

Thinking of last night and why he was here prompts me to ask, "Have you heard anything from your dad?"

"No."

"Well, that's good, right?"

He shrugs and says, "I guess. He is very stubborn and wouldn't ask for help, even if he was struggling."

I take a seat as I wait for breakfast and say, "That's sad. Will you call or message him?"

"I'll have to call him today to talk about the funeral." He tries to shrug it off as if it isn't a big deal.

"Do you need me to help in any way?"

"Not at this stage. I'll let Dad do it the way he wants to and just be there if he needs help, I guess."

I watch him serve up breakfast and I don't know why, but it's the sexiest thing in the world. Him in my place is one thing, and then to have him cook for me is the cherry on top. My stomach flutters. These feelings are new. I tug my lip between my teeth and keep my thoughts to myself.

"Good idea."

As we eat, I decide to ask about Candice. I don't want him leaving here without getting everything out. "So, Candice?"

He nods, squinting, and I can see his mind ticking, wondering where I am going with this conversation.

"She isn't pregnant with your baby. But she acts like she is? I don't get that."

He glances down at his plate and then pushes it away to give me his full attention. "Candice and I had an agreement."

I wince but bite my tongue, not wanting to interrupt.

"We agreed to it before we first hooked up. I grew up drinking and sleeping my way through my family problems. I partied every weekend and did nothing during the week. So, when I got the business, I had two choices: either stay drunk and sleep around or sober up and keep sleeping around in quiet. So I chose the second option. We met at the hotel, but it was only when I needed her. I know it makes me a cold bastard. But that was how I survived... until you."

"But," I shiver at the thought, feeling disgusting, and say, "you took me there."

An audible breath leaves his lips and a sadness flickers into his eyes and he says, "Yes, and I am deeply sorry for that dick move. I was initially trying to just fuck you because of my attraction. You know, thinking once you fuck, it will be over. But you, babe, are different. I can't stop thinking about you. All. Day. Every day. You have been the best surprise that has entered my life."

I bite down on the inside of my cheek, feeling stupidly embarrassed. He is the sweetest guy and I can't help but agree. "I thought I could just fuck you out of my system."

"Well, that seemed to work out for both of us." He chuckles and says, "But to finish the Candice story, she tried to claim the baby was mine. I'm super careful, so I knew it wasn't mine. I felt it in my gut. I had her get a paternity test, and it came back not mine. Like I said, I knew, but it was nice to hear the confirmation. She then wanted me to take the baby like it was my own. I couldn't do that. She needs to find the baby's father and let him know and decide."

My eyes are wide as he explains. I sit, shaking my head, my eyes as wide as saucers, and say, "Whoa, that's fucked. But I do also feel a little bad for her."

His face bunches up in confusion.

"Not knowing who the father is...That is sad."

He shrugs and says, "I guess." And I can tell he doesn't have any feelings toward her and I really can't help but feel sorry for her.

"Babe, I better get going so I can shower, call Dad, and then get ready for tonight."

I don't want him to leave, but I also know I can't hold him back when I'll see him tonight. His lips twitch and form a large, open smile.

I walk to the door with him hot on my tail and I pause, grabbing the handle and opening it. I lean my head on the side of the door as Joshua comes to stand in front of me, staring at me with puppy dog eyes and I feel giddy, like a schoolgirl with a crush.

I glance down at the floor before I peer back up. He steps forward and reaches out to stroke my face with his fingers, tracing the softest of caresses on my cheek to my jawline.

"I'll see you later," he whispers.

"See you soon." I fiddle with my tongue ring, rubbing it along my closed lips. His eyes follow my movement and I can see his chest rising and falling. I stop the movement with a pop and slam my lips shut. He shakes his head, probably trying to get his head out of the same direction mine is.

"If I don't leave now, I'm afraid I'll be fucking you against your front door. And I know I won't be leaving for another hour. You, my love, are a hell of a lover."

My love?

What does that mean? The endearment hits me like lightning bolt to my heart. I gaze at him, the sexual tension building, but I will not be the one to turn it down. I want more. I can't get enough of him.

He steps forward and I feel his breath tickle my lips, so I skim my tongue across the bottom one. He closes his eyes and groans, saying, "Fuck, babe. You're killing me."

He crashes his mouth to mine, and he pushes me to the wall. I have to drop my grip on the door to grab his face and meet his hard kiss. The passion pouring out of both of us makes me think there is every possibility my heart could get broken here. But I will take that risk because I know he is worth it. I can't walk away right now. I'm in too deep.

We kiss until he pulls himself off and says, "I'm going."

I nod, but I don't open my eyes straight away. I'm still in the post-kiss bliss. I slowly peel my eyes open and watch as he shakes his head. Then he steps through the door and I pull myself up and watch him walk out. A sigh slips out. That sexy man is mine and in a few hours, he will be back in my arms, but in his space.

CHAPTER 27

AVA

I WALK INSIDE AND close the door behind me. He is really something. I need to get my thoughts off my chest; I dial Gracie.

"Morning," I say, a little too cheery, when she picks up the phone.

"Are you okay?" she asks. My obviously merry mood is a little strange to her. I can't help being vibrant and happy after kissing Joshua.

"Yes." I laugh and continue, "I'm good. Just calling to debrief."

I walk over to the kitchen to grab a bottle of water. My mouth feels dry, so I gulp some down before I explain.

"Yeah, tell me... what is it? I'm intrigued now. You sound oddly happy."

I sit back on the counter, playing with the bottle lid as I say, "Joshua stayed over last night."

"Oh, whattt...lucky girl. He is hot."

"Even hotter in bed."

"Damn it. No need to rub it in, you bitch. I need some hot sex."

"You met his single friends..."

"Well, yes I did. They aren't my usual hook-up but I'm jealous of your hot sex and it's been way too long. I'm collecting dust. Help a sister out and set up a date."

I let out a big belly laugh. When I recover, I say, "Okay, okay. I will ask. I'm seeing him tonight."

"Where is he now?"

At the thought, I drop my head and explain.

Afterward, she says in a whisper, "A broken boy."

"Yeah, just perfect for my damaged heart."

"Hmm."

"Yes. I know. I will be careful. Anyway, tell me what's new with you."

I feel bad that lately I have been the shitty friend, always annoying her with my problems with work and Joshua.

"Same old. Oh, actually there was this ridiculous hot guy that came to the bar the other night. His car broke down, or so he says. But he was different."

I smile. This piques my interest. I tap my finger on my lip and say, "What do you mean? You can't just say that... tell me more."

"I don't know. He was older, darker, olive skin... maybe Italian? But his green eyes were piercing. And he just sat there drinking whiskey, staring at me. We barely shared a few words, but the electricity bouncing between us was weird...I sound like a fucking nut job," she chuckles.

I know exactly what she means. I say, "No you don't. I totally understand what you mean. So, you do not know his name or any way to trace him?"

"Nope. Idiot me was tongue-tied by him. I could kick myself."

"Damn it. I could kick you, too. You don't act like that over anyone. I wish I had been there."

"Me too. You could have asked him his name. However, he didn't seem like a man of words."

"Jeez, you with a guy like that... I think it might be better for him if you didn't find out his name."

"You bitch."

We laugh before we hang up.

I finish the rest of my water before I throw it in the bin and wander to the bedroom to make the bed. But as I stand in the doorway, staring at my bed, I'm hit with the memory of Joshua's large body lying in my bed, and my stomach does somersaults. He is hot. No, insanely hot. His arms draped delicately over my middle as we slept. Protective, loving, and warm. I'm officially fucked and on my way to being loved up. Fuck, who would have thought.

A few hours later, I pull up to the address he gave me. My eyes widen at his place. This condo would be worth a fortune. I take a few steps to his front door and press the doorbell and listen to it chime. I rub my hand down my front and a minute later, the door opens and his handsome face comes into view. I openly check him out and whistle. He is wearing a cobalt blue sweater and black jeans. How can he still look sexy in casual clothes?

He chuckles and says, "Come in, babe."

I step inside and stand awkwardly and don't know what to do. I play with my tongue ring, but I don't have to worry. He shows me the way we are now greeting, by reaching out and grabbing my middle, pulling me toward him. I stumble forward and his soft lips land on mine. I close my eyes instinctively and sink in to enjoy the kiss. My hands land on his solid chest as his hands glide down my lower back down to my ass and squeeze it. I pull back an inch and open my eyes. His gaze bores into mine. He pecks my lips and says, "Get your ass inside before I fuck you here with the door wide open for everyone to watch."

My mouth pops open but no words escape. So tonight is going to be his way. I smirk. *I'm so fucking ready.*

CHAPTER 28

JOSHUA

WATCHING HER MOUTH FORM an O is the sexiest thing I have seen. I have missed her. Her sweet scent engulfs me when we kiss, and her lush body feels so good under my hands. I only had her yesterday, but it seems like forever. Before she arrived, I was walking around, checking that every room was perfect. I have never let a woman come over, so this is a big deal.

I feel these deep, powerful feelings for her. Is this what they call love?

The desperate need to be with someone always? To think about them constantly? Want to protect them? To love them? Cherish them? Please them?

Because if it is, I'm in deep shit.

Ava is in my fucking head and heart. Her roots grow deeper every minute we spend alone together. It should scare me. Love from people has always been fake or a show. Never pure or real. But I feel it in my heart; it's different with her. I have to allow her in, even if I could end up hurt. I can't risk losing her.

We walk into the kitchen; she pauses in the doorway, taking in the state-of-the-art appliances. It's all white and sleek. Totally unused. I'm a lazy bachelor who lives on easy meals.

"Wine?" I ask while she continues to take in the condo.

"Please. This place is so modern and, I don't know, but it's surprising. Like the cream and white scheme doesn't seem like you."

I laugh, remembering how her apartment felt so different. But I don't feel like this place is cold anymore. Maybe it really was just that I didn't have anyone to share it with. I pour us both a glass of wine and hand one to her. We cheer and I sip before I say, "It felt calming at the time, but until you came here today, it has always felt cold. You bring such a warmth in here, and the calm feeling I was going for."

She bites down on her lip and I'm about to say something dirty when she throws cold water on that idea by asking, "How's your dad?"

I smile I love how she cares. She genuinely wants to know about him. She never stops surprising me. After I left her apartment, I phoned my dad on the way home.

I take another sip of alcohol and say, "He sounded okay. He was surprised I called. He was going to the funeral director's office, so I drove straight there."

She watches me, sipping her wine and waiting for me to continue.

"We began organizing the funeral. I sat back and let dad decide on it, as he knew her best."

I hate how we didn't have the relationship I wanted.

I swallow and continue. "But if he asked for my opinion, I shared, but otherwise I sat in silence. When we left, Dad asked me to call him tomorrow and run through the last of the details."

"How do you feel about your dad? Do you think there's a chance of a relationship?"

"Hmm. At the moment, I'm following my head, and right now, it doesn't feel right, diving straight in. I don't want to live with regret, so I'm going to slowly start talking to him... baby steps."

She nods and says, "That's fair enough. I'm sure he would be grateful for that."

Her face is so easy to read and the sadness on it is killing me. She isn't your typical young woman. She is a hardworking woman, trying to build herself a better life. When she opened up to me, I was shocked by how much she has had to go through. From the streets to trying to buy herself a condo in the city. That's the person I want in my life, someone to push me in the right direction. To encourage me and work with me to build a life and business for myself. Ava is more than perfect for that role.

"Let's go take a seat on the couch. Dinner will arrive shortly." Her face bunches as if asking *what have you organized*, but my lips are sealed. I will share nothing. She will have to wait and see.

I sit on the couch with her leaning back between my legs. Watching a movie feels unreal. I have never felt as good as I do right now. She sits between my thighs, totally at ease, but I am all too aware of how good her soft body feels against me. Except I'm sure she has felt my dick poking in her back. But I can't help it. She is like sex on legs. And my dick knows how good she feels. He will never get enough. I will never get enough. Her soft sighs and slight movements are becoming my favorite things. The bell rings and I wiggle myself from under her and rearrange my dick. I don't need to be opening the door with a massive tent in my pants.

I open the door to my chef. I have used him for parties here or at the office. He walks into the kitchen and I follow behind. I peer over at Ava and see that she looks bewildered.

I know she hasn't been treated like this before, and seeing her face lit up with joy is priceless. She will have lots more surprises, both tonight and in the future. I walk back to the couch, letting the chef do his thing.

"You hired a chef?" she whispers.

"Mm-hmm. Is that a problem?"

She shakes her head and says, "No, but a little extreme. You know I'm easily pleased."

My dick throbs at her and I raise my brows. She smacks my chest. "You know what I mean."

"I do. But this is a treat. I wanted it to be special."

Her eyes glow with something, and I just stare. She is utterly beautiful.

I cuddle up next to her on the couch and we return to watching the movie until our dinner is ready. The chef leaves and we sit down at the table. I sit across from her and top her glass up with more wine.

"This is special. Thank you, Josh." Her eyes are glassy and fuck, it punches me right in the gut.

"Babe, anytime. I love you."

Shit, the fucking words just slipped out.

Her eyes are wide and I can't take it back and I don't want to take it back. But now I don't know what to do. Please say something. Put me out of my misery if you—

"I love you too." A tear drops onto her cheek and I slide my chair back and walk closer to her. I swipe the tear with the pad of my thumb and run my hands through her hair, tilting her head back. I dust her lips with kisses. I want her now, so I pull out of the kiss and grab her hand. She pushes her chair out and follows me. We hold hands all the way to my bedroom. And inside, I peck her lips. I want this time to be slow—proper lovemaking, not fucking. I want to show her how much I love her.

I kiss a trail up from her shoulder to her neck at the same time I reach around and unzip her off-the-shoulder top. It drops to the floor and I suck in a breath. No bra. This woman rarely wears bras outside of work, and it kills me. In the best fucking way.

I stand back and let her take off my sweater and shirt. Her eyes twinkle in delight. She runs her hands over my torso and my muscles clench. I unbutton her jeans and slide them over her hips, where they pool at the bottom of her feet. She pushes them away and stands there in just a pale pink G-string and it's fucking perfect.

She touches my waistband and I let her un-button my jeans. They drop to the floor and I kick them aside. I'm just wearing my black briefs. I ease her back on my bed and I close my eyes, the vision knocking the wind out of me. Fuck, she is my kryptonite. Her hair fans around her and I kneel back and slide her G-string off slowly, tossing it to the side. I push down my briefs and stand back to remove them and grab a condom and roll it on. I then get back on the bed and hover over her. I kiss each eyelid and then her lips as I line up and gently ease into her tight, warm pussy. Her eyes flutter closed in pleasure, but as I rock, I need to see her eyes, so I ask, "Open your eyes. I want to see you, babe."

This slow rhythm is tortuous and hits me differently. Her walls clench and my balls grow tight. I have to hold myself back and wait for her to come before I can. I continue the slow pace, our gazes locked, and it's making my heart beat faster. Her nails are digging into my back, which means she is close. I'm using every ounce of strength I have to hold myself back.

"I'm coming" leaves her lips and she closes her eyes as she shatters beneath me and I thrust a few more times until my cock jerks and empties. When I stop, I gaze at her sedated state and smile. I kiss her lips repeatedly before pulling out and asking, "Did you want to shower? Before we actually have dinner?"

"Yes, please."

I grab her hand and lead her to the shower. We cover each other with body wash, my hands gliding over each curve. It's sensual and hot. I enjoy her soft hands on me and I love my hands on her. We get out and dress before heating our dinners and enjoying our meal. We pack the dishes away and wander back to my bed, where

I wrap my arms around her delicate body, cuddling her tight, and soon drift off.

CHAPTER 29

AVA

TWO DAYS LATER, I'M sitting across from Thomas, discussing our new design for an extension for an existing building when my phone rings. It's my cell and not my desk phone, so I don't rush over.

"Ava, your phone."

I wave a hand and say, "It's not urgent. I'll check it on my break because we are almost done here. You need to get home to your girls on time and it will be good to finish this so you can send it to the builder today and wrap it all up."

He nods and says, "This is true. Good thinking. Well, let's finish strong."

We continue, and afterward I walk back to my desk. I pick up my phone and see James' name as the missed call. My brows furrow, thinking *why is he calling?*

"I'm grabbing coffee. I will bring you back one."

"Thanks. I'll send this off. See you when you get back," he calls back.

I didn't offer Thomas to join me for coffee because I want to know why James called. I take the elevators and I'm lost in my thoughts. But as soon as I reach outside, I hit redial.

"Vixen."

I smile at the nickname and say, "Sorry I missed your call. Thomas and I were finishing a design meeting."

"All good. I just wanted to let you know that you have got the condo."

My mouth drops open in disbelief. I look around but not knowing anyone, I can't share the joy, but then a thought hits me and I say, "But I thought they didn't accept my offer. There was no way they would have dropped the price that much."

The line is dead silent, which for James isn't normal.

"Tell me," I push, knowing I can be a persuasive bitch.

"Fuck. He will have my balls for telling you this."

The hairs on the back of my neck stand up and my throat closes up. I take big breaths, trying to not have a wave of panic. I know who *he* is and I am at a loss for words, opening and closing my mouth, but nothing comes.

When I don't speak, James says, "But just know he did it out of love. You have brought him so much to him. This is nothing."

The way James is speaking, it feels true. I feel it deep within my heart that he is being sincere. It's a lot to process, but I really want to call someone.

"Okay. Er—thanks. I guess."

"I'll meet up with you so you can sign the contract."

"I'm walking to the coffee shop across the road now. Are you free?" I ask.

"I'll be there. Give me five."

"Wait. And James, don't you dare tell Josh. I can't wait to surprise him." My tone is light as a dirty thought enters my mind.

"You are a little vixen; I knew it. Lucky bastard. Catch you soon." The hang up tune sounds in my ear.

I bounce on my toes and call Mom to tell her the exciting news. Her delight and pride oozes from the phone and I can't believe how much has changed lately. I could never have dreamed of a time when I wouldn't struggle. This is the first time I truly will feel settled, and it's like I have lifted the world off my shoulders and I can breathe easier.

I text Gracie: *I got the condo!!! I'm off to sign the contract. I'll call you after work.*

Grace replies immediately. *Best news all day. So happy for you* :)

I meet up with James and sign the contract. He can't stay long, but he tells me it will be a sixty-day settlement I signed, and he leaves.

Now I'm strutting like a woman on a mission to Joshua's office, and as I pass Linda, she has a knowing look. She waves me close and when I lean over her desk, she whispers to me, "You and Joshua? I'm so happy. You two are perfect for each other. I don't know two people who deserve love more."

I feel bashful and gaze away, not able to meet her glowing eyes. The pride is oozing from her.

"Thanks," I say under my breath, unable to talk louder.

I walk into his office, knowing there is a fantasy I have been dying to have with him. He helped me get the condo, but he thinks I don't know. Well, let's make him apologize on his knees for doing it behind my back.

I smirk at what I'm about to do; he doesn't know what's coming. I walk into his office. The door clicks loudly behind me. His whips his head up, away from the monitor, and he watches me approach. I hit the button to frost his office walls. He swivels in his chair and then leans back. His eyebrow pops in surprise and he says, "What do I owe the pleasure for this visit?"

"Well, I had an interesting conversation with James and he told me I got the condo." I see his pupils dilate. *Got ya.* I roll my lips to stop a laugh from slipping. He is shitting himself. It's written clear as day on his face.

"You paid the rest. The bank refused to give it to me."

He sits up in the chair as I stalk closer, pretending to be pissed, making him sweat. I can see his mind ticking, trying to work out how to fix this. I watch his Adam's apple bob as he swallows. He opens his mouth and says, "I wanted to help you. You are the strongest person I know and I have never felt"—he taps his chest and then continues—"some weird fucking shit in here for a woman. I thought this company and being successful would make me happy. But I had that rather quickly, but then I still was missing something. I was lonely, and so sick of going home alone. And being around you makes me crave something I haven't ever let myself indulge in. I haven't felt this good, and I have you to thank. I have money, Ava, and I don't mean that to be rude. It is what it is, but I have you to thank for being a driven and ball-busting goddess. I want to give you anything you need. You make me happy and I want you to be."

I stare at this handsome fucked-up man I call my boyfriend, and if I didn't know I loved him before, well, I do now. But no words are coming out until I get what I came to do. Otherwise, I'll be a pile of mush and that's not what I want when I do this.

I clear my throat and saunter closer to his desk, rounding it; I run my finger across the desk, watching him sweat. My fingers cross his smooth black jacket as I walk behind him and run my hand along his shoulder, then stop, leaning behind him to speak into his ear. "Mr. Ward. You have been a naughty boy. You will need to be punished."

My breath tickles his ear, and I can see the rise and fall of his chest. He's enjoying this. This is only the start, baby.

I bite down hard on his earlobe and a hiss leaves his mouth. I pull back and smile and move to his other ear and whisper, "I'm not wearing any panties."

"Fuck, babe."

I chuckle and lean in to whisper again. "Nope, you will not get off... only me."

I spin his chair and his gaze locks with mine, and it is heavy with desire. I peer down and his pants are tenting from his erection; he wants me. His hands are gripping his office chair in a viselike grip. I'm loving bringing this man undone. I peek back up to meet his gaze and grab his chiseled jaw between my hands. The grip is hard, tilting his head in the direction I want him. His eyes widen at the move. I'm so horny I could burst, but this orgasm will be worth it. I peck him and move in front of him, his desk behind my legs. I move his jaw to the side and lean into his ear one last time and say, "Are you hungry, Mr. Ward?"

I pull back, dropping his jaw, and I hitch up my skirt and sit on his desk, opening my legs, and I know my sex is glistening with desire. It's aching and needy, and by looking at his face, I can tell he feels the same.

"Fuckin' starving," he growls and drops to his knees and doesn't wait as his mouth hits my core. I watch him in his suit on his knees eating my pussy while I am on his desk, and it has to be the hottest sight. His thick, strong tongue laps me and I close my eyes and tip my chin up to the roof, enjoying every nip, bite, suck, and lick. He loves this. He makes little grunts and moans and I feel myself contracting, trying to hold back. But when he inserts one finger, he thrusts it in and out in the perfect sync. He inserts a second finger and increases the speed of the thrust, and my spine tingles. He continues to pump and lick and I'm gone, unable to hold back. I moan as the orgasm hits me hard. My breaths are hard and fast.

When I come down from my high, I sit back up and open my eyes. His face is glistening with my juices and if I wasn't already riding high from that orgasm, I would get him to go for another round. But I want my man horny. I can't wait for the punishment tonight.

He sits back in his chair, as if waiting for direction. I slide off his desk, fixing my skirt back in place, and say, "I'll have to think about that apology, Mr. Ward. I better get back to work now."

The grin on his face says he liked the roleplay. I walk out of his office and return to my desk on a high.

I open my email and see he sent me a message. I tug my lip into my mouth and click to read it.

To: Ava Johnson
Subject: Meeting
Meeting: Ava,
My hand is twitching.
You better keep that outfit on tonight. I'll be spanking your ass for that stunt.
See you tonight.
Love,
Joshua Ward

My lip pops out from between my teeth and I smile.

I have completely fallen for Mr. Ward.

Epilogue

Ava

Six Months Later

I'm sitting with Joshua and his dad at our favorite local café, finishing my coffee on a Sunday morning. It has become a regular habit of ours since we share every weekend together and neither of us wants to cook. The breakfast plates are already cleared, leaving just the three of us to enjoy our coffees.

"What are your plans today?"

I look up into his dad's gaze and smile before turning to look at Joshua and saying, "No plans today. But I started design school this week, so tomorrow will be week two, and I will probably take it easy. Have a quiet night in."

Joshua squeezes my hand under the table. His face lights up with happiness. He is so encouraging of my further studies. We had argued initially over who was paying for the course; he of course wanted to pay and I didn't want to take advantage of dating the boss, but he had a point: It was for work, so we agreed on fifty/fifty. This keeps both of us happy.

He always shows me his love and pride, and I feel the same way. The company is growing monthly and I couldn't be more proud as his girlfriend. Since everyone found out at work that we are dating, they have been surprisingly great about it. I was worried at first that I would have been treated differently, but thankfully we are being received well.

"That's awesome, love. I think it will level you up and give you more room to move within the company."

"Exactly. I never would have thought I could use my creativity with work, but with Ward, I have so many options."

Joshua kisses my temple and pulls back, lingering to say, "So proud of you, babe."

Hearing those words will never get old. I love his words, dirty or kind. I want them all. They all make me feel cherished and adored.

"What are your plans, Dad?" Joshua asks.

My stomach flips at how he is trying to make conversation. I know this is hard for him, but knowing how much I miss my parents and how I would do anything to have them back makes him want to try. I would never push it upon him; I wouldn't want him to resent me. I just encouraged a coffee date once a month. His dad reached out a lot after his wife's passing and I know he wants to have a relationship with Joshua, so we agreed I would come and be the buffer. And so far, the way he acts when we leave the meet-ups has been great. It's like he is a child again. Deep down, I think Joshua realizes he can give his dad a second chance and that it's on his terms and that he can have him as much or as little as he wants.

We leave the café and walk home. Joshua is unusually quiet. I think nothing of it, just enjoy the walk, taking in the city noises. I still can't believe I live and work here. The only problem is the guilt I feel that work has taken time away from volunteering at the shelter. I get there as often as I can but it's not enough, I need to do more.

We walk upstairs to his condo and he opens the door; I step through and my hand covers my mouth at the sight. Rose petals have been scattered along the floor. I follow them and I can only hear my pulse in my ears, beating wildly. I know Joshua is following because I can feel my back heating as I move. As we enter the kitchen, I see the table set for a romantic dinner, but the rose petals are in the shape of a heart directly near his glass windows overlooking the city. I pause, but he takes my hand and walks me to the middle of the heart.

I watch him walk off in disbelief, and when I turn around, my hands still cover my open mouth. I blink and my vision becomes blurry and I shake my head. This can't be happening.

Joshua is down on his knee with a box open and the most simple, elegant, pear-shaped diamond ring sparkling under the warm lights.

"Ava Johnson. Ever since we bumped into each other and you looked into my eyes, I swear you could see straight through to my broken soul. You have changed me into a man who has to spend every day, every hour, every second with you. Please do me the honor. Will you marry me?"

How did I get to be so lucky to have a man who loves me this hard? I will never take him for granted. My life is his.

I nod and say in a choke of tears, "Yes." I stretch out my shaky hand as he glides the ring onto my left hand. He stands, and he kisses me, and then we hug tightly.

"I love you," he whispers into my neck.

"I love you too."

The End.

If you enjoyed Joshua and Ava get ready for more in this world. James is Here

Do you want to see Ava with Sarah in a bonus scene? Read Here

If you have any problems accessing it, please send me an email at: sharonwoodsauthor@gmail.com

Have you read Thomas and Jennifers' story? If not Click Here and read their love story.

Also By Sharon

The Gentlemen Series

Accidental Neighbor

White Empire

Complete Standalone's

Doctor Taylor

ACCIDENTAL NEIGHBOR

JENNIFER

This has to be the world's slowest moving line. The shivers running up my arms into my bones have me rethinking my outfit tonight. Cold wind whips around my bare thighs. My teeth chatter, and I shuffle forward. My friends are waiting inside Three Dots Bar and I'm late for my best friend's twenty-first birthday celebration.

It was a struggle to make it here on time, and that was before I had to stay over at work filling in paperwork for a child that had an allergic reaction and vomited on me just before the mom arrived. Loving my job makes these times bearable. I'm scheduled on the late shift at work this week and getting ready for a big night out takes time. The line moves—thank God—and I reach inside my bag for my ID card.

Shit. The contents of my purse spill onto the pavement, and I quickly squat down to gather my belongings when I hear a rip. I suck in a breath and freeze. My tight tartan yellow skirt has a new thigh slit.

"Great," I mutter as I scramble to pick up my lip gloss, phone, and wallet.

"That's what happens when you stuff too much into a small bag," a deep male voice comments. I see his black shiny dress shoes and I know he is standing above, watching me.

Wanting to see his face, I rise, careful not to make the situation worse, and tug at the end, trying to add the illusion of more length.

My gaze focuses on the voice's face, and I feel dizzy staring back into a set of dark, brooding eyes. I watch his eyes squint from a smile, causing creases to form near them. His teeth are straight, white, and perfect. And his brown hair is tousled neatly on top of his head. My hand is twitching to see what it would feel like. What is wrong with me?

He slowly and seductively slides his gaze downwards over my black bodysuit and over-the-knee boots. And I feel stripped but intrigued by this handsome man. I need to know his name. Before I have a chance to speak, he is turning and walking off inside the bar.

Finally, I make it to the front of the line, but my relief quickly turns sour. The bald bouncer eyes me with heated desire, his stare lingering on me, and I quickly avert my gaze and fight the urge to roll my eyes because I cannot afford to piss him off. I need to get into the bar. My phone vibrates in my hand. 'Olivia' flashes across the screen. I hit decline but type out a quick text.

Jennifer: *I'm about to get inside. In line now. See you soon, birthday girl.*

Olivia and I have been friends since kindergarten; she is the most supportive friend you could have in your life.

"ID, sugar?" The bouncer asks.

"I'm twenty-two."

"I see." He drools and my skin crawls at his unwanted flirting.

Once inside, I'm surrounded by tall wood tables and long booth seats. Sconces with glass globes on the walls create a cozy yellow hue. The stench of hard liquor is evident, but the soft music playing through the speakers in the ceilings keeps me from running outside and into a taxi back home. I'm trying to spot my group when a screech comes from my left.

"Jen! Jennifer, over here!"

Olivia waves her arms above her head, the biggest smile lighting up her whole face. She looks radiant in her emerald-green dress and if it was sparkly and had wings, I would think she was Tinkerbell with her blond hair curled to perfection.

My mood instantly lifts, along with the tension I was carrying on my shoulders. Olivia, my little pocket rocket, is everything. I wave back, stepping across the worn wooden floors to join the group. Olivia, cheeks flushed from already having a few, or more, drinks, jumps up from her chair and throws her arms around my neck.

A laugh slips out of me, and I hug her back. "Happy birthday. I can't believe it's finally here."

She bounces on her gold heels, green eyes wide and glassy. "I know! I am so fucking happy you're here. Let's get a drink."

She stumbles, and I grab her arm to steady her as a giggle slips from her mouth. "Are you sure you don't want some water first?"

She tips her head back, shaking her head vigorously from side to side. "No way, Mom. I'm fine."

I smile, but don't believe a word she says. "Okay, but if you vomit, do it near someone else," I say. "I've already had vomit in my hair once today."

A few minutes later, we squeeze up to the bar where suited bartenders dash back and forth in front of the bottles of alcohol lining the rows of wooden shelves behind them.

A blond bartender rocking a black vest strides over to us. "What can I get for you, ladies?" he says in a deep voice.

Before I can order our drinks, Olivia cuts me off. "Oh my God, I love your accent. Is it Australian?"

"Correct." His eyes roam her face, and a corner of his lip rises.

She twirls a lock of hair around her finger and flutters her eyelashes at him. Olivia is extremely flirty. It's part of her charm. Men fall for her at the drop of a hat, and women are jealous or want to be friends with her. Personally, I envy her carefree, speaks-whatever-is-on-her-mind attitude. I don't have an ounce of it, keeping how I feel locked tightly away.

He finally takes our order, and they chit-chat while he prepares our trademark turquoise drinks. I take the opportunity while she is distracted, to search for those dark eyes from outside. But with a good peer around and no luck,

I sigh and return to listen to Olivia invite the bartender to join us when he's finished, and then we wander through the crowd, back to join the others.

When we arrive at the end of the table a few minutes later, I finally get to see who turned up tonight. Olivia's brother, Jackson, is on at the end of the round booth, already standing up to pull his little sister into a side hug.

I spot and wave to our good friend Katie, who's sitting next to the space Jackson just vacated. A few of Jackson's friends are seated in the booth as well. Tyler, Cody, and ah... shit, Nathan. We hooked up once when I had too many drinks at Olivia's.

The guys shuffle further in around the booth to make room and I slip onto the seat next to Tyler, Olivia slides in after me. They throw a few hellos my way before they're back to their beers and banter.

"I thought you weren't going to make it!" Katie says from across the oval-shaped table. Her hair is up in a bun with two pieces out, framing her face, the green headband in her hair making her blue eyes pop.

"Ugh, don't even get me started."

The last thing I want to do right now is think about being covered in vomit. "I love my job, but today was just not my day."

"Oh, hon. Well then, a good drink is exactly what you need," Katie says soothingly.

"Darn right it is!" Olivia smacks her lips on my cheek and laughs before declaring we all need to do shots.

Oh God, what have I got myself into tonight?

Jackson returns a few minutes later with a large tray of clear shots, placing it on the table before handing each of us two shots.

Oh, not good.

We all raise our first shot. "Happy twenty-first birthday, Olivia!" we shout and clink our glasses together.

I'll definitely regret this later.

I throw the shot back before I have time to psych myself out, the liquid burning a path down the back of my throat. Screwing my face up, I grab my cocktail and take a long sip, chasing it down.

The second shot isn't any easier than the first, and I can already feel the alcohol working its way through my system. This is why I don't do shots. Give me a nice glass of wine or cocktail and I'm good to go. Although, I must admit, I'm definitely feeling relaxed.

I'm on my third trademark turquoise, the buzz of alcohol well and truly in my veins. The bar's vibe has hit a new level. The music is louder, and they have moved some of the tall bar tables to make a bigger dance floor.

"Hey, I'm going up to the bar to see if I can get some food," I shout, but nobody pays me any attention.

Jackson leans in close and whispers something in Katie's ear, a lazy grin on his face. Katie giggles, a blush spreading over her cheeks.

Well, this is new.

My stomach growls, and I need to get to the bar for some food because my head feels light from the buzz of alcohol. Olivia joins me and we set off through the crowd that is now doubled. We squeeze our way to the bar, then wait behind patrons ordering.

"Just grab me a drink," Olivia yells.

"Are you sure?"

She pops a brow at me. I lift my hands in surrender.

I watch as she heads farther down the bar, already distracted, as the people in front of me move away with their drinks. I step forward and lean on the bar, reading the menu once more.

I flip it over and scan through the drink menu, wanting to try something new.

"Oh, honey or say my name," a deep sultry voice says beside me, close enough I can feel his breath on my cheek, and I suck in a sharp breath at the familiar voice. It's him.

My head whips in that direction but connects with a hard jaw. Ouch. I peer up into the most magnificent set of deep-brown eyes.

My mouth moves, but no words come out as I rub my head to soothe the ache. The slight buzz from the alcohol is helping dampen the pain, but isn't helping the flush creeping across my skin.

I watch his mouth move and realize he is talking to me. Shit!

"Sorry?" I whisper, my eyes still locked on his stunning face.

How can a man be this hot? I don't think I have ever met a man on this level. I still can't form any words. His beauty takes my breath and words away. I just continue my stare until he chuckles.

"I was saying Oh, Honey or Say My Name are excellent drinks."

He moves forward to lean across me, pointing at the menu. The alcohol thrumming through my veins makes my movements slower than usual as his spicy vanilla scent fills my nostrils, causing them to flare and take a deeper inhale. Shit, he smells good.

My skin prickles with goosebumps and I blink, snapping my thoughts back to the here and now. Get a grip, Jen!

"Ah, I see. I understand now." My voice comes out husky, so I clear my throat, moving to the side so I can face him better. I lean my arm on the bar for support. "Which one would you say is better?"

Am I flirting?

I cringe inwardly, but it's not enough to stop myself in this tipsy state. He is evoking a behavior that is foreign but also refreshing. I didn't think I had desires for an older guy, but this man is stirring me up inside.

"Hm, tough call. It depends." He tips his head back and taps his chin, his handsome face etched in concentration. "Let me ask you some questions."

I nod back, unable to say anything. My focus catches on the movement of his finger, which is all too close to his full lips. I want to feel them crushed against mine. I bet they are soft and taste amazing. But I'm not bold enough to make the first move.

"Light and fresh or citrus with hints of sweet?"

Oh, right. He was asking me questions. Focus, Jen.

"Definitely citrus with a hint of sweet." My voice is still husky, but at least I'm forming sentences.

"Vanilla and honey or honey with spices?"

Thinking of his sexy scent, I respond without a second thought. "Honey and spices." His lips tip up. And maybe I'm being too transparent. I glance down at the bar before meeting his gaze again.

"And your last drink question." He rubs the five o'clock shadow on his jaw. "Sherry with dried fruit or peaches and lemonade?"

"Easy—peaches and lemonade."

"Good choice." He nods and waves down a bartender. "I'll grab a Redbreast Lustau, and one Say My Name." He winks at me.

"What is it with the names of these drinks? Redbreast?" I blurt.

I roll my lips inward so no other embarrassing words slip out.

He shrugs and throws me a lopsided grin. "I don't know, but clearly they were drunk or horny... or both."

With the mention of the word, my eyes lower to his lips and his tongue comes out to skim across his lower lip. I'm so transfixed with the movement I don't realize I've caught my lip between my teeth until his thumb reaches out and tugs it free.

"Please don't tease," he murmurs.

I freeze and close my eyes at the heat burning beneath my skin.

What is happening to me?

Normally, I only attract playboys who want to have fun for the night, not the older, successful, sexy man.

"Here you go." The bartender places our drinks on the counter.

My mystery man drops his hand and pays, before leaning on the bar, his attention solely on me, which doesn't bother me at all. I want it.

I want more.

I reach for what I assume is my drink, given its colorful appearance compared to the amber whiskey-like liquid in the other, and take a gulp.

A deep laugh leaves his chest. I don't care because I need to cool myself down. I've never reacted to a man like this and feel like I am about to combust.

"Could I order a bowl of fries—delivered to my table?" I ask the bartender, trying to remember the table number, and desperate to get control of myself. "Table four."

The bartender nods, and I take another sip of my drink. "Mm, this is so yummy. Thanks. Even though it would mortify my mom I accepted a drink from a stranger."

I could kick myself for my childlike statement. I must be turning him off now.

"Well, I would have to agree with her there. You shouldn't. But we aren't strangers." He picks up his glass and takes a drink. "I'm Thomas, but most people call me Tom."

"Hi, Tom." I like the way his name rolls off my tongue. "Jennifer... but people call me Jen."

"Beautiful," he says in a way that I'm not sure if he's referring to just my name.

My cheeks flush hotter and I glance away from his prolonged eye contact, needing a distraction. On the dance floor, a few couples dance seductively, kissing. Totally not helping to distract my mind.

"Have you been to Three Dots before?" he asks.

Being this close to him, I can tell he is older than me—probably mid-thirties, judging by the eye creases, the confidence, and the conversation. Older guys have never attracted me to them, but there is a spark between us I can't deny.

"Actually, no. I rarely go out. I work a lot and I prefer to stay home or have dinner with a glass of wine with my friends." I glance around the bar, fiddling with my hair. "You?"

"This is my first time here too. I can't normally go out, but tonight I'm with friends celebrating a work promotion."

My brows frown at his comment. "Can't?"

He rakes his teeth across his bottom lip. "Would you like to dance with me?" He doesn't answer my question, but I figure it's rude to push a stranger to talk.

"Yes, I would love to."

I finish my cocktail in a few guzzles while he downs the rest of his drink in one pull. The alcohol buzz gives me confidence when he grabs my hand, pulling me to the dance floor behind him, leading me through the crowd as bodies press all around us, dancing to the music. The last few songs have changed from upbeat to slow, and a dim light over the floor highlights the sweaty bodies all around us.

He pauses in a section of the crowd, spinning me around to face him, stopping me in my tracks. "Are you okay?" he asks, staring down at me.

I nod.

My palms sweat and my heart races inside my chest. This pull toward him is a new feeling for me, but I want to explore it. Explore him.

He skims his fingertips over my forearm, setting the skin on fire. I move my hips to the music. I am not a dancer, but being around Thomas is making me brazen.

I check him out from head to toe, taking in his muscular frame covered in a tight black long-sleeve top and dark low-hung jeans, finishing at his black shoes.

The song changes to "Positions" by Ariana Grande, and Thomas closes the distance, so we have only an inch between us. His hands snake around my stomach to my lower back, causing my insides to flood with heat. Reaching up, I caress his muscled shoulders, skimming my way until my hands link behind his neck.

We move to the beat, our bodies flush. He is taller than me, yet cocoons me perfectly, and I crave more—more closeness, more touch, more of everything he can offer.

I gaze into his heated dark eyes while my heart flutters and beats wildly in my chest. He leans forward, his hand moves to the back of my head, and his full lips take control of mine. When I part my lips, his tongue plunges into my mouth, tangling with mine. He tastes of mixed spice and dried fruit. I groan at the flavor.

My hand thrusts into his hair, pulling him closer, meeting his intensity with hunger. He moans and slides his hand down a little further, settling on my lower back.

I break the kiss and take deep, shaky breaths. His eyes are heated and heavy-lidded. And an idea pops into my brain. I contemplate it for a minute, but the way he is looking at me mixed with the way my body is reacting, I give in to the desire. Grabbing his hand, I find a dark hallway and he must sense what I want because as soon as we are out of eyesight he pushes me up against the wall, and captures my mouth in a savage attack swallowing my gasp into his mouth. His large body covers mine, his hands buried deep in my hair, and our tongues twirl together in a frenzy. I feel his erection hitting me through his jeans, and I move my hips to rub myself on him, chasing friction on my clit. After a few strokes, he lets out a growl and it causes him to snap. Yes. His hands move out of my hair and advance to grip my legs, lifting them to his hips, and I lock my ankles over each other behind his back, spreading my pussy over his cock. Our lips are still sealed and our tongues still exploring.

Without warning, he grinds himself hard against me. Breaking our kiss, I tip my head back on the wall with my eyes shut and whimper. The friction on my clit is like a lightning bolt to my body, waking every part of me. He does it again and I moan.

This feels amazing.

He leans forward and trails soft kisses and small nips up my neck, and when his skilled mouth reaches my ear, I feel his breath tickle. "Shhh princess. I need you to be quiet. Unless you want to be heard?"

My eyes pop open.

Holy Shit.

My mouth opens and closes repeatedly, but my brain is misfiring. I squeeze my eyes shut again and shake my head.

"That's what I thought. I will make you feel good. Just relax," he whispers.

One of his hands leaves my hip to dust across my ass, down to squeeze it and then move over to my quivering pussy. Where I'm already wet and ready. I hold my breath with anticipation. He drags his finger under my panties, gently grazing it along my opening, and I hear a hiss leave his mouth. "You're already wet."

My breath releases, and I pant. "Yes."

My pussy is aching, begging for more touching. His thick finger finds my swollen clit. He circles firmly, and I arch my back off the wall, trying to get more pressure. My body is climbing quickly and when he inserts his finger, my body shudders, welcoming the intrusion. He thrusts his finger in and out, rubbing along my wall. My body convulses and I grab his shoulders, digging my fingers in and grind down, chasing the orgasm that I know is building.

He enters a second finger, and a pinch of tightness is felt for a second before my body welcomes the intrusion. With two fingers he moves faster, and it isn't long until my walls tighten around him and my orgasm ripples through my body, causing me to feel faint. I'm shocked by what I just did but also by how much I enjoyed it... and him.

He pulls his fingers out of me tenderly. Which surprises me after what we just did. I open my eyes and lift my head off the wall to see him studying me with a starved look. My throat squeezes and I watch him bring his fingers to his mouth. They glisten with my slickness and he licks them clean, groaning. "You taste sweeter than I imagined."

I gape at him, transfixed by how sensual this image is. But also shocked by his words.

I move the leg that he is still holding up back to the ground. His hands move to my waist, and I smooth my hands down my skirt, making sure I'm all covered again.

This should feel wrong, but with him, it didn't.

It felt good.

The only doubt entering my mind, is the fact he's older and more experienced.

"I think I need some water. Uh, it's boiling in here," I whisper.

"Let's head back to the bar, shall we?" He unexpectedly leans down and pecks my lips softly before he leans back, smirking at my mouth hanging open.

Thomas grabs my hand to make our way back to the bar. When we approach, I realize I haven't seen Olivia in a while. I look down the bar to the last place I saw her, but she's not there. Maybe she went dancing or back to the table. I decide I really want to check and make sure she is okay, considering she consumed a lot of alcohol tonight for a small person.

I glance back at Thomas. "Do you mind grabbing me some water? I need to find my friend. It's her birthday tonight and I should really check in on her."

He nods with a smile. "Of course."

I glance down at our joined hands and watch as I slowly remove mine, feeling cool air on my palm. I really wish I didn't have to go right now. I clench my hands.

"I'll be right back," I whisper.

But when I go back to the bar after finding Olivia, I drop my head and murmur, "He's gone."

Acknowledgments

My husband you're my rock. And my two blessings, my children. Thank you for allowing me to write and watch you grow at the same time.

All my beta's, friends and family, without each of your support, I would be awfully lonely. I'm so happy to be supported by a tribe. Just know, I will be forever grateful. Love you all.

Tee or some of you know her as T. L Swan. Thank you for always supporting, encouraging, and giving me advice when I need it. When I picked up your book years ago, I had a dream, and I reached out and you answered me. I will always be forever grateful to you, my Margarita loving queen. Love you!

My readers, thank you for supporting me and purchasing my books. You are supporting my dreams and without you, my career wouldn't exist.

Thank you.

ARE YOU A SHARON SWEETHEART?

To keep up to date with new books releases, including title's, blurb's, release date's and give-aways. Please subscribe to my newsletter.

Want to stay up to date with me? Come join my Facebook reader group: *Sharon's Sweethearts* This is a **PRIVATE** group and only people in the group can see posts and comments! Join Sharon's Sweethearts

ABOUT AUTHOR

Sharon Woods is an author of Contemporary Romance. She loves writing steamy love stories with a happy ever after.

Born and living in Melbourne, Australia. With her beautiful husband and two children.

http://www.instagram.com/sharonwoods-author

http://www.facebook.com/sharonwoods-author

https://www.tiktok.com/@sharonwoods-author

http://www.sharonwoodsauthor.com